# CAUSE & EFFECT

JEREMY BOBROWSKI

Jon Mohni

Thanks for the support!

D1521399

ISBN: 145386623X
ISBN-13: 9781453866238

# DEDICATION

This book is dedicated to my wife, all of my friends and family, and, most of all, to my parents. Without all of their help and support this book would never have been created.

# JUNGLE LOVE

The Sun's first rays of the day splintered mercilessly between the sweeping, bowed leaves of banana plants, torching previously tanned legs as they stalked the old dirt trail. Short glances upward acknowledged towering trees and brush that shot skyward in an attempt to touch the calm stillness of a blue sky set as a finish line to the heavens. Bare legs covered only by short, khaki-shorts skimmed the brush along the side of the centuries-old dirt path. Overgrowing undergrowth littered the path attempting to overtake property previously within its possession. Sweat stains on her crusty old t-shirt outline a much-appreciated jog bra she had picked up in some street market in San José. She had broken into a jog in order to remain precisely on time, and it mattered little to her that the logo sewn on her bra was probably not the actual brand.

It was a small dirt trail, a path where paw prints outnumbered footprints, and it lay right where he said it would. Despite the fact that she'd gone over the map a thousand times, she hadn't actually graced the path's dirt until now. The many hours spent in preparation for the event and in practice out on the boat with maps and stopwatches and calculators flooded her memory. With the blasting caps in place, all she had to do was pull the triggers and then watch the Earth swallow him.

Her chest and lungs heaved under the heavy humidity. Her nerves no doubt quickened her pulse as well. She felt the jungle around her and listened to its sounds of alarm at the wake of her presence. Birds not instantly recognizable scattered overhead, and a billion beady little insect eyes monitored her, but most continued to work at the task at hand.

Slightly in a daze from the three miles she had jogged she welcomed the small clearing she came to, which contained a giant mound of dirt that was to be her cover. It was her perch, a bird's eye view to the end of an era, and the small mound of fresh dirt just to the right was where he had hid the wired detonators. Despite her excellent physique, her pits and chest dripped wet with sweat and dirt. When she had finally stopped running, she felt the perspiration pouring down her back to the top of her khaki shorts. She grabbed a dry handkerchief from the left front pocket of her shorts and briefly padded her forehead, but saved most of the leftover dry areas for her palms which were now the most important tools on the mountain. With her back jutted into the mound of mud and dirt, she squatted and cooled a bit. A tall tree shielded her thighs from the laser beams of scorching sunlight. She guessed it was a hundred twenty degrees or more.

Peering down just over the mound of mud, she saw the factory. It was your basic cookie-cutter big box, save for the elongated smoke stack sending out millions of poisons an hour into the upper atmosphere, where they lingered and infected. It stood a thousand feet below her, where it was almost entirely concealed by the two small mountains. A feeble attempt at hiding the evidence from God. Mostly this was on purpose, she thought—out of sight, out of mind. For pushing this one past only a few prying eyes, some crooked official got a handshake full of cash and a McMansion somewhere south on the Peninsula. Perhaps on the beach.

There was a lone access road carved out between the two adjoining mountains, and a calm, harmless river that crawled next to the concrete blemish. The road, mostly dirt, was to be paved in the spring. The board had originally ruled not to give its managers four-wheel drive on their company cars as a cost cutting move, only to find the road completely impassable during the rainy season. They fought off the jungle that surrounded it with lawnmowers and earthmovers and backhoes. Heavy machinery as well as toxic chemicals helped produce a well-manicured front lawn in the middle of the jungle. The river was there, too, which was where they dumped the chemical by-product, poisoning the surrounding Earth.

The factory, barely eighteen months old, had already been accused of causing the alarming number of birth defects from the two villages just a few miles away. The evidence was right there among the surrounding population in the form of cleft palates and other such deformities that magically appeared once the factory began production. But even though it hadn't exactly made it to the front page of the New York Times yet, the story would perhaps have a happy ending. Her group would see to that. There would be some amazing before and after pictures emailed to the Times in the morning, when they were free and clear. She pulled the two detonators out from the small mound of fresh Earth just in front of her, brushed them off a bit, and removed the duct tape that had covered the safeties.

Peeking back to the trail, she saw a brooding jaguar that she had obviously woken on her route in. Sleepy, and gaunt, the Jaguar stretched out his two front paws in the dirt of the trail. He let out a voracious yawn and picked himself off the rest of the bed of leaves he had made that morning. After casting an angry look her way, he then sauntered down the trail in the opposite direction, skipping back into the brush a few hundred feet away to look for solace.

She had worn the shorts anyway, despite his protestations. She wanted to show off her legs. In action. He would be watching. She thought he would think her beautiful. She hadn't shaved them much lately, but they still passed for beautiful and were well tanned from all the time out on that boat. Whatever hairs that were visible were frosted blond by all the sun. Sitting there, propped up against a large mound of mud, things landed or tried crawling on her occasionally, and despite the fact that most things out here were not venomous, they were generally unsightly.

She allowed herself a few solitary moments inside her paradise. The silence is spoiled by the sound of a door opening, and she cautiously peered over at the factory below. She watched as Joe escorted the lone employee (some middle management import) with a taser, until he climbed into one of the canoes rather clumsily. She had secured the canoes from her village friends the week before. They were handmade and remarkably sleek—as if you glided on top of the water on a piece of paper. Joe had secured the last employee remaining. They had to remove him for his safety and in order to avoid stupid, careless mistakes. She turned back to her Eden to admire the few remaining moments of peace and quiet left in her life.

*Christ, it's beautiful here*, Jessica thought. Pulling the handkerchief from off her neck, she wrung it out and then dabbed at her forehead and wiped her palms. There could be no slipping now. She would never see this jungle again, and while it was about to rain mud, and bits of the Earth would be harmed, the world was about to get a bit brighter. A few remaining years of youth lay upon her face despite the miles she traveled. She wiped her hands again. He said she fit in here, in the jungle, amongst all of God's beautiful, shielded creatures. He knew her well. He knew where she belonged.

She hated the pre-game speech, but this morning he told her it was her responsibility now. She thought they sounded preachy and always held a hint of lunacy. This factory did more harm than good, and it was time to strike a blow in the Earth's defense, she had said. It was a factory that's version of pity was to hand its workers and the poor surrounding villagers pennies. It was time to make the bad guys go away (at least from this land). They had all known what to do and what their jobs were as she stood addressing them. Those tasks had not changed, at least not for a while now. And this time he stood beside her...and there were cheers.

Her watch beeped once, telling her it was almost time. She closed her eyes to imagine him...

He moved swiftly within the factory, gliding in between the sedate machines, swift and purposeful. The ting of empty gas canisters echoed among the silent machinery as he hurled them into each corner one by one. There was the distinct, acrid smell of gasoline being showered over the metal machinery. She watched him give the finger to the photo of the company president on the wall as he passes. The picture sat in a smart frame, no doubt inspiring awe to the company workers. But not today. The dam that had "accidentally" been destroyed ensured no village workers would be making it in today by swallowing the lone access road with water. His pulse quickened and his mind moved faster after he checked his watch, knowing it was almost time. It quickened even more after he noticed the padlock on the door to the smokestack.

He approached the opening, and in one move grabbed a steel rod the size of a baseball bat from off the top of one machine and, with one swift

down stroke, struck the lock from the door. He pulled off his t-shirt, exposing back muscles that rippled back and forth as his lean body jogged through
puddles of gasoline. Kneeling in the entrance to the smokestack, he tossed
his shirt to the floor in order to soak up some of the gasoline, then wrapped
his shirt back around the steel rod. Grabbing hold of the ladder and rope
Joe had flung down, he began his trek upwards towards the sky. There was a
debate as to who had the worse task: him climbing the smokestack with just
a small ladder and a rope, or Joe sitting in a canoe with that middle management type for an hour as they rowed to safety. From the bottom of the
smokestack, a clear blue patch above was his bull's-eye. It grew fast with the
climb up the small service ladder borrowed from a maintenance closet, but
once he ran out of space on the ladder, the ensuing climb up the rope slowed
things and his hands stung like he was strangling a hive of bumblebees.
As badly as he wanted to drop the rod that held his shirt, he does not. The
engineer said the smokestack would hold against the mudslide. He hoped
so. The spectacle will be grand.

Back up top, she slid the safeties off the detonator and marveled at the
two triggers and how they reminded her of the remote controls for her elec-
tric train that she had played with as a child. It was the set her dad used to
prepare for her every Christmas. She'd play all damned day with that train.
Watching mountains of gifts grow in the background as Mom and Dad
finished wrapping. It would have been an easy life. To stay in that house.
It would have been perfect. A perfect house…a perfect family and a perfect
life. But she knew she had the strength for more. She was blessed. On the
day she was leaving, she told her dad that it was just something she had to
do. He fought it. But one day, she thought, he'd realize just how tough she
could be.

Things had not gone according to plan on that day. She was still a kid
then and it hadn't been her plan anyway. Perhaps he was on one of his many
business trips and had miraculously recognized her. She had seen him out of
the corner of her eye as her face bit into the concrete, held there under a cop's
boot as cold metal sealed both of her thin wrists. She still managed a smile
and what passed for a "Love you, Daddy!" out of the corner of her mouth.
The police in riot gear maced the rest of her compatriots, but not her. The
rain mixed with mace, and there was chaos. Her long, beautiful, peroxide-laden

blond hair saved her a beating she thought. Still, she had been black and blue for a week after being thrown into the paddy wagon. Suits cheered during their incarceration. The worker bees would be allowed back to their desks in order to go back to toiling away at life that much closer to obesity. She peered through a small window in the paddy wagon in search of a suit not clapping, but she could not find her father. A defaced billboard or two (dozen) prominently displayed across the city served as a momentary distraction for the worker bees. The onlookers applauded the beating, apparently in support of the *Listeria* they had been eating. It was at the fast food trough and hidden between two small buns that they chowed down on. She may not have seen him again, but she knew who bailed her out of prison that night. It was her first and only time in handcuffs (consensually or not). She swore to him it would be her last in a rare letter home giving thanks.

If all went according to plan, tons of dirt would be pushed a few hundred yards, the result of just a few hundred well placed sticks of dynamite and a rainy season on record as one of Costa Rica's worst ever. The local workers were all gone now. That left only the part about the wanton destruction of property. *We're burying the evidence*, she thought. *Burying and burning it from God's eyes.* The shaft lay only five or six feet across, enough room for the smokestack to jut out from the ground and allow enough oxygen inside to fuel the fire that would burn the machinery into molten metal clumps of useless mass. There would be no more product here. No production. And no negligence. A statement, sure. *You are not wanted here. You are not wanted. You've damned Earth with your residue and by-product and poisons. You are not wanted.* Every vein pulsed with hate within her. She looked across the valley at the mountain one last time and said a quick prayer. Soon it would rain mud. She seethed and gritted her teeth. Seconds ticked closer. The engineer said the force would not damage the smokestack. Another prayer was said for him and his climb. Her watch beeped twice, and then she pulled the triggers.

# SUMMER BREAK-IN

*DAVID HOBBS – AGE 21*
*August, 1995*

Shot glasses clink together ceremoniously, sending clumsy echoes that reverberated back and forth from the bar's patio section. From the surrounding marketplace, tourists briefly took note of the further salute to drunkenness from an intoxicated trio. Choosing instead to concentrate on combating the high heat equipped with their pocket-sized battery powered misting fans, tourists flocked past the hopeful locals running the small shops and stands in the market, who can only defer to soiled handkerchiefs and shirtsleeves.

Blasting down upon the Yucatan peninsula, the Sun's rays invaded a small Mexican town that most people didn't know about yet. Shielded only by a small thatched roof, the gang of three endured the late afternoon heat at the small bar just off the dock. The cruise ships were just beginning to put in here and the resorts were going up faster than you could find English speaking travel agents. It used to be only a few real fishermen would stop. Nowadays, the locals stockpiled merchandise in preparation for the sweaty, bloated tourists.

Relief from the heat was sought from a bottle of tequila provided to the three sailing buddies by a waiter that showed up during injuries in the soccer game on TV. Displays of public drunkenness ensued as a tribute to a good sailing trip. They'd managed a number of days partying with the intent of avoiding all thoughts of the upcoming school year. With shot glasses raised yet again, the tequila bit the backs of their throats while smiles and cheers still go forth from a small, crickety wooden table. More chips and salsa are ordered.

Within the market, bits of broken Spanish are thrown about as Americans attempt to barter down their remaining souvenirs for their friends back home. And while they cross names off their lists, tourists hand over stacks of funny colored pesos (funny to them). The shopkeepers supplied their goods and scurried to the back of their store, or in some cases hut, and quickly made the sign of the cross. David Hobbs observed all of this as a twenty-one year old and through a haze of late afternoon tequila shots.

Opting for a table on the patio, the crew of three observed many transactions that day. And there was a view of the Gulf of Mexico on one side and a jungle with some rather sizeable mountains jutting up from the landscape on the other. Mostly though, David Hobbs acknowledged, the table was chosen in the hopes of monitoring the beautiful ladies walking through the marketplace: Those that were there in Mexico to work on a tan, or those that were tan and just there to work. It was the boat crew's next to last night in the land of resorts and burgeoning tourist traps and then it would be straight home. Unfortunately, they'd have to give the boat back in Miami and catch a flight back to Chicago.

But there'd be time to think out there on the water. Time to think about the internship David had just finished. Time to think about the last year of college and the potential job that waited for him when he was through. Mostly though, David thought back to all the pretty account girls he had worked with who teased him for being some green intern over this past summer. He wondered when the women wouldn't seem so temporary. David knew full well that with a little time and effort, once he pulled in the dollars, he'd have his pickings of those same account girls. He heard the whispers. David was an attractive young man. Revenge from all the teasing he received this summer would come in the form of their underpants on his bedroom floor next year when he was full time at Graham and Hoffman Advertising.

It was easy for David. He knew he was taking things for granted. But he'd busted his ass all summer at that internship and he deserved a break before going back to school. Once he graduated, there'd be nothing but responsibility...and life. David lifted his shot glass once more and joined his two crew mates as they poured back the fire that stung their throats like swallowing a handful of bumble bees. *Here's to responsibility,* he thought.

David knew he was a much better sailor than his two current mates. He knew that they knew, which was why they called him "Skipper" on this brief little jaunt to Mexico, despite the fact that it was the boss's boat, and that one of the mates was the boss's son. The proof lay in between his boss's own words when he left his internship.

David stood at attention in front of his desk while his boss, Lou, sorted through a file cabinet. The boss peered up above his cheaters acknowledging David's presence in his office.

"We're good for the Mac next year, right?" Lou requested through the difficulty of reading his own handwriting on a file jacket.

*He was referring to the Mackinac Island Regatta. Piece of cake*, David thought.

"Yes, Sir, of course. I'm very much looking forward to it."

"Yeah, well, you keep it up and you'll be second in command in no time. Those boneheads don't know their way around a boat for shit. They grew up in the Midwest."

"I grew up in the Midwest, Sir," David responded rigidly.

"I'll be damned, Kid. It's in your blood, isn't it?"

"Kinda," but that was another story, one not to bother the future boss with.

"Well, you sure as hell were a big help this year. And not just for the Mac. Kid, you've got some great ideas, and you are by far one of the most intense individuals I've ever worked with. You stick by me, and you'll go far in this company."

"Thank you, Sir. It has been a rewarding and enriching..."

He cut the speech off that he's heard a few dozen times.

"Why don't you do me a favor: You got a week or so before going back to school, right? We've got some storyboards that need to go down to our Miami office. I'd feel safer if they were in your hands. Why don't you take them down there and meet up with my son, Jeff. Take the boat out for a week or so. He'll have it all prepped by the time you get down there. Just do me a favor and teach him a thing or two about sailing, would ya'? I swear all that kid wants to do on the boat is smoke pot and hump that girlfriend of his. Hell, that's about all he wants to do when he's off the boat. You, David...you're not like him. You're much more...focused. And cut that "Sir" shit out."

He wasn't allowed to say much more. This was a business.

"See Janice at reception before the end of the day. She'll have your plane tickets. Go grab the boards from Al in the cutting room. He may not be done yet so don't piss him off by just standing there looking over his shoulder."

David's memories eased his mind back to the impending doom of another school year (the last thankfully). Now, sitting alongside his boss's son and his boss's son's girlfriend, sweating tequila in the blast furnace that was late summer Mexican heat, David suffered the fog of fresh drunkenness. Thoughts of school and classes drifted away with his sobriety.

David sat at the table basking in his daze of drunken thoughts and listening to the random elocutions thrown aloud from the Boss's son. Exhausted from arguing against Jeff's views on the government's laws against marijuana for the better part of an hour David's brilliant blue eyes that dotted a recently tanned face searched the marketplace and eventually wandered to her. The sight of her shook him from his lonely daydreams and drunkenness. There through a marketplace crowd, in between the locals and the tourists, was an absolute stunning vision that jolted him and drew him back to sobriety. David watched her stroll through the crowded market, careful of the worn out cobble stone streets that were in much need of repair. Not at all tan by sun worshipping standards, she wasn't pasty white either. Wandering through the market to observe, strolling past certain displays to admire the art among the vendors, she would occasionally pause to look above her as the local women watered plant boxes in the windows above. David realized that she knew the neighbors all watered their plants together at the same time so they could chat. This...exquisite creature was obviously there to do anything but purchase some trinket. She watched and observed things. It was completely opposite to what David was subscribing to that afternoon, and this rare pretty girl was a complete surprise. She looked back out at the marketplace and faced it for a moment. David succumbed to his shyness and avoided eye contact as he sat under the tarmac of a thatched roof with two drunken boobs who counted the minutes before their next roll of a joint or roll in the hay.

A short-sleeved white button down was tied loosely above her belly, exposing the slightest bit of taut skin at the waist and, with only some buttons fastened, revealing a chest covered by a black bikini. She was tall and thin, healthy it seemed, and with shoulder length, straight hair that was naturally tuxedo black, pulled back loosely with a few long bangs darting down sharply. She was conscious enough to place those bangs precisely in the correct spot to know that she looked exquisite. A turquoise sarong covered her bottom half, and if the bag of shells she carried was any indication, David guessed there was a black bikini bottom underneath and nothing else. A large beach bag caressed the top of a lone bare shoulder. Thankfully no obvious tattoos accompanied her superb body. Classy and confident, she strode from the market in David's direction. This one was far different from the arrogant account girls he'd worked with over the summer, David noted. The air of class was something the tourists had abandoned once the floral print shirts were freed from their suitcases. This girl looked like a photographer should be following close behind her, taking pictures for some magazine spread.

David, as any young man of twenty-one would naturally admit to, fought the urges of lust just about every moment of every day. The virility that beat in his blood and the desire for the prowl grew strong in him. The hunt...was on, he thought. Looking over his shoulder now as she passed him, his eyes dutifully covered by the Ray Bans, he realized his mouth was agape, and he closed it immediately for fear of looking foolish. David then acknowledged his present company was all he needed to look foolish. A quick departure from them was necessary. Thankfully one was provided.

It was just for an instant, but after the plant boxes in the windows had been watered and the chitchatting women had all gone in, her eyes shifted directly to David—if only for a second, she had noticed him, perhaps even studied him, albeit briefly, but the recognition of his existence was there. That was all David needed.

A wry smile cracked the corners of her lips just after she'd caught him staring at her. Intrigued by her, David pursued his options as she passed the patio bar.

The teasing ensued from his mates followed by short giggles.

"Well?" asked the boss's son.

"Well?" asked the girlfriend.

"Well, what?" David replied.

The two choked back marijuana-laced laughs.

"You just can't let that go, my man!" the boss's son admonished.

"Yeah, Man, you gotta go after her!" the girlfriend advised.

David turned to watch the back of the crisp white button down continue to wander through the marketplace.

With purpose he had not before demonstrated, David burst from the patio in pursuit, nearly toppling the old wooden chair after him.

"Excuse me, miss? Um, miss, hey, wait."

*Anxious. Too anxious,* David thought. He even grabbed her arm. As she turned to face him, he noticed she was still smiling. *Tone it down some, Spaz,* he thought.

"Yes?" she asked, glancing down at his hand on her.

"Oh, good, you speak English," David said, relieved he wouldn't have to amble through his broken Spanish.

"Practically everyone speaks English here...now," she said.

David let go. Her arms folded in front of her protectively. A small mole dotted the corner of her mouth, and it looked beautiful on her.

"Well, that's good for me, I guess."

David couldn't take his eyes off of her. She wore just a slight bit of eye makeup. Standing so close to her now it seemed to David that with every exhale she breathed beauty in to the world and to those surrounding her.

"I guess..." she said, and paused. "Well?"

"Well?" David asked ignorantly, still breathing her in.

"You stopped me. I was walking through the market. Is there something I can help you with?"

"Oh, right, right, sorry about that. My name is David, and I, uh, I saw you just now..."

"And?" she demanded.

Her patience waned. David was losing her.

"Well, I saw you saw me. I mean, see me. I saw you...see me."

Her foot toe-tapped with fresh annoyance and impatience.

"I'm afraid you're going to have to do a little bit better than that," she declared.

She walked away from David who could only offer a stare. After a moment, David was able to shake himself free from the Tequila grip of nonsensical banter so that he could chase her further. *This one is tough*, he thought. David jogged up to her.

"No, what I mean is, you looked at me. I caught your eye."

She stops again to look up at David.

"Is that all you got?"

"Well, no, to be honest I just kind of rushed over here and am making this up as I go along. Normally I'm pretty good at this sort of thing."

"Not today," she said and started to walk away again.

"Well, what I meant to say was that you're kind of unexpected here, ya' know."

She stopped, and a curious look falls on her now as she turns back towards David.

"You know, someone...beautiful. I mean, we're kind of surrounded by bellies here, and I can't get the smell of Coppertone out of my clothes."

"Go on," she inquires.

"And you, well, you look beautiful. Like you belong here. Like it's you who belongs here and not all these... Tommy Bahama shirts."

"That's better," she said, and her arms fell to her side.

"Is it? Well, it's true. You spend enough time here and your brain gets kinda lazy. Like you're on some kind of permanent vacation."

"Well, not just a pretty face and glib repartee. You've actually got some perspective. Are you sure it's not the tequila?"

"That probably has something to do with it. You're really going to make me work at this, aren't you?"

"I wouldn't have it any other way. Go ahead, give it a shot."

David rubbed his hands together in preparation and noticed he was perspiring.

"Where ya' from?"

"All over," she responded quickly, "strike one."

David, frustrated, acknowledged lackluster attempts weren't going to work.

"All right, I've got it. The construction company that's putting in those pricey condos up on the mountain? The ones that are going to have the unbelievable views. Up there on the mountain making that dent in the jungle, right? You're the daughter of the CEO and you're here to take in the sights."

She exuded an audible sigh and rolled her eyes. She looked down to her feet, and an angry look shot across her face. David knew what happened next.

"No, genius, strike two," she said gathering herself while beginning to walk away.

"All right, other way around, then. You're one of those hippie, do-gooder types working at the habitat for humanity putting together the living spaces outside of town for all the Indians and villagers displaced by the construction of those condos."

She sighed again, took two steps and then stopped.

"So what if I am?"

"Ah, ha!" David exalted in a moment of self-congratulation, "I got it! A little worried there for a moment, I'll admit. Boy, you don't really look like one of them hippie-types. I mean, you smell good."

"And what about you? Summer vacation with the frat brother and his girlfriend?"

She nodded back to the patio table where David's two crewmates rolled a joint.

"Off sailing around the world one summer. Getting those last licks in before you head back to that really, really tough east coast University of wherever. Getting ready to bitch about the days where you have to sit in class for three whole hours?"

"It's the Midwest, not East Coast," David corrected the only inaccuracy. "I'm from Chicago."

"I should have known with that accent. That mouth is used to chewing on pork chops and deep dish pizza."

"I hate deep dish pizza. How'd you know I had a boat?"

"I saw you and your, uh, crew, pull in the other day. Heard you, really. Don't hesitate to reinforce the American stereotype, will ya'?"

"Well, what about you? That bag of shells doesn't mean you've been building homes for the poor all day."

"They're gifts for friends. And those poor people are innocent villagers from a tribe that has lived on that hill for hundreds of years, in that jungle, and now it's being destroyed. Besides, I'm allowed a day off for a mental vacation. What? You think it's nothing but granola and patchouli oil?"

"Sort of, yeah," David admitted.

"You want to know what it's like, David? Helping others as opposed to kicking it on Daddy's sailboat in the Gulf of Mexico?"

"It's his daddy's sailboat," David said, intrigued, and nodded back to the bar, "and, yeah, I do."

"Ok, meet me at the site tomorrow. I'll show you what an honest day's work is like and that us do-gooder, hippie-types are all right."

She turned to leave.

"Wait," David said, "what's your name?"

"It's Jessica," she said with a slightly noticeable nervous twinge while shaking his hand. "I'm Jessica. See you tomorrow, David?"

"Sure."

They both turned, and while David smiled, he thought of something else.

"Oh, hey, what time tomorrow?" he asked.

"Our work day begins when the sun comes up, Skipper."

Tough, David thought, he liked that. He liked her. The interest was definitely there to stomach the early a.m. wakeup call. He turned to see her gliding away purposefully through the market. David got a glimpse of her rear end as Jessica walked away. Then her head turned back to him catching his ogle. They both pitched innocent smiles in one another's direction.

\* \* \*

Daybreak and thoughts of Jessica forced David from his sleep. He took a look out to sea as his feet hit dry land, and he hurried to meet his ride. He was met by a quiet market and a lone shop owner sweeping up in front of his store. A stray tourist power-walked across the cobble stones and nearly broke an ankle. Darkness still covered the town, but David was afforded a view of the Sun's rays reaching in from the sea dutifully. A local fisherman that David had befriended drove him to the work site.

At the work site, abuzz with moving people all about, David took orders and looked around for Jessica. She was there but in another group. David got a sheet of instructions on what they were responsible for that day. He was also given training on some tools that he was already familiar with. The sound of mitre saws buzzing and hammers banging away clogged David's ears. He and Jessica both snuck sappy stares at one another throughout the morning, and David rather enjoyed watching her work up a sweat. Jessica wasn't fazed one bit. She passed two-by-fours to carpenters with ease and worked hard.

They pushed and pulled all morning amid the menacing rays of a merciless Sun, David sweated the toxins out from the previous day's debauchery. The heat continued to bear down upon the group once the clock struck one. David could barely pick-up a nail gun without gloves because the metal roasted in the day's heat. Despite the sweat dripping from his body, the heat still made him feel heavy and exhausted like he was sinking into the ground.

Pleased by accomplishing something of importance for once this summer, David stepped back a moment to look at the frame going up and smiled to himself. A water break in the early afternoon allowed Jessica and himself to finally get a chance to speak to one another alone.

"So, you been working with these people for awhile?" David asked.

"Seems like it," she said solemnly. Jessica tied a bandana around her forehead and scratched dirt away from her eyes. "It ain't enough though."

"What's that?" David asked her.

"These houses."

"It looks like there'll be plenty of space for a family…"

"I'm not talking about space!" Jessica said and smacked David's forehead playfully.

"What did you expect?" he asked.

"Respect. Some respect for a people's culture and a village that has been around longer than the t-shirt shops in that market."

David noticed a necklace of small shells around Jessica's neck and guessed that they had been the shells she had picked up from the beach that previous day.

"It's something," David tried.

"I guess it is," Jessica said, sadly, turning to look back at the mountain. Dump trucks overflowing with earth and all sorts of shorn bits of foliage severed from centuries old roots careened down the mountainside. The trucks carting payloads down the dirt roads wound their way up and down the mountainside road, blasting mechanical sounds and emissions at everything in their path. Birds scattered from the tree lines in tune with the smog bellowing from exhaust pipes.

"It really bothers you, doesn't it?" David asked.

"Yes, it does. I'm bothered by the whole god damned nerve of it. People can just throw money around and have an entire village removed and placed into...sanitized track housing."

"I'm sorry," David said, putting his arm on her shoulder compassionately.

"You don't have to be sorry. You said you wanted to help out, right?"

"Yes, I did."

"Good. We need help."

One of the team captains walked over interrupting them.

"Couple of more waters for the newbies?" he asked, presenting them with big, beautiful bottles of crystal clear water. Jessica ripped at the cap on her water and gulped from the bottle. She pushed David's into his bare chest. His t-shirt had long been abandoned due to the drenching sweat he had worked up.

"Did he just call you a newbie?" David asked.

"Maybe he just doesn't recognize me," Jessica said and shrugged her shoulders. "Come on. Break time's over."

Jessica tussled David's blond bangs that flopped about in the Sun. The team captain blew his whistle. They both guzzled water and went back to work.

* * *

Quitting time brought another whistle. Muscles not generally used by David throbbed and ached as he put away a nail gun. His hands and back stung as he stretched towards the fading Sun. Tiny slivers of wood lined his palms. His feet felt like they'd burst through his boots at any moment.

"What's the matter, softie?" David recognized her voice already, "Tired from being on your feet all day? Thinking about pushing paper in that fluorescent dungeon?"

"Well, as a matter of fact, I was just taking a moment to realize how oddly satisfying all this hard work was."

"Stick with me. I think I can keep you satisfied."

It was her first double-entendre and most certainly not her last. David smiled, appreciating her sense of humor despite the long day of work. They both smelled awful. Layers of dirt and dust soiled their skin. Jessica turned and walked back to her group for a debriefing and celebration. David ignored his group but continued to monitor the interaction that was going on between everyone in the fabricated village. He recognized it was the first time in a while he'd seen people meeting together to create something positive and worthwhile.

After a few minutes Jessica walked up and sat on the ground next to him Indian style, cupping dirt from the ground with her suntanned hands. Shifting it from one palm to the other carefully so as to not lose a single grain or tiny pebble of the precious Earth she was holding, Jessica looked around to see who could be watching.

"Thanks for coming today, David."

"It was worth it. I feel...good."

"Well, we're certainly on our way here. Homes for people who already had homes. Look at those trucks going up and down that mountain. I counted twelve different trucks today, David. Yesterday it was ten. Last week it was eight."

"You can't stop expansion. Look on the bright side, if it weren't for some shit bag developer and a couple dozen condos we probably never would have met in this tropical paradise."

"It's not expansion. It's a scheme prompted by someone's greed to have some miraculous view for a few months out of the year. Never mind the fact that it was someone else's land."

"I'm sorry. What can I do to help?"

"For starters, you can buy me dinner tonight. And I want one of those huge margaritas that are so big you get to wear that big dumb sombrero with it."

"I can definitely do that. And you may not be the only one in a sombrero."

"I need a shower first. And so do you. Can I shower at your boat? It'll be faster."

"Certainly," David said, sensing an opportunity. "I just gotta figure out how to get us back to the dock."

"I've got a moped. I can take us. I always come prepared, David."

"I guess..."

"There's just one little stop we gotta make first."

David hoped it was a stop to make out.

The moped chugged and churned up a dirt road that led up the mountain. The road had been recently carved out through jungle and brush, and Jessica avoided the wide tire tracks in the road that were laid there by massive trucks. Donning an expensive pair of sunglasses that looked like they belonged to a fifty year old rather than some twenty-something Jess steadied the moped as it dodged debris. They held each other close on the small moped, and the jungle swallowed the two figures. David hoped that Jessica cared little about his sweaty body holding her so close. From a glance in the rearview mirror, David noticed her smiling.

The jungle was something foreign to the tourists in the resorts below. Perhaps a few snarls from large cats and other predators resonated at night as far as the all inclusive bar where the Tommy Bahamas hung out. Perhaps they were drowned out by the blender. David was seeing it all firsthand now. And as they got closer to the compound, larger machinery lay in the jungle in preparation for further destruction. Jessica seemed relaxed until they got to the front gate of the compound where the main demolition on the mountain was being done. A lone guard slept in front of a black and white television in a small office. A fence surrounded the compound where the trucks were parked. David wondered whether the barbed wire on top was intended more as a deterrent for humans rather than predators.

"I just wanted to see why we were here, David. Ya' know, get a little look-see at the evil doers."

"Are they really that evil? Or is it just that they have money and can do whatever they want."

"From what I've seen, that's one and the same."

Jessica stared at the idle dump trucks in the compound and the smile vanished from her face. Her feet crept away from her sandals so that bare naked toes could temporarily grace the soil and dirt path.

David, in a weak attempt at comforting her, "It really bothers you. What they're doing to this place, doesn't it?"

"More than anything."

"So, you're telling me if you were some spoiled brat you wouldn't want a house in the hills overlooking the Gulf of Mexico?"

Jessica stayed silent for a moment and then said sullenly, "What makes you think I'm not a spoiled brat, David?"

The conversation ended there. Jessica still had a sad look on her face. Before she cranked back on the accelerator, she planted a quick peck on David's cheek. A kiss for both acknowledgment of a job well done today and for the effort to console her, he thought.

"C'mon, let's get back to your boat."

The jungle was beginning to wake as the scooter charged away. Going downhill was easier, and David tried not to push all his weight into the back of Jessica. David sensed her mind was elsewhere now.

Twisting and turning down the hill, the moped jostled in between massive tire treads and branches that had been broken from the taller trees. Stray garbage wrappers littered the ground. David watched birds with massive wingspans flap across the sky as they scouted the ground for prey. Bushes and branches from within the jungle moved sharply but without any appearance or manifestation of the source. David marveled at all this as the Sun fell and stars began to fill a clear sky.

* * *

Standing in the main cabin, the sound of the shower teased David. The room had a twin bed (nearly always occupied by the two "humpy" kids until now), a shower in back, a loo, a dresser, and a small fridge with a bar. David begrudgingly stood guard while Jessica showered. Freshly shaved and gathering up his second wind, David had wandered down to grab his charts and maps in preparation for the trip back. But now, he realized, she was here, the figure he'd been staring at for the majority of the day, lifting brick and mortar and wood, performing hard labor earlier, and now completely naked, just a few feet removed. One opaque glass shower door lead to paradise. Jeff and Caroline made faces at him from above deck through the porthole. They even breathed on the glass and drew little hearts with arrows through it. David gave the finger to the two idiots and drew blinds over the porthole. Looking at the door of the shower David tortured himself by imagining what part of her body the water was now dripping from. He didn't want her to think that he was in the master cabin just to make sure she didn't steal anything or perhaps to get a quick peep at some skin.

David continued to pretend to study the charts and realized that the water had stopped. There it was, revealed to him in the mirror on a tiny dresser. He caught just a brief glimpse of her bottom as she toweled off meticulously, and he quickly looked away. She was skinnier than he'd thought, David acknowledged as he continued to hang close by. He couldn't afford to let some girl he'd just met yesterday walk away with something valuable from the boat. Though currently, besides the boat, the most expensive thing on it was probably David's wallet, which contained all his credit cards, or maybe it was the pot that the two kids had brought with them. He didn't feel all that perverted because he hadn't purposely looked and truly had gone down there for the charts. He was glad to have gotten a glimpse of her. Knowing Jessica and the can-do hippie attitude she sported, she probably wouldn't have cared anyway. David wondered what she was like in bed.

"It's a beautiful boat," David heard her say.

"Thanks," David said, probably too loudly, "It's not mine though."

David hoped Jeff and Caroline had returned to their prep work. They were supposed to be shoving off at six a.m. David did not expect to see her walk out into the bedroom in nothing but a towel, but she did.

"What's that mean? I wasn't supposed to use the shampoo?"

"No, no, you're fine," David said, looking away purposefully, afraid of eye contact for the moment and afraid he'd stare her up and down too much. "I just mean that, I don't own it. It's my boss's boat. Well, future boss really."

She had taken a long shower. The water would have to be topped off before leaving. Jessica walked up to David.

"Um, do you mind?"

"Mind what?" David said, desperately trying to look away from the cleavage that stood not too far from his face.

"My brush."

Blushing and embarrassed, David moved slightly aside. She ran the brush through her hair.

"Nice mirror," she said. David blushed even more.

She stroked her hair with the brush a few more times, and David moved the charts away so they would not get wet. He'd seen this game before, but he wasn't getting the sense that she was easy. Interested, yes, but not easy. Jessica wanted David to get a glimpse of the goods, which was all right. She moved quickly to her clothes on the bed. Before coming aboard, David watched her grab them from the storage compartment under the seat of her moped. It looked as though she had everything she needed to live stowed away in that moped's storage compartment.

"Yeah, I was interning at this agency in Chicago all summer. Worked out pretty well."

"Well, you must have done well if the boss gave you the keys to his boat."

"Well, I think he wanted me to give Jeff some pointers on sailing."

"Did you?"

"I did the best I could. He's not too interested in sailing."

Jessica turned around and dropped her towel to the floor and moved quickly into her clothes. David barely had time to look away but was afforded another brief glimpse of Jessica's glorious rear end. She continued to stroke her hair with the brush after each layer of clothes was applied.

"Advertising, huh?" she asked.

"Yeah, advertising."

"That's what interests you?"

"Yeah, among other things."

"Other things? Like those bitchy account girls just out of college in designer suits and full of points to prove to their male bosses."

"Those girls? Those are hobbies."

"Ah, something to spend a little time on."

"Yeah, just a little time."

"Looking for true love down here in Mexico, are ya'?"

"I don't think you can look for true love. I think it just kind of finds you."

Jessica put her brush down for a moment and looked over at David from across the cabin.

"I agree," she said.

Decked out in a tight black lycra top, her still-pristine white button down was now accompanied by black capri pants. Jessica had applied very little makeup and added nothing to her hair. She didn't even blow it dry. She looked delicious, David thought.

"And I also agree that it is far past the time you take me for dinner."

"After you, please," David said and motioned to the ladder leading to the deck.

Jessica climbed the ladder with a familiar ease, and David watched as both buttocks shuffled past his face. She was comfortable with her surroundings and not clumsy at all on the boat. There couldn't have been that much hot water for the length of shower she took. She didn't complain one bit. Despite her hair being wet, David had no doubt that it would look perfect by the time they sat down at a table.

Caroline and Jeff said their good-byes, and as David and Jessica disembarked from the boat, Jeff and Caroline snickered aside to David. "Shoving off at six, Captain?"

"Aye-aye," he said.

David and Jessica strolled over the crickety wooden planks of the old dock towards Jessica's scooter.

"Oh, let's walk into town," Jessica pleaded and took his arm in hers. "I like to see the lights."

"Whatever you like, my dear." It was just a short walk, and David pressed his aching muscles to move further on.

The lights from the town's restaurants grew closer as they walked. Jessica and David listened as the waiters yelled at fellow kitchen staff while maitre d's begged them to sit down as they passed each restaurant. And why not, they were a beautiful young couple that would make their restaurant look good and popular. David felt the restlessness of the night stir in his body. He hoped there would be more than just drinks and dinner with his new friend.

Jessica had chosen a much nicer restaurant than they'd originally planned, but that was okay with him. Sadly there were no large sombreros, but they both appreciated a nice meal. He'd remember sitting outside with her, here, in Mexico, once the winter hit the middle of Iowa. As the wind whipped through empty plains, David would long for the turmoil of the city.

Jessica ordered fish, and David admired how quickly she devoured her meal. She looked even more…attractive…after her shower and now that she was cleaned up.

"Any more astute observations about me you'd care to share?" Jessica asked, gulping down a bit of her margarita. She was forward and playful at dinner. The conversations had been fun.

"Well, you play the part of the renegade very well."

"Thank you, I try."

"And you're a woman of few words—when you want to be."

"What's that supposed to mean?"

"Nothing, just that every time you answer a question of mine it seems…planned. Thought through, I guess. Like you need to know exactly how you're perceived. For instance, tell me, do you have family?"

"I have a family."

That was all Jessica offered.

"You see, right there. By answering that way I still know nothing about you. You're very guarded, aren't you?"

"Yeah, well, maybe I just don't like strange men knowing all my secrets."

"Am I strange? Or do you just have a lot of men following you around."

"No, no, you're not strange. Not at all. And I don't have a boyfriend if that's what you're asking."

The bill arrived, and David paid dutifully. Jessica thanked him.

"Come on, let's get outta here. I'll walk you back to…where the heck are you staying anyway?"

"How about I drop you at the boat? We can take my moped."

"Didn't we walk here?"

Outside the restaurant where slender sidewalks were stuffed with sweaty tourists, David felt the restless night air fill his lungs. Sure enough the moped stood parked triumphantly in the first stall in the parking spaces just outside the restaurant. David acknowledged he had quite a bit to drink, but he was certain that they had walked. He was also certain he'd felt a hand on his bottom and that maybe someone was trying to pickpocket him, but it was just Jessica brushing up against him as they mounted the moped.

"Hop on, we've got one little stop to make before I drop you."

"Another stop, eh? Hope this one's a little more exciting than the last."

"Oh, I'm sure it'll fire you up."

David hoped this time it was to stop somewhere and make out.

\* \* \*

In fact, they'd just gone back up the mountain. This time it was too dark to avoid the potholes and tire tracks so the trip was a great deal more turbulent. It didn't slow down Jessica one bit. Her driving was considerably faster. David hugged Jessica at the waist and was afforded ample time to notice how skinny this girl was. Muscles still moved and twitched in her back with each winding turn up the mountain, but David wondered just how many meals Jessica had been skipping lately. Perhaps she was just trying to look good in her swimsuit. She didn't strike David as the kind of girl who'd let her image bother her or the kind of girl that hung out on the beach all day.

The jungle sensed them and watched them invade. David could feel a million eyes on him, but felt it less and less as they approached the compound. The trucks stood idle within the fence, protected, unsuspecting, and dormant. Silent metal beasts replaced living breathing ones. The smell of used machines and diesel fuel choked the thick jungle air and hung there for David and Jessica to take in. The clunky moped rolled to a stop at the gate.

Jessica turned around and looked straight at David.

"What's wrong?" he asked. "Why are we here?"

This was definitely not make-out time. Jessica got off the moped and walked directly up to the security guard who was waiting for them at the gate.

"*Puedo ayudarte?*" or "Can I help you," asked the guard, but in not such a very nice tone.

"*Si, estamos aqui para a ver los camiones.*" or "Yes, we're here to see the trucks."

"Eh?" David responded.

"*Que?*" said from the security guard, or "Eh," and he drew his gun.

"I said my friends and I are here to see the trucks. Now, please put your gun down and open up the fence." She had said so in Spanish.

"*Muevete, Chica.*" Or "Go away little girl."

"Listen, I just want this done the easy way."

And then Jessica looked back to David who was still stunned.

"Uh, Jessica, what are you doing?" David said, befuddled.

"My friends and I are here to see the trucks."

"What friends?"

Jessica whistled once. Folding back the leaves from tall trees and bushes and tiptoeing out from the darkness of the jungle and into the moonlight-flooded compound, a dozen or so half-naked men came into view. They carried spears and bows and arrows and wore war paint on their faces, looking as though they'd seen the Earth and lived on it for centuries. It took a few of them to sneak up behind the security guard and disarm him. The fat security guard scoffed when a bow and arrow was pointed at him and his pistol was taken away.

"Not to worry, Sweetie. It was never loaded," Jessica said.

Jessica, it appeared, knew her way around the Smith & Wesson as she dropped open the loader showing the empty chambers to David. She then chucked the pistol in the jungle. Out of the corner of his eye David watched as the Indians worked fast, removing the guard's keys and opening the gate. They apparently were not concerned with David. Each one passed him by on their own mission objectives, which were seemingly very well rehearsed. One of the Indians approached Jessica and whispered to her in a language unknown. She nodded. It seemed things had gone from interesting to insane pretty quickly.

"Is this pretty common for all your dates, Jessica?" David asked.

"Only the good ones," Jessica said, but still projecting her serious side. There was work to be done.

Jessica was happy to see David was still keeping a sense of humor about the whole thing. He wouldn't for very much longer, she thought. Jessica's focus returned to the security guard. The Indians held the front gate wide open.

"*Sientese, por favor. Pon los manos arriba.*"

"Um, Jessica, what is it that you're doing exactly?" David asked.

Jessica and the Indians walked into the compound to get closer to the trucks. The night's sky was lit only by a partial moon, but there was enough light to see the Indians handing Jessica bottles they had retrieved from the storage compartment of her moped. Each bottle had been wrapped delicately in a celebrity magazine.

"Would you believe wanton criminal destruction of property, and maybe just a little bit of arson?" Jessica replied.

Jessica counted heads. One of the Indians dumped a barrel over near the trucks and gasoline began roaring in waves past each truck's massive tires. Then he came dutifully running back to the group and they all stood semicircle at the entrance.

"Well, are you coming?" Jessica asked from the middle of the semi-circle. She stopped at the entrance, waiting for an answer from David. Matches were struck and the flames waited anxiously to adhere to the rags outside the glass bottles filled with gasoline.

"I can't," David responded.

"Why the hell not?"

"Because it's wrong."

"Wrong-schmong, David. Was it wrong when they kicked these people out of their village? Was it wrong when they brought the bulldozers up here? Hell, you're already an accomplice, David. Might as well have some fun and watch some metal burn."

David sat down, defeated, next to the security guard. He noticed for the first time tonight that the necklace she'd been wearing was made of the shells she'd picked up from the beach the other day. He also noticed that every Indian was wearing a necklace that was similar.

Jessica walked back to David and sat down to talk. "Listen, David, the damage being done, it's negligible. Their stupid trucks are going to be covered by insurance."

"That doesn't make it right! Jess, do you have any idea what will happen to us if we get caught? We'll be in a Mexican jail for years. And that would be the best we could hope for."

The security guard made the sign of a throat being slashed. One of the Indians held him down.

"Hell, David, was it right to just push these human beings out of their homes? It was their land. Do you have any idea how long they've been living on this mountain? Away from civilization and perfectly happy doing so?"

"They'll get new land."

"But it's not theirs, David. Don't you get it? They'll just be shoved aside the next time! We cannot let this go unpunished. It's an idea! A philosophy. New construction is pointless when destruction is necessary."

"Who's philosophy is that, Jess? What group are you from? Listen, I don't dig chicks with records. And I'd like mine kept perfectly clean."

The Indian and the security guard watched David and Jessica. The rest kept striking matches waiting for the okay from Jessica. David smelled the gasoline and watched the moonlight bounce rays off the slick surface that floated just beneath each truck.

"David, I have work to do," Jessica said as she rose. "And you can help me."

David sat in thought. Backlit by the moon he could see she was smiling. She was happy doing this. One of the Indians brought Jessica a bottle. Apparently they had used empty beer bottles.

"Decision time, David. You said you wanted to help."

"Help, yes. But you're talking about burning this place down."

"These people need someone to stand up for them. Just a little shove back that's all. Then they disappear. No one gets hurt. Just a few trucks get torched, and a message is sent."

David sat and continued his thinking. The margaritas weren't helping. She was so damned sexy out here, in this unknown land, in the middle of a jungle. He wanted to stand up, grab her, and kiss her right then and there.

"What was there a sale on Molotov cocktails or something?" he asked.

"Beer bottles tossed on the road from the truckers. I thought it was a nice touch. You don't think I'm overdoing it, do you?"

"No, not at all. Why would I think that?"

Jessica held out her hand to help David off the ground. Finally, reluctantly, David took it.

"Atta boy," she said knowingly.

They walked into the entrance of the compound and held hands. An Indian walked the security guard away from the compound and into the jungle, away from any danger.

"Want to do the honors," Jessica said and handed him her bottle.

"Why not?" David said. "A little arson never…"

"Would you feel any better if I told you that you were helping to save the world?"

"It might."

Jessica flicked her match and lit the rag.

"Watch your hands when you throw it. Aim for the grill. These suckers are going to burn all night."

It was a perfect strike. David heard the glass shatter and fall. The innocent fire dripped off the grill of one of the trucks and into the pool of gasoline. Then, Jessica mumbled something in some other language which apparently meant "now." At once, Molotov cocktails flew in the air like fireworks. Glass bottles twinkled in the moonlight for a brief moment only to come crashing down on to metal. Liquid fire spread immediately over the transporters of dead Earth. One by one, each truck bathed in flames.

Jessica moved swiftly into the jungle past the huge dense bushes and drooping leaves of a palm tree. David stepped cautiously inside as well in pursuit.

"No scooter?"

"Sorry, but we're hoofing it down the mountain."

Watching feet and legs dart in between trees and branches, careful not to stare too much at her behind, David heard her instructions, "Step only where I step."

"Ok," he offered simply.

"And touch absolutely nothing."

David thought he had sweat a lot at the worksite. Now, sucking wind and almost continually wiping sweat from his forehead, he almost begged her to stop. Even at night, the air and the ground were moist, but he was too busy concentrating on following her to breathe correctly. David thought he'd been in good enough shape but was embarrassed now. Jessica didn't even break a sweat. *Nimble, too*, David thought. She knew exactly where to move, and David followed, mimicking each footstep as best he could. The moon gave them some light, but occasionally tall trees covered them. David noticed Jessica monitor the sky the entire way down the mountain. While not quite a jog, it was certainly a better pace than a brisk walk. David guessed they had moved for an hour before Jessica let him catch his breath. It couldn't be much further, he thought.

"You're doing fine," Jessica said. There had been little talking throughout their trek. David guessed it was to conserve their energy, or perhaps it was not to disturb the inhabitants in the jungle.

"Really?" David questioned, "I'm huffing and puffing. You're barely breaking a sweat."

She was being kind to him. He had tripped and fallen on his face half a dozen times. They finally stopped when they broke into a small clearing.

"Take a seat on that tree limb, David. Take five."

He did so and was careful not to sit on something that might bite or sting. She continued to scan everything that moved.

"Is this all part of the usual tour?" David remarked, watching some animal slither up an enormous tree trunk very close to him.

"It won't be much longer now. To your boat. And, by the way, we could have taken the scooter, David."

"Well, why the hell didn't we?"

Jessica turned from the sky and looked back down to David sitting, sweating, on the tree trunk. She chuckled a bit.

"Because I wanted you to see this. I wanted you to feel this. All of this." Jessica motioned to the jungle surrounding them. David gave an obliging look to his surroundings that wasn't entirely skeptical. It was beautiful and serene. Probably her Eden, he guessed.

"Not exactly a grand escape plan coming from you?"

"You sure? Look at this place. When you're away at school, daydreaming during some boring lecture, you'll think about this place. There are things in this world that are far more pressing and concerning and more deeply moving to look at than bank accounts and client forecasts."

Looking down to his feet, he watched an iguana the size of a Chihuahua scurry past his feet, and he chuckled at the absurdity of the situation. Perhaps she was correct.

"I know this is a wild guess, but I take it you're not exactly here for habitat-for-humanity, are you?"

"No, I'm afraid not, David. I'm sorry I had to deceive you. But I had to know for sure if you'd help me."

David stood now and began to pace.

"Oh, yeah, you know, I'll just chalk it up to all the illegal activities I've ever performed in my life. You know, jaywalking, uh, tee-peeing my neighbor's house when I was a kid. That's pretty much it."

"I know you, David. I know you've been studying your entire life. I know there's something in you. It burns you. And you just keep pushing forward hoping to forget. I can feel it, David. You've done everything anyone's ever asked of you. Take a little time for yourself, David. It's an adventure, for chrissakes, enjoy it! Besides, the fire wasn't exactly the help I was looking for anyway."

David slowly realized his oversight. He hadn't looked at what had been there all along.

"The boat. It's the boat, isn't it?"

David smelled the fire and the smoke that was charging through the air. It wouldn't be long before the smell hit the town. *Might even be able to see it,* David thought. And when he looked back to Jessica, he knew. He knew for certain that they would see the fires that burned a dozen trucks that had taken away that village's land. People would see it from miles away.

"I'm all alone here now, David. I need your help, yes. But I wanted you...to help me."

"Wanted me?" David said dejectedly.

"Yes, wanted you. You can help me. You have a good heart, I know it. You can help me get outta here."

"It's going to look a little suspicious, don't ya' think?"

"Nobody knows me, David. I'm a ghost here. I've been living with the Indians for six months just in preparation for this night."

"Six months of planning and you don't have an exit strategy?"

"The six months I spent with them was to learn from them. This little stunt was just the end of my stay. The Indians are ghosts, David. They'll be on the other side of jungle by now. The other side of the country in a week. You've come this far with me, David. All you have to do is bring me aboard."

"I bet you're an excellent swimmer, aren't you?"

"Yeah, I'm pretty good," Jessica said, looking a little embarrassed.

David paced and sighed in between each quarrel. He was impatient with her, and she knew.

"What about your friends. Can't they help you?"

"It's kind of a test. I'm supposed to earn my stripes."

"Going to be kind of tough after the stunt we pulled. The police will be all over the place."

"Not if we leave tonight. Right now."

"You've got this all figured out, don't you?"

"I'm sorry, David. I can't take chances. Come on, we don't hurt people."

"Just their millions of dollars in equipment and machines."

"Their ideas. What they did was wrong. We were just sticking up for the people that were already there."

"Who's we?"

Silence. Nothing.

"Well, that figures. Am I endangering my crew by having you aboard? Any preachy, wise-ass do-gooder types going to meet us out in the middle of the ocean and hi-jack my boat?"

"Nope, like I said. It's a test. I have to find a way to get back on my own. And we don't hurt people, David. That security guard is in a bar right now watching the soccer game."

"So you thought by taking advantage of a college boy you could make your way out of here."

"No, it wasn't like that. I wanted you to help me. I liked you, David. From that first time at the market."

David harrumphed and still felt taken advantage of. Jessica moved close to him and put her arms around his shoulders. David still wasn't buying it.

"At least you know what I stand for, David. I won't trick you anymore. I won't lie. I won't deceive you. Nothing but the truth from here on out."

David smelled the fire burning and looked down upon Jessica.

"How'd you know I'd show up at the work site today?"

"I just knew. I knew you liked me, too, and that was why you chased after me in the marketplace. It felt to me, like, you were sort of meant to be here. To help me."

They stared into each other's eyes, and David took too long to act.

"You can kiss me, now, David."

"I thought you said not to touch anything?"

"Just shut up and kiss me, please!" she said.

Lips met warmly, and they fell into each other's arms. Within their embrace, they met the smell of the fire's intense smoke filling the thick jungle air, and they kissed harder. Their tongues found one another, and their mouths joined for an eternity. Hands and arms fumbled about shoulders and backs in search of bare skin. David wouldn't let go. He had wanted her, and he had finally gotten a hold of her.

\* \* \*

Feet stomped down an old, rotting wooden dock hastily, and the sound jostled Caroline and Jeff from their slumber aboard the *Bejeweled*. David held a few gallons of water, and Jessica had a bag of hastily chosen groceries from the all-night market. Caroline and Jeff woke up to a fire smoldering in the mountains.

"Time to shove off, gang."

"What?"

"Move!" David shouted at them. He helped Jessica aboard. Jeff and Caroline roused from the deck at once.

"Dig the groovy lightshow, David," Jeff said rising up letting out a long stretch from skinny arms.

"Yeah, I dig," David said, taking one last look at it before his work started on the boat. David admitted that even though it was just a heavy-duty make-out session up there, it was certainly the most interesting place he'd ever made out with a girl: a jungle mountainside outside of small town Mexico, while a fire which he started raged, consequently chasing him from the country.

"Jess, I don't suppose you know your way around a boat?" he asked.

As he said this, David looked aft and saw Jessica untying one of the moorings.

"Let's boogie," she said happily.

David knew he shouldn't be surprised by this. He was even pleased.

"Good, good," he said. Eventually he took his position behind the helm in order to steer them the hell out of there.

She was right. The damage would be negligible, and there'd probably be a dozen new trucks up there in a week. But the tourists saw the fire. They would ask questions. They would find out what happened. They would smell the smoldering dump trucks as they went to their frosty pools in the morning in a hurry to reserve their towels and lounge chairs. Perhaps a few tourists would even care. He looked to Jessica who sat at the rear of the *Bejeweled* next to Caroline. David watched her look back to the fire. She held back tears with a look on her face that combined a mixture of sadness and joy that just seemed to capture her.

"I don't suppose I need to offer you a life preserver?" David asked, walking over to her and embracing her.

Jessica shook her head no.

"Of course not," David said.

She'd want every inch of the Earth's beauty surrounding her at the time of any near-death experience, he thought. Besides, she was an expert swimmer.

"You miss them already, don't you?" David asked.

Jessica nodded and looked up to him for help.

"I think you're starting to get me, David," she said with tears flowing.

He nodded, grabbed hold of Jessica, and held her close in the darkness that was accented only by the fire which they had started up there on the mountainside.

*  *  *

An hour later, the first of a few police lights could be seen scaling the mountain road. David and all sailed away unharmed, safely. Caroline and Jeff stared in wonder at it after having just lit up. The remnants of the fire filled a skyline with a plume of smoke that shot into the sky like ink. Eventually receding into the horizon, David watched as Caroline offered a poke to Jessica, and she refused. Jessica had then gone below for the binoculars.

"Unless the Mexican police force has started outfitting their cars with water hoses, there's not going to be a whole heck of a lot for them to do," David remarked.

"It'll burn out eventually," Jessica admitted, "There's nothing left up there but dirt."

"And if it doesn't?" David asked.

"Then let it burn," Jessica said wickedly. "Let the whole damned thing burn right down."

Jessica stood beside him and put her head on his shoulder while he steered. Her hand reached around his waist, and she held him safely. David wondered exactly what it was he was doing. Perhaps he was falling in love.

# HERE'S THE PITCH

DAVID HOBBS – AGE 32
Summer, 2006

Flinching from the recoil of the imaginary five o' clock bell, the "clock-ers" forced their way towards cramped elevators. Hustling white collars and working girls exited their office buildings under the cover of dusk and hurtled themselves into their routine commute, sprinting about the city, clogging street arteries, destined for the major expressways or overcrowded public transportation. Trains, cars, and buses hauled worker bees all agog with the fresh frustration of a workday concluded and filed away somewhere negligible in their consciousness.

Sufficiently fed their daily deficiencies by a boss or co-worker, they took retribution out on a crowded bus, muttering under their breaths and thrust-ing elbows at the vulnerable ribcages of fellow innocent straphangers (not totally by accident) as they argued and shouted at one another. Train pas-sengers on their way to the suburbs sought solace from a can of beer, which they cracked open before the train even had a chance to depart the station. The city's subways ripened with bodies baking in the underground heat. Commuters in rumpled clothing, exhausted, and waiting impatiently for the "L" on the platform, fanned themselves with newspapers. Outside on the streets, tailgating begat middle fingers and expletives launched at strangers, while further frustrations mounted, and brake lights lit the expressways like an angry airport runway.

David Hobbs realized these were people with families, he guessed, all with their own sets of different problems. Who knew procreation would speed up your race to extinction? David just didn't give a damn about all that. He chose to limit the stress in his life by not involving himself in family whatsoever. There would just be work, and that was all. There would be no surprises and nothing to shock him. The last time David saw something that surprised him, he was watching some kid right out of college in a shiny new suit buy a fifth of vodka at the convenience store in the building across the street from Graham & Hoffman. David shot the kid a look as if to say, "Just a little something to get through the interview, eh, Kid?" But that wasn't the surprising part. The surprise would come when he walked into the reception area to greet his three o' clock interview and saw the kid there waiting for him. How fooled David could have been if he hadn't seen it. There were arguments from the board about David not actually seeing this superstar whiz kid drinking or smelling of alcohol, but David knew. And he felt bad for the kid. He felt bad for the hypocrisy of it all. At the thought of his own bottle that floated around a spare pair of loafers tucked inside a desk drawer. David reluctantly gave this prized whiz kid an interview. *But aren't we all optimistic in our twenties?* David questioned. He couldn't remember.

Observing all this, David Hobbs journeyed to the bar, which was either three or four blocks away. He couldn't remember exactly what street it was on. It was the first sweaty commute of the summer, and the all-important, image-conscious David acknowledged the jacket was perhaps overdoing it, but he sacrificed himself through a thin layer of sweat in order to look good. For David, the only thing he sought after outside of work (besides sex) was the closest bar stool.

David watched the foot traffic surpass him as he made his way to the bar. It was time for one celebration or another, and most of the important people from his company would be there. The surge of foot traffic that David fought against pushed past him in search of shortcuts through buildings and alleys and side streets, faster bus routes, and detours around construction, anything to save themselves precious seconds. David just hid behind his black suit and a pair of sunglasses and let go a few exhales as he walked leisurely against the ground rush. But today there was actually cause for celebration. Oh sure, it was so-and so's birthday or something, but

David was coming off a successful new business win. It wasn't everyday you could land multi-million-dollar, blue chip clients to your agency's roster. The only thing that remained was securing a few signatures on the dotted line. Having put a couple hundred million in the company's back pocket along with the pending announcement of summer hours and morale was about to go through the roof. David could look forward to long lunches in the bar. Most importantly, when the AJ Quality Retail account signed the contracts in the morning, it'd be the nail in the coffin for David's certain ascension to the board of directors. Maybe not this summer, but definitely by next Christmas. In the sixty-five year history of the company, no one could ever claim being a board member at thirty-two years old. *Not too shabby,* David thought. Hell, he already had an Executive Vice President's salary with nothing to spend it on but bar tabs.

David could let loose a little bit after the stress of the pitch. Perhaps he'd stay just sober enough to hand in the signed contracts to the Graham & Hoffman lawyers in the morning. Then he'd be able to continue the party. No doubt word had already spread about the win and David wouldn't find it too hard to accept the credit. *So it would be a good night*, he thought.

The bar was just another block away and David forced himself against the throngs of nervous-looking, sweaty commuters headed for their homes. David watched them drop candy wrappers to the sidewalk and toss cigarette butts on the ground while a multitude of police cars burned hours of gas lapping city blocks announcing their presence.

A summit of global corporations meeting to discuss their effect on the environment was taking place. Apparently some people still weren't pleased with what was happening to the planet and were taking it out on the corporations and individuals that were responsible. Burly, tough Chicago cops that would not be fucked with stood on street corners and studied David and the rest of the swarm. To David, it appeared they were looking for somebody.

What was all the rush for, this mad dash, David asked himself. He had already sold his soul to his company in search of the almighty dollar and a hefty title, so a conscience was unnecessary. Once he was able to admit that he had long abandoned his soul, he felt less guilty sitting on all those bar stools. David felt that, ultimately, life was just about killing time before death anyway. Going out on top was David's goal, no matter who he had to step on to get there. And who cared if death came at forty-five or eighty-five. David hadn't planned on dealing with his family's long history with arthritis. Or cirrhosis, for that matter.

At work he was taught that you bleed loyalty for your brand. Whatever it was that you might be hawking. It transformed you like a vampire taking the first gnaw on a fresh neck. The job transfused your old blood with a new, corrupt version. Dying for the brand made sucking in a salary that rivaled most third world countries' GDP seem worthwhile. But even the paycheck seemed secondary now. Relief came after the walk into the office, usually fighting the hangover. It came in hiding underneath the bed of fluorescent lights, working on inconsequential brands, and trying to figure out new ways to sell people crap they didn't need. And from there on, you left your blood to the company, transfusing it in sweat and angst and phone fights with the press and lawyers and contracts. Thankfully from the new business side, David's role allowed him to sell his soul multiple times over and for whatever prospective client that lay out there for the taking. They bled him dry over and over. Wins mattered. No one pitied David when accounts chose rival agencies. No one slapped David on the back and said, "Don't worry, champ, we'll get 'em next time." When everything was done to excess, there needed to be success. Failure was only fuel for rumors and an opportunity for hangers-on to garner support. Thankfully, David very rarely lost. *Sell your soul for the almighty dollar time and time again*, David thought. It used to be that he had a whole heck of a lot to sell. Not anymore, it seemed.

And there it was. His current state of affairs summed up on a brisk, sweaty walk to the bar. It was make the board of directors, which, with the contract signing tomorrow would be well within reach, and beyond that, there wasn't much else to do in life, was there?

He reached the bar, where he would celebrate somebody's something or other. There'd be time to torture himself with planning and foresight later. It was the booze that beckoned him, and he realized that someone was either coming or going, and it didn't really matter who it was anymore.

With the shutting of the door, the bar was closed off to any sort of natural light, and fresh air quickly became a commodity. The smell of crusty ashtrays flooded David's nostrils with stale smells of desperation. Bartenders clobbered down pint glasses upon coasters on the large oak bar. Neon light pierced the air, and rapid conversations impeded absorbing any one of them. David entered the bar and began his victory lap. He made his way inside in search of his crew, his coven of assistants, which consisted of twenty-something girls. He had given them strict orders to secure a booth. The long, narrow bar took up most of the space inside the first floor, offering precious little room to maneuver around young women. Occasional contact with a cheek or two was unavoidable (and generally quite pleasurable even if the contact was completely accidental). David finally got an answer as to why they were all there when he saw the balloons and a large "good bye and good luck, Charlie" sign posted above the bar. David stood and wondered at the sign and whether or not he'd really live long enough to get one himself. Someone patted him on the back, suddenly relieving him of any thoughts of the future.

"David, hey, you came! Thanks!"

David couldn't quite remember the man's name, but he knew he sprang from accounting.

"Yeah, yeah," David said, "wouldn't miss it."

"Well, we'll see you around, I guess, right?"

"No, no, I was just coming in," David admitted not too caringly.

The annoying person pauses too long at his side, and David found the silence uncomfortable. Thankfully the stranger finally broke in, "Well, we've been through a lot of battles, David. A lot of wars."

"Yeah, sure, sure," David scanned the bar. He spotted his crew in a booth not far from the bar. It was one that held a prime vantage point for the entire bar. He had taught them well.

"Hey, I heard we were pretty close on the AJ Quality Retail account," said the man, still finding things to say to David.

"It's a done deal. We start work next quarter. The client will be in tomorrow morning first thing to sign the contracts."

"That's great, David. Good for you!"

"Yeah, I'll see you around, huh."

David, disinterested, bored, and afraid to be seen with this person, left the man quickly to make his way through the crowd. Faces approached him, moved past him slowly, and stared at him as he went by. David ignored the throng of uninteresting people until finally he was forced to stop. Some young kid had grabbed David and hugged him while shouting, "Summer hours, woo!" David wondered how long the kid had been here. In between the laughing and chuckling David lifted a shot glass from an unsuspecting waitress's tray as she went. He hadn't seen a drink since lunch, and the whiskey warmed him.

Spotting the coven of young account girls that he had hand picked out of college, David smiled and walked over to the booth that they had secured. Karen, the eldest of the three at thirty, started, "I don't know why you wanted a booth. You never sit down for very long."

"Doesn't matter," David responded, "It looks good."

The girls slide in closer to one another as a largely out of shape David forced himself into the booth. Stephanie, at twenty-five, was next in age. And then there was sweet, sweet Emily, who was barely twenty-three. He had scarcely tasted her lips when she spouted that she still had a boyfriend who was back at college. David almost burst with laughter; he told her that when she was ready he'd be there. They all worked hard. And David worked them hard, showing no remorse. That was the idea. To beat the hell out of them and see which one passed.

"Did you say good-bye to Charlie?" Karen asked.

"Who?"

"Charlie in accounting. It's his going away party. You know, the reason why we're all here. I just saw you talking to him."

David takes a slug from a cold beer, which was just placed in front of him by a familiar waitress. "That was Charlie?"

Karen and Stephanie sighed disapprovingly. Emily showed no feeling, simply staring off into space. Emily was a bit ditzy. It showed when she was presenting in front of large groups. But Emily was great at grunt work, and David needed a soldier for that. Not to mention the fact that she wasn't too hard on the eyes, and she wore expensive perfume that David liked smelling when he walked in to the office each morning. It was usually the first scent that his numbed sense of smell would begin working on each morning. Emily was staring off into space, and David realized she was probably thinking about the long distance relationship she'd been in. She'd need just a bit more time, David thought.

"So, we thought you were babysitting Thomason tonight," Stephanie said in reference to the new client that would be signing the contract in the morning.

"No, he said he just wanted to chill out by himself. Who knows? He's probably got a chick in town."

Stephanie was a brain, but Karen combined it all: good looks, intelligence, and cunning. She'd be replacing him eventually, and David questioned whether or not that would be done so willfully. Karen was an exceptional lover. The best of the three, he surmised.

A brief announcement from the CEO (who was rarely seen) yielded stifled yawns throughout the crowd, and David noted the fact in case he has to give the same speech someday. Summer hours are indeed confirmed, and cheers ring out. Then, tactless as ever, the CEO asked if someone would like to say a few things on Charlie's behalf.

No one volunteered. The bar was ridiculously silent.

"I would," David said at last, vaulting up from the booth and pinching Karen on her upper thigh, unbeknownst to the crowd. The crew at the table stared at each other, mortified by what was about to take place.

"Listen," David started, grabbing a fresh beer from the bar, "I know there comes a time when you and I are pounding out a presentation, or a report, or some analysis or whatever..." David could thrive on drama, the pitch, the sell, and all the eyes peering up to him. The attention, the spotlight was right where he liked to be, with it shining brightly upon him. "...and we may not see that light at the end of the tunnel. And we just say, 'Fuck it, I'm done. I'm toast. I can do no more work this evening. Tomorrow is a new day.'

David slowed the pace some as he strolled the length of the bar. Past the creative teams drawing giant penises on cocktail napkins. Past some other account teams arguing about design flaws in the new conference room. Finally, he reached the section of the bar where accounting was hanging out.

"But I want to tell you about Charlie and what I know of him in that situation..."

Back in the booth David's girls scrutinized his performance.

"What's he doing?" Emily whispered, leaning in, seemingly interested in the events surrounding her.

"He's either sinking, or swimming." Stephanie conceded.

"He'll swim," Karen responded. "He'll always swim."

They leaned back in the booth to enjoy the rest of David's discourse.

"And when most people would just chuck it and go home, Charlie would come to me and say, 'David, I'm here for you. We've got a battle to fight. And a war to win.' Isn't that right, Charlie?"

"You bet," Charlie offered to David and the crowd.

"Well, we fought a lot of battles. And we won a lot of wars. And it'll be tough to see him leave. To go…"

David hadn't any idea where Charlie was headed. Hopefully it wasn't terminal cancer. David quickly found Karen's face in the audience for help. She mouthed the words clearly, "Back to school."

"Back to school. For Heaven's sakes, it's great for you…and bad for us. But here's to you! To Charlie!"

David held his beer high. The bar saluted and announced in unison, "To Charlie!"

David saluted himself by taking the beer down in one long gulp. Others joined him. Charlie tried but failed. Many a back slap and intoxicating hug followed David's speech. Charlie was convinced that he was loved and appreciated. David, getting dizzy from the rapidity of shots and beers that he'd machine gunned over the past few minutes, eventually found his way back to the booth.

"Thanks for that," David said, "I owe you one, Karen!"

"You've owed me one for as long as I can remember."

"Well, put it on my tab then. Come on, name another boss that lets you drink for free. Eat at the best restaurants. Go out to the hottest clubs…"

"And work my ass off hung-over as shit the entire next day," Karen responded. "That would be you."

"Well, you're damn good at your job hungover or not," David praised.

"I suppose I should just take my compliments when I can get them."

"Darn tootin'," David said.

David raised a fresh shot to his mouth. As he felt the sting of the whiskey touch his lips, he devotedly chased it with a cold beer. In a few minutes the sting wouldn't be there, and hours later complete numbness would ensue. Through the rare moments of sobriety, when guilt pinballed through his sober consciousness, he thought of her. Of Jessica. It was before the drinking caught hold of him and wrestled his senses away. David fought the sadness that swallowed him. He imagined Jessica pleading for him to return to her and he tried like hell to rid the past full of memories from his brain with all the booze he could find. And he thought back to all the times she lay next to him and he was happy. There were no memories that he relived now. It was all just a steady stream of one semi-conscious life.

"David," the CEO said, patting a liver spotted hand on David's shoulder, "thanks for bailing us out back there with Charlie."

"Oh, no worries. It was fun."

David warned his brain to stop slurring words, if indeed he was.

"Did Thomason ever sign that contract?" the CEO asked.

"He'll be in tomorrow morning to sign. I assume with his lawyers."

"Good, that's great news. Let me know when you have the signed contract. PR is ready to go. Hey, you gonna do the Mac this year? Or are you going to give us old timers a break like last year."

David had cut himself off from the race to Mackinac Island, the largest freshwater race in the states. It was something casual for David now, more a booze cruise than anything really challenging. David muttered something about being away, and the CEO eventually left David alone.

"You know you took me here the first day I started at G&H," Karen waxed. "You've put on a few pounds since then."

David had stopped monitoring his weight gain. It was an unwinnable war, and he just didn't give a damn anymore.

"Yeah, well, how am I supposed to find time to exercise when I'm entertaining all the time?"

"Or drunk all the time," Karen declared.

Another round of shots eventually landed at the booth. David thought for sure Stephanie was behind it.

Karen said, "I've got to go." She impatiently fights her way from the booth.

"Karen, wait," David stands and grabbed her arm as she passes, stopping her in her tracks, "Will I see you later?"

"I'll see you later," Karen said curtly and snapped. "Good-bye, David."

David plopped himself back down in the booth. Upon surveying both Emily and Stephanie, they seemed quite disinterested with him for the moment. Stephanie and Karen were good, close friends. Emily as well. But they warred when it came to David. The liquor continued to warm him and leave him uncaring. It pushed aside memories into a pile of sloppy drunken thoughts laying about some unkind heap, drowned in alcohol and deposited in the back of his mind. More and more David's consciousness sent information to that space. And more and more David enjoyed its residence there.

* * *

A few short blocks away, just across the street from the Graham & Hoffman office building for that matter, a homeless lady decked out in a mass of crusty, old clothes shuffled down the aisles of a convenience store, grumbling at the products to the left and right of her which she knew she could not purchase. The night manager, a boy in his late teens, took note and stood dutifully monitoring each mirror so that not too much product would disappear under his watch. A large physics book and a car magazine joined him on the counter. The teen watched as she pulled a cereal box from its appropriate place on the shelf. He watched as the bag lady spoke to the crazy looking animated bird on the front of the box.

The teen manager interjects upon their private conversation, "Listen, lady, if you're not going to buy something, then you've got to get out."

More grumbling at the cereal box emanated from the mass of clothes that moped up and down the aisles. A lump of humanity stood hidden under rags and what were once respectable forms of clothing. Small, slender fingers poked free from underneath a long sleeve and find the seal on top of the cereal box.

"All right, that's enough!" the teen manager said and hopped spryly over the counter. It was too late to be arguing, and he had homework to catch up on.

A smile spread across the bag lady's face. With her back turned to him she used the mirrors above to monitor his approach. Her hand stealthily deposited something inside the cereal box. She quickly folded the top down and put the cereal box back on the shelf.

"That's enough," the teen manager said, grabbing a hunk of clothes and finding only a rigid and wiry shoulder blade to grab onto. "It's time to go."

One last smile was sported for the cameras above, and her middle finger goes up in front of her chest, away from the teen manager's sight, only for the cameras and whoever might be watching later.

The manager adjusted the boxes of cereal so they stand straight, tall, and undisrupted. He hustled the mound of clothes (silly for such a warm day, he thought) towards the exit. She willingly conceded and soon found herself ejected from the corner store and walking quickly down the sidewalk in the quiet night air. She stole a quick glance to monitor the store clerk, but then her line of vision moved more obviously to the workout center above, where a jogger pounded a treadmill. The manager watched the figure move away from the store and resumes his interest in his car magazine for the moment. He exchanged the magazine for the large physics book.

Much further down the street and with much more pep, the homeless lady crossed the Dearborn St. bridge. The pile of robes and dirty clothes finds the Chicago river. Breaking into a jog now, with the homeless lady disguise completely removed, the figure is revealed to be a young, elfish-looking girl in her early twenties, with a thin, gaunt face and short, spiked hair matted down from sweat. A skinny frame reveals shoulder blades that poke through the top of a sports bra. At first glance one might suggest the girl is anorexic or possibly even malnourished. She took short quick steps down the street until she found the correct alley. She moved spritely and knew the course expertly although they'd never gone through a dress rehearsal for fears of being identified through the surrounding buildings' cameras.

Very quickly she receded from view. Inside the alley a black van waited. A nod of her head signaled the absence of a tail and the side door of the van jerks open allowing her entrance.

"Matthias, put that fucking gun down already," barked a voice from in back of the van.

The command is obeyed. Guns lowered. The van's engine exploded to life.

Back at the store the teen's eyelids fluttered in front of the physics book. A bell electronically wired to the back door stirred him from his soft slumber. The teen manager was behind in class. He scolded himself silently for procrastinating. A fresh customer stalked the aisles vigilantly. It was the jogger from upstairs; he had been coming in each night for a week straight. The man that had been pounding away at the treadmill popped his head inside the refrigerated coolers, grabbing a red colored sports drink. He did this each night he was in town. He was famous for jogging. He was famous for rigid schedules at the conferences. He kept his personal schedule rigid, too. To a fault.

Placing the sports drink on the counter in front of the kid with the textbook, he scraped coins from a waterproof Velcro wallet from inside his tracksuit. There were still notes from the conference to go over. The sugar would do him good this late at night. He hated the thought of going through his notes from the conference but knew that it was necessary. Receiving the change from the kid behind the counter, he saw from the front window a blacked-out van pass the store slowly, and he took note to mention it to building security in the morning. The important man in the tracksuit took his change and walked back towards the rear door down the cereal aisle.

A short, quick explosion that lasted no longer than it takes to pop a blown up paper bag, hurled glass, concrete, and plastic through the front of the store. It was a crude, messy, and powerful blast. At this time of night there was no traffic to impede body parts tossed into the street. Car alarms blared instantly and obnoxiously as plastic bags dripping with blood rained from the air. Liquids poured from the store out to the sidewalk as beverage machines spewed their brew through shattered plastic laminate. Blood dripped liberally from the front windows' jagged, splintered glass. Bits of both bodies mingle together messily, caught by the pointy chards of glass hanging there limply. There is not much fire, but the explosion is heard for a mile. Obnoxious and alarming sound waves bounced back and forth off the facades of the Loop office buildings bearing startling sounds not previously heard in these buildings' lifetime.

\* \* \*

Returning to the booth after greeting a still-going-strong horde of well-wishers, as well as accommodating a much-needed trip to the bathroom, David staggered freshly numbed from a shot and a beer. Perhaps it was luck that David fell into the correct booth. There sat the two remaining recruits, molded in David's vein. And that was the way he liked it.

"Where have you been?" Emily questioned.

"Just briefing the creative team on what's coming up for next quarter's work with this AJ Quality Retail account. I think. Either that or I just made a great connection for pot at the office."

"Very professional," Stephanie said.

The music apparently grew louder as the night progressed. In reality, David was just drunker and felt like he had to talk louder. David looked to the crowd around the bar and sized up the endowments, looking for his one girl on this one night. It was a decidedly younger crowd that remained. David noted the approximate ages and wondered what he'd been doing when he was their age. Young and stupid. Willing to do anything for a beautiful girl. Or perhaps he was working back then. Bringing his attention back to the booth, he found a mop of hair that belonged to a young boy, maybe twenty-one, who was passed out on the table.

"Who's this?" David asked.

"Intern," Emily responded quickly, doing her best not to showcase the slight slur.

"Well, what's he doing here?" David asked.

"Said he had some package for your new client, Thomason. It's right here. Seems like he had a few at the bar waiting for him to show."

Stephanie pulled a large FedEx box from underneath the intern's arm.

"Jeez, what is he? Eighteen? What's he doing in here?"

"He's dedicated, David. Didn't you used to be like that?"

"Yeah, well, I guess I could just hold my liquor better."

"Mom must be so proud," Stephanie remarks.

"When I see her, I'll ask her."

"Well, I'm off," Emily said, "Steph, you coming?"

Stephanie shot a glimpse to David. He shook his head no.

Emily, quiet and depressed in the office recently, would probably spend all night talking to her boyfriend at college on the phone. In all likelihood she would spend the rest of the evening after that crying into her pillows. Or perhaps it would be a combination of both. The two girls jockeyed the rough, crowded bar, appropriately saying their good-byes. David, left virtually

alone save the passed out intern, dodged more questions from curious pas-
sersby about his ambition towards the Mackinac Island race this year.

While David avoided these questions, he let his eyes examine the crowd.
The bite and invincibility of youth had been lost from him for some time.
The fake excitement provided by work no longer pushed him. The youth
inside the bar, with so much to see, and so much to be disappointed by, just
kept slapping each other on their backs. They threw casual winks and flirty
exchanges back and forth, ambling forward in age. David presumed he'd
just keep bringing in business. *Keep making the company money.* But David felt
the cold and callous, uncaring inevitability of old age. Everyone here cared
little of his accomplishments, David noted, as he watched the CEO leave
with a young woman who was not his niece. David recalled his theory about
killing time before death and suicide.

"Well, Kid, I'm going to see Thomason in the morning, so I shall
relieve you of this box and deliver it in person."

David seized the FedEx box and tucked it inside his shoulder bag.
Exiting the booth, his legs a bit wobbly, he felt the room spin. It was all
smiling and laughing now amongst the crowd while David further ignored
inane questions about sailing. They were either sucking up to him or needed
advice badly, the giving of which wouldn't benefit David, so why bother?
Stiff and stoic, far from sober, he wandered the crowd, laughing at jokes he
didn't understand and from people he didn't even know. It goes on like this
until he finds a skirt he likes, on a body he approves, and a face he can't quite
recognize (very likely an account girl from another agency). She's young.
A tight behind shuffled with the music as it moved through the crowd.
One last shot and a beer is fuel for the rest of the evening. The fog of a surreal drunk surrounded him. The FedEx box is quickly forgotten but safely
stored in his bag. He felt the back slaps as he moved through the crowd.
He smiled and moved towards the skirt that continued on. Turning around,
she said something to him, inaudible, but he just continued to follow her.
There's a couple that's close to sex near the men's room. They are all hands
and tongues but still have their clothes on. David realizes that it's himself
and the girl, the skirt, upstairs in a closed off section of the bar. It is not an
account girl. It is the waitress that had been eyeballing him all night. She's
young, he can tell, because she's a sloppy kisser. No matter anyway.

The explosion traveled through the loop rattling the plate glass window near the front entrance to the bar. The sound is mostly drowned out by the deafening banter. David briefly took note of the disturbance and attributed it to the background music. A small flash is seen by people at the bar as it reflected off of storefronts blocks away. The crowd would hear the fire trucks and ambulances a few minutes later as the loud sirens sent piercing shrieks throughout the night.

# GO FISH

*DAVID HOBBS – AGE 21*
*August, 1995*

Stirring from a slumber that had been infused by the smoky, charred embers of tattered clothes, David awoke from unrepentant nightmares of massive skyscrapers burning to the ground. At some point in the middle of the night he and Jessica had disrobed (separately) and tossed their smoke-encrusted clothes overboard. Floating away in the Atlantic, the night covered the slick of gasoline that lay secreted atop the water, trailing the barely visible pile of left-behind clothes. It was their only evidence from the aftermath of a night of fire in the jungle. Dutifully, Jeff and Caroline had relieved David at dawn, and he'd slept soundly for most of the morning.

It had been a glorious start to their getaway. Realistically they knew there would be no one chasing after them. Even overestimating the communication measures and procedures that lay between customs and the Mexican police force, the *Bejeweled* had plenty of time to get home. David and Jeff both concluded that even if the policía had bothered checking the manifests and logs at their port, they'd be well beyond Mexican waters by then. Given the security guard's propensity to hang in bars for three to four days at a time, there likely wouldn't even be a description of Jessica and David handed over to the U.S. coast guard for at least a week. And it was awfully dark out there. Four more days and there wouldn't be another boat in sight until an hour or two before they hit the port of Miami.

The quiet calmness of the sea was welcome. Once fully awake, David gathered together the day's tasks and duties inside his head. The safe, secure rocking of the sailboat was conducive to David's thought process. There'd have to be a plan formulated concerning Jessica. Looking over to one of the empty cabins that lay aft, it seemed she had woken first. Perhaps she was topside giving hippie lessons to the two humpy kids. The night carried their clothes far. Jessica had commandeered a pair of jeans shorts from Caroline as well as a few t-shirts from David, which she hadn't bothered asking to borrow.

What to do about Jess? Where would she go once they hit customs in Miami? Would the story end there? *Where will she go? Where is it that revolutionaries go?* David let the issues stir in his mind while he woke. He awoke even further when he heard Jeff shout, "Man overboard."

David's pulse fired through his veins as thoughts formed of a drugged out Caroline lying motionless in the water below. His mind rehearsed CPR as his feet stomped up the ladder leading to a big, bright Sun. Jeff and Caroline stood at the bow pointing and laughing good-naturedly. As David approached, he could see what it was they found funny. There, naked in the sea, swimming about the Ocean, was Jessica's pasty white butt bobbing atop the water.

"Just what the hell do you think you're doing?" David asked her from a few feet away. Jessica was treading water now, and just far enough from sight that David couldn't see any other of her other naughty parts.

"Exercising. Come on in! The water's refreshing!"

David frowned, and she could tell he disapproved.

"Don't you know there are sharks out there that'll swallow you whole?" David asked with genuine concern.

"Not me."

David watched Jessica swim about and withheld a comment about sharks' impartiality to skin and bones. Her pale butt bobbing up and down from time to time amused him, and David observed the sense of freedom that surrounded her. Swimming naked in the ocean seemed like she was merely appeasing Mother Nature by performing good deeds. Jessica smiled and splashed water at David playfully.

"Come on in!"

"No, thanks. We've got to keep moving."

"Aw, don't be a poopy-head."

Jessica smiled suggestively but sensed her time in the water was limited. Her bare shoulders and arms gently and gracefully spread through the water as she approached the boat.

"Who gave you orders to drop anchor?" David asked and looked in Jeff's direction.

"She said she was going swimming, Captain," Jeff shied from David apologetically. "There was no stopping her."

"Yeah, that seems to be a recurring theme. Next time, leave her behind."

"Ya' know, I'm right here. I can hear you."

"Speaking of behinds...well, that's good you can hear me then because I won't have to say this again. The next time you pull something like this we're not waiting around, you hear me? Now, get back in the boat." David pulled a small aluminum ladder from its mount and dropped it over the side for her. Jeff and Caroline continued to laugh at Jessica's daring.

David turned around and traipsed back down the ladder to the master cabin, mostly to give her privacy as she toweled off and put her clothes back on. David could hear her grumble as his face hit the pillow, "I'll break you yet, David Hobbs!"

David shut his eyes and tried not to imagine her above deck. Carefree and naked. Bare skin sucking up potent rays of sunshine. An imaginary, seductive look perhaps tossed his way in search of his embrace, her arms locking around his frame seeking security. Another hour of sleep drowned out any further thoughts of her.

* * *

A serene and peaceful afternoon was interrupted sharply by a constant *thump-thump-thump* of a noise coming from above deck. David and Jeff, looking up from the chart table and through one of the portholes, noticed Jessica's legs active. Besides the sticks were some of Jeff's father's fishing equipment that apparently had been dug out from a storage locker. It seemed Jessica had taken it upon herself to break out one of the crusty, old fishing rods while they were anchored.

David and Jeff stood topside now to check on the commotion. Jessica's biceps flexed each time she snagged what looked to be rather large groupers. *Good eating*, was David's first thought. Peering into the storage cooler off to the side, David noticed piles of beautiful, lengthy grouper that Jessica had landed.

"You know those have to be twenty inches when they're out of season," David said.

David, giving the fish she pulled in another look, realized they were easily thirty inches. *Monsters*, David thought. Caroline stood next to Jess with a pair of pliers and piles of bait at the ready. The pliers didn't seem to be necessary as Jessica unhooked the fish with ease.

"Yup," was all Jessica could say while removing the hook from the fish's mouth in one stroke. She never stopped moving while she was on the boat, and she worked hard as a crewmate. Perhaps not quite as experienced as David would have preferred for a crewmate, but it was obvious she'd seen time on a boat. Jessica picked at the bait Caroline would hand her in order to find a good sized chunk of cut up squid. She'd pause only to take in brief, brilliant glances towards the sea or to examine a school of fish going by, but that was all.

"You brought your own squid?" David asked.

"It was at the market," she countered. "What can I say, I like to fish. Is that okay?"

David and Jeff watched as Caroline picked through each fish in the cooler and tossed the smaller ones back over the side. David inspected the cooler to see half a dozen of the prettiest grouper you'd ever see bathing in crystal clear ice cubes.

"Must be a nice reef underneath," Jessica remarked.

"Sonar didn't show anything," David admitted.

"Just lucky then," Jessica said and gave a shoulder shrug. "We'll have some good eats tonight." Her eyes never veered from the fishing line.

She'd have to go back at some point, David considered. What the hell, David thought, why not come right out with it, "So, uh, what exactly are we going to do with you?"

Jessica fiddled with the fishing pole nervously.

"You mean little 'ole me?" Jessica said and smiled sheepishly. Then, much more serious, Jessica turned to David and fought the Sun in her eyes. "You can dump me. Just get me five miles or so from the beach. I can take it from there."

Jessica tossed another grouper back in the sea. David frowned, insulted, and said, "I don't think so, Toots."

Jessica stopped fishing for one moment to look at David.

"I don't want you in any jeopardy," she said shyly.

David, putting aside thoughts of harboring a fugitive responded, "You've got a passport, right?"

"Yes," she had said too quickly, "I have a passport."

David thought better of it.

"Let me rephrase that. You've got a legal, legitimate passport?"

Jessica offered no response and turned back to her line.

"Figures," David said. "Well, we'll make it work, won't we?"

Jessica looked back to David through the Sun, recognizing his admission.

"As long as you're okay with it. Looks like you're stuck with me."

David got brief nods from Jeff and Caroline, which were then accompanied by smiles.

"Well, can you tell me why it is I keep letting you walk all over me?"

"Because you just can't resist me, David."

Jessica placed her fishing pole aside, walked up to David, and threw herself in his arms. David liked being around her. The feeling of her touching him. He didn't want her to leave. He could feel her energy and the sense of ease surrounding her infect him.

"Perhaps not," he said.

The boat continued to sway in the face of the wind and anchor setting. Jeff marveled at the fish that she had caught, and Caroline stared at the bucket of bait. David and Jessica stood joined in an embrace aboard a boat in the middle of the Gulf of Mexico. A summer Sun warmed their bare skin, and their hearts began to burn wantonly.

\* \* \*

Below deck, David stood at the chart table and kept an eye on the legs of Jeff and Caroline as they stood at the helm. As the Sun had set, David had been relieved, and now he was charting their course. The slow methodic rocking of each tack eased David's nerves. He hoped sleep would come soon. It would allow David the freedom from thinking about how to approach Jessica.

The sound of the hatch closing disturbed David from his thoughts. Wondering if it was Jeff with further questions regarding the course or Caroline rifling through her knap sack in search of a lighter, David turned his head for verification. It was, in fact, Jessica who'd come below. Reeking of the sea and the salty air with skin burned from a torching Sun, she approached him slowly. It wasn't until he sensed her breasts immediately next to him, nearly touching his back, that he decided to swivel around to face her.

Instinctively she would be curious as to their whereabouts, but that was not why Jessica had gone below. She ignored David when he began talking about wind speed. In fact, she had not uttered a single word since entering. She just stared straight into David's eyes as she moved closer. Her eyes, failing to even blink, blasted away at his defenses. They both knew that it was time.

David stood and faced her. Refusing to wait for her plea this time, he immediately pushed his lips onto hers. Jessica withstood the force and eventually matched it with her own intensity. Their tongues thrust into one another's mouths, and the sounds of silence were broken only by sharp grunting noises as they kissed their way to the master cabin, knocking things off shelves as arms and legs flailed wildly. Finally, upon reaching the bed, a "here let me" was spoken as David helped Jessica anxiously remove her t-shirt and bikini top. Jessica sent out a moan as his hands fumbled about her bare breasts.

David tried to be gentle and caring, which was how he was taught to be, at least the first time, with any new lover. Jessica, however, was on a mission, and they paused briefly only for the condom application. They had been roaming about the bed together madly, and it was Jessica who steered David away from foreplay and straight to intercourse.

For David, it didn't feel so much a mad dash to finish, but more a celebration of relief from pent up frustration. They were a team now and had both been forced to let their guard down for one another. To David's surprise, it was Jessica who finished first, not long after she had climbed on top of him. She rode him gently at first, playing close attention to his cues, and she moved with him wonderfully. When David finished, Jessica's face fell on to his chest, and they both heaved and panted.

"Good God, that was nice," Jessica said rolling off of David and reaching for a water bottle by the side of the bed.

"Yes, yes it was," David admitted. "Please, if I..."

"No, no, it's me who's sorry. It's been quite a while, David. Yes, quite some time since I'd done that."

Still modest, and in case Jeff and Caroline couldn't help but peep in, Jessica curled up next to David and reached for the covers. Safely and securely set in his arms, Jessica slept soundly for the next couple of hours. David remained by her side, forcing Jeff to take another shift. Turning to look upon her now, David rationalized the appeal of it as Jessica exhaled soft purrs of breath onto him as she slept. Eventually sleep captured David, too, and the nightmares and constant thinking and processing of thoughts did not come this time. Instead, he just slept.

*  *  *

Later, it was she who woke him. Coming back from the head. David watched her pull on a pair of Caroline's jeans shorts and then adjust her bikini top in the dark. A light from David's watch told him he had about forty-five minutes until the Sun came up. David joined her at the foot of the bed fully intent on probing a little further.

"So, you're too classy a girl to be the love child of hippie parents. What's your story?"

Jessica acknowledged David's question with a quick answer. She'd predicted he'd pry.

"I was Daddy's little girl until, I don't know, something just clicked within me. I just got tired of seeing people on TV needing help. I decided I'd be something else."

"I suppose Mom and Dad didn't take it too well," David broke in.

"No, certainly not. But, one day, oh, God knows when, we'll speak again."

"I'm sorry," David said genuinely and placed an arm around Jessica, which she seemed to welcome.

"Oh, I guess it's all right. I'm not sure how I would take it if I saw my daughter leave in a black van one day, leaving an entire life behind."

"You ever think about going back to…" David realized he hadn't asked her where she was from.

"Ohio."

"Oh," David said. "You ever think about going back?"

"I can't. There's a job to do, David. I believe."

Jessica sat a little sullen and forlorn.

"What about you? Do you have any fun ever or is it just study, study, study in preparation for that tough job in advertising."

"I don't know. I guess I'm good at sailing. Been doing it since I was a kid. But there's more to life than sailing."

"Looks like we've both made sacrifices. Funny how we met, I guess."

"Yeah, it is."

"But, that's what life's all about, isn't it, David? Sacrifices. Sacrificing yourself for what you believe in."

"And sacrificing yourself to a gun that may have been loaded?"

"We knew it was not."

"But if it were? If that security guard decided to pull the trigger on you last night? Is it worth sacrificing yourself?"

"It's a war, David. That's how much we believe."

"That's silly."

"You just don't get it!"

"Teach me," David argued. "Teach me to 'get it.' I don't know what you people are about. We're stuck with each other for four more days. Enlighten me as to your ideas and ways of the war."

"I'll teach you more than that."

David and Jessica rolled back on the bed. This time it was David who was on top. He entered, and this time they were slow. And the sea took them, rocking back and forth in a quiet night. Soft moans and grunts in one another's ear as they made love on the sea.

\* \* \*

Elbows nudged David from a sluggish sleep. Jessica pulled at David's gawky toes until he was fully awake. Jessica stood at the foot of the bed completely naked.

"The first thing I'm going to teach you is how to let loose. Come on!"

Jessica turned around and darted from the main cabin.

"Where are you going?" David called out.

"For a dip. Follow me!"

Giggling up the ladder, almost losing her footing, Jessica hogged the sheets until bare toes touch the guardrail. She offered a quick nod to an early sunset. Bare skin graced the pure air of an immense ocean meeting the tides of open water. The cold water shocked the system. A second splash joined her just a minute later. The cold water was refreshing to her, as she'd been warmed by all the lovemaking.

Barely a full moon traced between the clouds and threw down shadows of Jessica exposed to David down below the surface of the Gulf. David watched her from below as she floated about the surface. The anchor line stretched far into the quiet ocean below. And as he swam up from below David caught her in his arms. Jess fit the model for flawlessness. The water's waves lapped at their bare skin. David, with his self-discovery still intact, found out how much more she cared about most things and how little he cared about everything. He watched her arms tread water pleasurably amongst the soothing gulf's waves, her legs scissor kicking gracefully below the surface. She hung upon his arms and danced with him in the water, offering kisses to his lips amid breaks in the waves. David tweaked her mischievously and further splashing ensued. Jessica shrieked and laughed playfully.

\* \* \*

Back in bed, dry now, both naked bodies lay cocooned under the sheets and housed with scents of salt water and sweat. Jessica's head lay nestled in between David's chest and arms, and she yanked at his chest hairs each time he nodded off.

"Is being what you are as romantic as they make it look like in the movies?" David asked. "Being a...what the hell are you anyway?"

"It's not me. It's not one person. We're a group of people who believe in holding the corporations in this world accountable to the environment and the waste that they disperse all over this world."

"Kind of like acting like police for the world's garbage men."

"No, and I'll thank you not to mock me. We're just out to show corporations that people are watching what they're doing, and they're not going to get away with it any longer."

David thought for a while. "Tell me all the places you've been," David asked of her. He held her tight and secure and sent the tips of his fingers to her bicep tracing lines in her muscles.

"It's not as romantic as it may seem, David. Some days I need to look out a window to remind myself where I am. Sometimes even then I can't figure it out. But we're smart, David. We're really smart. It's not like before, when it was just retribution or revenge. We learned from them. We learned to be better. We can catch them in the act now, David. Research, study, observation, reconnaissance, it's all there for us. It's work...and then we act. And hopefully, we change the world in the process."

Jessica took a brief moment for composure and continued, "It's the dumping and the polluting and the nobody giving a damn. It just eats me up inside. It's agony seeing what's being done to this world."

"There are consequences. There are fines and lawsuits."

"That's right, there are. And they still try and get away with it. Well, we don't let them."

"How many of you are there?"

Silence from Jessica. There would be no answer.

"How long have you been at it?"

"Since right before college. This was just an exercise. My first solo performance. But, I've been in a few fracases in my life, David. I was with some pretty bad people before, and I learned my lesson. This group, we're righteous and honest people, and we've got leaders. We're not out to destroy the world. Just change it."

"And the Indians? You were just sent there to do some damage?"

"Right," she said, "they briefed me on the way. Hidden below deck on some massive freighter I watched everything and read everything there was about the case. And then, they told me to 'do some damage.' That was right before they pushed me overboard. With nothing. That was my initiation. Real romantic, huh? And all we had to do was read the papers, David. We're a small group, really, but we can see everything. You're smart, David. You can help. You can be a real help."

"I have my future already."

"What? Some crummy advertising job after college?"

"At least it's a future. Let me remind you that you had a gun pointed at you a few nights ago."

"Come on," Jessica said, "don't be that guy. Don't be the man who just sucks life and consumes and digests and shits on the world. You could be a tremendous asset."

"Oh, and what would my initiation be?" David asked.

"You need to lighten up, man. You're carrying around enough angst inside you for the *Queen Mary,* let alone this here boat. You are one insanely intense guy!"

"Yes, I've heard that."

Jessica had no immediate reply. She knew one wasn't necessary and that her argument had been quelled for the moment.

"It was a damned fine thing you did, David. Brave."

David remained silent apart from a few overly dramatic sighs at his further recruitment.

"I threw a Molotov cocktail. Please. If I hadn't have done it, you would have. So what?"

"You struck a blow for peace. Those people had their homes plowed down by a bulldozer."

"It seems to me that history has you revolutionary types ending up working for the Man, maybe smarting in some slum of a foreign jail cell out of ignorance, or dead by your own organization's hand or some sloppy mishap. What's it going to be for you? What happens when that new recruit ends up a madman?"

"Oh, I know firsthand about that, David. We clean up after ourselves, though. We hold everyone accountable for their actions. Including ourselves."

In bed, as the hull swayed back and forth, they drifted in and out of sleep between the interspersed bouts of furious lovemaking sessions. In between there was sleep, and they held each other tenderly. Jessica broke a lengthy wordless pattern of silence.

"I can get away for a while, David."

David, without thinking, offered, "Laying low is what they call it. Why don't you come back to school with me?"

Jessica failed to respond quickly enough for David. He pressed further. "You can stay as long as you like. I have my own apartment. Come on, you can make friends with the hippie crowd, and you'll fit right in."

"Right, those wannabes…"

"Well?" David demanded.

"Sure," she said readily.

They celebrated by making love. The lines and shapes of each other's bodies began to seem recognizable to one another. It propelled them to further intensity. They'd also begun to learn what one another liked best and where they liked it.

Eventually they broke for dinner. David had shown Jeff how to appropriately filet a fish. It was almost a shame seeing Jeff practice on the beautiful grouper that Jessica and Caroline had caught. Retreating to the master cabin for a night at anchor, both couples enjoyed one another's company relaxed and at peace. Jessica could still smell the galley which reeked of olive oil, garlic, and breadcrumbs. After a stretch of lovemaking filled with grunts and groans, it was Jessica who formed the first complete sentence.

"Remember what you said to me about falling in love?" she asked.

"I remember," David said with sweat still lining the back of his neck.

"You said that you can't just go out looking for love. That eventually it finds you. Well, I found you, David. And I think you're falling in love with me."

David responded a bit blankly, the only way he could, "I believe you're right."

Their bodies continued to rock together with each wave the callused sailboat soared through. Mostly though they just held each other close that night. David stroked fingers from the top of Jess' scalp through her hair, running his hand down her back and just to the top of her bare bottom, which put her into a calm doze. An occasional creak from the teak and fiberglass bending and swaying with the wind and sea broke between their heavy breaths. Finally, silence and sleep arrived for David, and rest for Jessica.

# LETTING GO

*DAVID HOBBS – AGE 32*
*Summer, 2006*

The arrival to the 21$^{st}$ floor was an exodus from an elevator filled to capacity with fellow, carbon-copy advertising professionals. Immediately the bevy of fluorescent lights with their unnatural illumination doused David Hobbs and the sunken, bloodshot eyes he carried. This morning's hangover was a head splitter, a jack hammer unleashed upon his brain, and his tardiness was not atypical for the average starting time of the advertising executive (refer back to the jammed elevator). More annoying was the fact that he was faced with forced "Hellos" and "Good mornings" from the usual throng of sycophants and just plain-old nice people. Mercifully the door to his office signaled the end to the morning's commute (a bleary taxi ride desperately hoping not to puke) and the annoyances of all the well-wishers. David took note of the fluorescents that blazed away in Stephanie and Emily's offices, but Karen's persisted to grasp the darkness. Perhaps she had found someone else finally.

A solitary brass lamp laying about the old oak desk did what it could. David's stocking feet quickly found the edge of his desk, and he reclined back in a leather chair that he inherited after the funeral. Shaky hands dislodged the stubborn top to a bottle of Tylenol, and he quickly poured a dozen or so out onto the desktop which he fully intended on finishing before lunch. An icepack pulled from the mini-fridge is applied to a forehead that still hears the echoes of the bass from the techy club music that the waitress played during sex. David's sense of smell begins to return. It is signaled by the smell of Emily's perfume invading his nostrils as quiet confirmation. Blinds that may well have been permanently closed shield the world from David's eyes. Thirty minutes of rest or so was allowed before the client was expected. Shortly thereafter David could take the contract up to the lawyers triumphantly and while they were inspecting each line item David would take the express elevator to the nearest bar.

David's office was a cold, dark sanctuary away from the outside world. His minions knew not to bother him until the phones started ringing. Memories from last night's furious lovemaking interspersed with today's consciousness. A roommate complaining about the music and their romping noise. David flushed the toilet on purpose when the roommate was in the shower this morning.

David's phone beckoned with the CEO's name on the display and a red light flashing incessantly. He had known better and turned the ringer off. *Interesting*, David thought, *the CEO this early*. Accolades, perhaps. Perhaps not, his gut told him.

"Yes," David managed as he found his voice and the speaker button.

"David, can you come up to my office right away, please?" the CEO stated, more of a demand than a request. There was nothing else.

The hallowed halls of the 22$^{nd}$ floor beckoned cordially as each of David's oxfords settled in to the lush carpeting. Much nicer than the low grade industrial stuff spread out around the rest of the building, David observed. With his eyes closed, he imagined what life would be like up here. An executive kitchen, his own private bathroom, and an assistant that actually worked hard awaited his move up one floor. David thought that the imagining part wouldn't have to last much longer after that contract was signed. Awards lined the sacred hallways, and David kept a silent count by nodding to each bit of business that he had a hand in bringing in to G&H. Mostly they were print ads from yesteryear, and hopefully soon they'd be replaced. Out with the old, David rationalized, just like with the rest of the old coots roaming the floor.

Assistants usually wary of David's advances offered fleeting looks as David passed the jumbo offices in search of the large corner that overlooked most of Chicago. Lawyers David recognized and usually regarded with welcoming smiles buzzed about the adjacent offices of the board members. David got more strange looks.

The CEO sat similarly to David's position just a few minutes ago. Feet up. Ice pack applied to head.

"We could have done this over the phone," David remarked gently, entering the behemoth of an office. "I was in the same position just before you called."

"Sit down, David," he said and removed the ice pack. A curt response. *It must be something urgent*, David thought. *Something new perhaps?* David didn't get that feeling. He cursed at the cobwebs leftover in his head while a ceaseless pounding tortured his brain. *Like a racquetball bouncing around up there*, David thought. David fed himself motivation: think clear thoughts. Clear thoughts and provide answers when you can.

"Looks like your night ended similarly to mine," David chided, attempting to break the ice in the room. The CEO, perhaps fifteen years his senior, enjoyed his roost at David's last boss's expense. It cost him dearly. It occurred to David to mention the FedEx box still safe and secure in David's shoulder bag. He again forgot about this as he studied the CEO's silver hair and wondered when he himself might go gray.

The CEO walked slowly over to his office door and closed it swiftly. His office was the opposite of David's. Light was everywhere. He had barely looked at David. He studied his thoughts, his words, inside. He was being careful. He had gotten less sleep than David which was very little to begin with. He rubbed his eyes as he moved over to the corner of his desk next to David in the chair. David noticed a hitch in his step. The CEO ached as he sat down on the corner of his desk. Hip pain. Whoever she was, she must have been hard on the old man last night.

"The contract, David," he began, "Thomason and his boys. They didn't sign it?"

"Well, I don't have it yet. I was expecting them at ten."

"You don't understand, David. They're not going to sign it."

"What?"

David, practically jumping from his chair, grabbed at the CEO's phone on his desk.

"I'll get Karen over to the hotel to go pick it up. I was going to give them a half hour and..."

"Thomason is gone. Left on a plane late last night. Before he left he signed a contract with Fisher Steel. It's in all the papers. Graham & Hoffman looks pretty bad."

David put the phone down to listen. The CEO threw the collection of papers in David's lap.

"No, no, this can't happen. He made the announcement after we finished with them yesterday afternoon."

"Well, it's a difficult situation, really. In your state it must be difficult to understand."

"What is that supposed to mean?"

David fought the urge to swear at the CEO of the company he'd been working for his entire life.

"What it means, David," the CEO began, "is that they're gone. Thomason. The account. The business. The money."

The CEO let that sink in. David's face lost any color, and for once he had nothing to offer. The conversation, the words that frequently flowed with ease had dried up in fear and terror and hysteria.

"And that's not all."

"What more could there be?" David asked begrudgingly. The pain in his head had grown from a slight pounding into an alarm bell.

"Karen's gone, too."

"What? Karen? My Karen?"

The CEO, finished with the easy part, rose from the corner of his desk and limped over to the comfort of his leather chair and the safety of his desk in between the ferociously angry David.

"Yes, your Karen...is now with Fisher Steel. It seems one of the items she took with her was Thomason."

"This can't happen. There are legal ramifications here that we can fall back on."

This was completely unfathomable to David. A client stolen from him. Karen had better hope he didn't see her at any of the 4As parties this summer.

"Yes, we're investigating that, David. But, the fact remains that it happened under your watch. Two losses at once for G&H, unfortunately. Something I just had to give a statement about to the press."

Sitting up here in the clouds, in the CEO's office, David realized the point to this conversation still needed to be made. Everything before this could have very well been done over the phone, yet he was supposed to be here.

"I taught her everything I know," David admitted sadly. It was dawning on him how much the loss of one of his team members would hurt him.

"We're aware of that," the CEO replied, rubbing at a forehead worn by stress lines.

"Fisher Steel is a good shop. They're not us. They don't have the manpower."

"No, not yet. Not until they raid some of our ranks."

Corporate cannibalism. It was inevitable once big accounts started moving around a city.

"And it's all because of the careless mistakes you've made on this pitch, David."

The point to his being up here, in the office in the sky, had just been revealed, David thought.

"Well, the board members and I just had an emergency meeting."

"What are you talking about? Do you have any idea how much business I've brought in to this company?"

"That was then, David; this is the here and the now," the CEO said rather irately. "And you fucked up. Royally. You fucked it up. You let Karen take that business, didn't you?"

"What? I didn't know anything about that."

"Right, but you do admit to having a sexual relationship with Karen, correct?" the CEO asked with his cheaters on now and looking down upon David. There was no way out.

"No, I mean, well, I was nailing her on the side, but I wouldn't call it a relationship."

"Unfortunately that's how we're looking at it."

"We" meant the board of directors, but this was all his doing. David was a threat. Too popular and too good. David felt his stomach drop, and he grasped for a safety branch to keep him from falling.

"I would never sabotage one of the G&H clients over some piece of ass. That's not me. I've worked here too damn long. I care too much about this company."

"Don't bullshit me, David. You care about yourself and that's all. No matter. I spoke with the board and that's how we see it going down. Listen, I know things have been rough for you since Lou passed. It's been rough on all of us. Take some time off. Go get your sea legs back."

This was more generic small-talk from the powers that be. They didn't give a shit about Lou. Hell, they practically dug his grave for him. It was time to stop being so nice, David thought.

"Fuck you," David said. He stood up and paced by the window.

"David, I tried to do this gently."

From the floor to ceiling windows David scanned the city and a sky that lead to a non G&H world. *So this is what it looks like when guys toss themselves over the side. This is what it feels like, too.*

"You know damn well Karen did this on her own. And you know what? I'm proud. I'm fucking proud of her. I taught her. I brought her up. And that shit took moxie. And it took guts. Good for her she got one fucking account. Her name will be shit all over town in a few hours. Hell, she probably went to the hotel last night to bang Thomason personally while he signed Fischer Steel's contract. I'm fucking proud of her."

The CEO turned to his desk drawer and grabbed a thick chunky manila sealed envelope. He tossed it to the edge of the beautiful oak desk. David could still smell the ink from the sharpie that had written his name in big bold letters on the front of the envelope probably less than fifteen minutes ago.

The CEO lit himself a cigarette.

"What's this?" David asked.

"It's your package, David."

The realization to the point of the conversation and the actual elimination of his job were two different things until now. Upon convergence, David realized his life was ending right before his eyes.

"Unfortunately for you, David, its time G&H cut all our losses. You're done here. And if the papers this morning are any indication, then you're probably done in Chicago as well. Good luck to you wherever you land. But you are out at G&H, David Hobbs. You are over and out."

There it was. Papers signed and sealed dictating how much severance and profit sharing he would be receiving on a month-to-month basis. And that was it. An envelope sealed with the lick of some admin who printed out the paperwork in HR not fifteen minutes ago. David grabbed the envelope that summed up his entire life.

*** * ***

David left the skyscraper and performed the businessman's walk of shame. He held one box with his very non-descript personal belongings. It was the walk of failure, like going to the corner of the room and putting the dunce cap on. At thirty-two years old, walking into the same building day after day for thirteen years, destroyed after one phone call from the CEO. He had been given an out. A chance to stay. But it would have been torture. Word was already out probably. The giant ego known as David Hobbs had been brought down. He wouldn't have been able to stare any employee in the face. There would be no position of power anymore. He'd have been a lame duck. They wanted him gone.

Now, with sobered blood and walking down the street at ten a.m. on a Friday morning when he should be upstairs partying, he noticed cabs aplenty but decided to walk home. Why not face the humiliation of his fellow straphangers? The FedEx box rested neatly inside his shoulder bag, which David had forgotten about when turning in his ID badge. David's world outside his body moved at lightning quick pace. Inside he burned and stalked towards the lake. This was a stoic walk. Go to the lake, he thought. To the lake. Watch the waves and be calm. David Hobbs was now a beaten man, a zombie. Devastation and loss consumed him, and he felt like a vein had been opened. He didn't know if he should kneel down in the middle of the street for a good cry or light one of the city's garbage bins on fire and throw it through the plate glass window of the G&H lobby. His life had ended in a few short minutes. The Sun blasted down brightly upon him. It blinded him. His last question to the CEO was a reminder of what it was all about: "So, this is how it works," David asked.

"Yes," the CEO responded, "this is how we work."

# SURF'S UP

*WILL FROST – AGE 23*
*June, 1992*

Straddling his surfboard, Will Frost traced his thumb over each depression and thanked Mother Earth for the serene waters of the Pacific Ocean. Perched atop his custom Merrick, alone in an alcove just outside his friend's small beach house, Will swore at the dents he'd put in his old board. Never-ending, sun-bleached, blond hair forced its way down to his shoulders. A lengthy, six-foot-one inch, taut frame of ageless wonder sat fixed under youthful skin. Will fantasized about fifteen solid feet of whitewater, his head planted in Liza's bare bosom, and Kenny and Dooby rolling a fatty. Will had always been described as a low-key and pleasant dude. Just about the only two things he cared about surrounded him day and night. He had good friends, and he surfed just about every day. There wasn't even anything especially stressful in his life right now. It was just that he'd grown short with everyone lately, and he questioned himself this very morning as to why that might be happening. What once was a usually quiet and reserved young man had recently switched to a fierce fighting machine that tore everyone a new one. He'd been in an especially foul mood recently. He was so easily set off that Liza and Kenny had stolen his board from him one night, and Dooby airbrushed a small "Have a nice Day" smiley face on top. Still, out here all alone, he seethed. Will was a beautiful human being, but he knew inside that all was not right. Will's anger sought the surface constantly, now wanting to be unleashed. Will laughed at that stupid smiley face and admired its reassurance. It reminded him of the person not to be. He took deep breaths, closed his eyes, and looked to the Sun that was just rising.

*Water is calm as hell today*, Will thought. Even the pot wasn't helping take away the edge anymore. *Just keep your eyes closed and let everything wash away*, he thought. He thanked the Ocean for its calmness. His feet kicked in the water underneath his board. They itched terribly, and Will was scratching at them constantly. Perhaps it was just the polite school of friendly fish that had encircled him, pecking away at his toes looking for food. Pulling his feet up closer to the surface for inspection, Will noticed the blood. All the scratching had torn away the skin on both feet, and the fish had been tearing at the bits Will had scratched loose. Figuring that all the blood was sure to attract the attention of the three local sharks, Will decided to paddle back to the shore and take care of his wounds. The sharks were named Larry, Moe, and Curly for obvious reasons. It often looked as though they ran in to each other, rather comically at times.

Will could barely feel the water on his skin. Never much of a wet suit guy, he'd taken to wearing one ever since the rash developed. It had started on his feet and made its way up his back. Will wished he could stay out on the water forever, despite the numbness and tingling in his feet. Making his way in finally, he'd heard his name being called from the shore.

Liza, Kenny, and Dooby welcomed him from the shore, waving back and forth, smiling and laughing. As he paddled in, Will began to wave, too. When he grew closer, he noticed that they were actually lined up together screaming in agony. They rolled around the sandy beach, shrieking in pain as limbs began to fall off. Will tried to paddle faster, but couldn't quite make it to the shore. He heard his name called again, but this time it woke him.

"Mr. Frost, I'm sorry, do you need a moment?" the judge asked, "The jury is ready now."

Will was the only one who'd made it out of the hospital alive. Soon after the four of them were diagnosed, Will watched Liza, Kenny, and Dooby melt away in intensive care after months of pain and suffering. They died surrounded by plastic wrapped hospital walls and irritating whirring machines. They wouldn't even let Will give Liza a good-bye kiss.

Will nodded to the judge in approval.

The jury awarded Will and the families of Liza, Kenny, and Dooby one hundred and fifty million dollars. Considering that the four friends were the only family they'd had for the last ten years or so, Will had just become a rich man. Liza's parents had left to follow the Grateful Dead around some time ago leaving the beach house seemingly for good. Liza had never heard from them and they never came back.

Will remembered the day they told him. It was a month or so after the day he'd gotten out of the alcove with bloody feet. It took an entire team of doctors hidden behind the safety of bio-hazard suits to address him. Amazing, Will thought, by what started out as a silly little rash. The doctors spoke to him about his condition, telling him what he would and would not be able to do. *As if they knew what Will was capable of*, he thought. They kept talking, he kept listening, but he thought about how Liza and Kenny might have taken the news. Dooby probably didn't know any better and would have asked them when lunch was. Finally, one of the doctors ripped off the helmet to the bio-hazard suit, and said it, "Will, you're going to die."

He would fight it. Just fight it off. Before they found it, all the doctors had no answer for Will's sudden change in attitude. They guessed it was depression. They referred him to some psychologist who he never visited. It didn't take long to find the toxic effluents and other wastes being dumped into the Pacific, with much of it gathering in their alcove, courtesy of the local greeting card company. The card company, apparently not content in robbing Mother Nature of her trees in order to produce "Thank You" notes with cute, little cuddly kittens on them, was dumping dyes, inks, and other such wastes into the Pacific Ocean. The alcove, their entrance to their surfing world, had been a bath of poisons. It was a place they had entered almost every day for the last ten years. No wonder the sharks never bothered them.

When Will got back to the beach house after getting out of intensive care, he looked at the carcasses of Moe and Larry among dozens of other fish that had washed ashore. Curly's dorsal fin still bobbed up and down well away from the shore. Curly continued on, especially ferocious attacking various fish. Will could see the battles and the thrashing. Curly was taking out his bereavement on every living thing he could find that was possibly guilty for upsetting him. Will admired the tenacity and strict adherence to such a colossal master plan. *If Curly could keep on trucking, so could he*, he thought.

The lawyers for the defense didn't even blink at the amount. Will reckoned it was insurance money he'd be getting. The greeting card company wouldn't even be fazed. It'd be a minor blip to their bottom line.

Will's doctors told him to spend the money quickly.

"At times, you may not be able to walk. Other times you may feel perfectly fine. But the fact of the matter is, Mr. Frost, that your skin is going to stop growing. Basically, it won't be able to keep up with your lesions."

Will was destined to become a human skeleton. He'd bleed to death eventually from an open sore. Will recalled how Liza and Kenny melted away in a month. It took Dooby longer, and he moaned in pain most of the day towards the end.

Will gagged into his bowl of cereal one morning when he saw the CEO of the greeting card company on the news blame the accident on sabotage. Everything about the case screamed of senseless inhumanity towards Mother Earth and fellow man, and now it had been made worse by the failure to assume responsibility. It was unethical, and the EPA would surely see to fines for all the damage done. But there was no punishment to fit the crime. Will was sure the greeting card company had a way around that as well. The greeting card company would be slightly inconvenienced for the three deaths, soon (or maybe not so soon?) to be four. The CEO at the greeting card company would be available for comment after eighteen holes of golf.

The courtroom was cold, and Will left his bandages on. His attorney had advised him to take the bandages off on the stand so the jury could see the progression of the discoloration and the sores, but Will refused. So far, no one had seen Will's face.

Upon leaving the courthouse, looking very much like the invisible man, Will guessed, the press pestered him.

"Mr. Frost, how does the jury's awarding of the one hundred and fifty million dollars help you?"

"My problems can't be fixed by a jury," Will said, being lead down the steps of the courthouse by his lawyer.

"What are you going to do with your share?"

"I promise the money will go to help Mother Earth be cleansed of all its impurities."

Inside the limo, alone finally, Will pulled the bandages off revealing no bruises or discoloration of any kind. The lesions on his face had gone into remission. The doctors had said they might go away occasionally, but their return would grow worse and worse each time. Thus far, his face had been completely hidden. Once-blond locks of brilliant sunshine colored hair had been ruined by the dyes and transformed to a ridiculous frosty silver shade. From the darkened windows of the limo, Will could spy the defense lawyers' Mercedes. He had asked his own driver to follow it temporarily. Following them to an outdoor café, Will watched as the lawyers presented the papers that would provide Will with the multi-million dollar award. They never even offered a legitimate settlement. The CEO never even bothered to get up. He just signed his name and kept on drinking his latte.

Will stood on the dock near the alcove. He watched Curly shuffle around a mile out or so. Curly was intent on destroying everything in his path. His dorsal fin rising above in salute to Will. There was pain, but no tears could come. Perhaps that was a side effect as well. Will stood and watched the Sun set above the water he would never set foot in again. Curly continued to circle out there and dart in and out madly. Everything that Will held dear, his friends, the water, his surfing, had been destroyed. There'd be no more fifteen-foot whitewaters, screaming for a horizon after getting knocked underneath the sea, grabbing hold of knotted up sea grass in desperation, finally getting that first full breath of air. The Sun left the horizon. Curly's dorsal fin continued its patrol, and Will registered his anger once more. Upon leaving the dock, Will unfastened each light bulb lighting the path to the end of the dock, leaving only the darkness.

* * *

The fiberglass and plastic cooler, just large enough to stow a human being, lay on a dolly presented in the middle of the beach house living room. It was a difficult cooler to find, but the wholesale marine store found it for him and wished him good luck on his fishing trip. Apart from the few leftover bongs that Will kept for sentimental reasons, the rest of the beach house had been cleaned out and disinfected many times over. Will could smell the surf even now and knew that it was still foul. Now, with a bit of a limp from the pain in his feet, Will marched to the dolly and opened up the top to the cooler.

Upon opening the lid, the chum Will had purchased polluted the living room air and nearly made him gag. No amount of incense or hashish would ever get rid of the smell of dead fish and blood. But this room had died long ago, Will thought. Soaking and marinating in the chum was the CEO to the greeting card company. He was duct taped at his hands and feet. His mouth had also been taped shut. Will didn't want to hear any more from this man who would be responsible for his death. He offered muffled screams, but Will addressed him.

"I can't wait," Will began patting at one of the CEO's less bloody splotches on a bald head, "to see the company's stock prices once they find you."

More muffled screams and pleas from the eyes of the CEO. There was blood everywhere, splashing about, puddles formed on the carpet in the living room.

"Of course, given Curly's anger at seeing his friends die, they'll probably be finding bits and pieces of you for a month."

Will wheeled the dolly with great difficulty to the dock. Over his shoulder he carried thick, brown, leathery rope that had seen many days in the Sun. More screams, and Will checked the beach. No lights on in any of the nearby beach houses. No one to stop him now. It was almost dawn.

"Now, now, we're just going to feed the fish. One great, big fish."

Will stopped the dolly close to the edge of the dock.

"I'm not sure if Liza or Kenny would approve of this, but given the fact that you're a coldhearted bastard and the fact that they're not exactly here to disapprove..."

Will scooped up some of the chum and started splashing it into the ocean below.

"Curly, I'd like you to meet the man responsible for the death of our friends."

Just as the Sun hit the horizon, spreading light forth, Will could make out the unmistakable triangle of Curly's dorsal fin sailing back and forth among the waves.

Will took the rope and tied a knot around the duct tape and another around the CEO's hands. The other end was tied to the end of the dock. Will plopped more bloody chum into the water.

"Let's see just how pissed off Curly is. Now, I'm not sure if I measured this right, but if I did, it'll probably be pretty quick."

Will kicked the immense cooler over, clumsily, on its side and the strength it took to do so made Will's chest heave with shallow breaths. The CEO's body fell over the side of the dock amid chunks of chum. Splashing below him, fish guts provided the landing pad for the lower half of the CEO's body submerging in the sea. Will heard the unmistakable crack of the CEO's arms dislocating from their shoulder sockets.

"Hmm, half right, I guess," Will said mildly upset he had added wrong but not at all surprised. He looked over the edge of the dock and saw that the CEO squirmed and wiggled helplessly.

At the smell of blood, Will watched Curly's dorsal fin careen towards the dock almost immediately, darting underneath the water sharply. The CEO screamed and kicked endlessly. Exactly what he shouldn't be doing, Will thought, but then again, nothing could save him now.

"You took everything from me! Now, I will take everything from you!"

Will heard the CEO go quiet. The shadow of the twelve-foot, man-eating missile falling upon him sent the CEO into shock. For a half second, Will cringed and felt a few pangs of guilt and doubt about what he'd just done. And then he looked at the skin peeling off of one of his calves.

"All yours, Curly."

After a few moments of thrashing, the CEO went silent. Will watched Curly shoot away with the CEO's legs. His upper body was lifeless, hanging there in front of the Sun. Curly chomped twice on the mass of bloody stumps, and the legs disappeared. Curly came back soon after, just circling the hanging remains. Will pulled out his knife. It took him fifteen minutes to cut through the thick rope. The CEO's body fell and bobbed up and down on the surface, pale and lifeless. A corpse. Curly stole it from Will's view in one quick swipe, dragging it underneath, where Curly gnawed a half dozen times on the chum-soaked corpse.

Will thought it best to leave. Turning back and walking down the dock, he caught his last glimpse of the beach house and of the alcove and of the surf he would never see again in this lifetime. He entered his new, blacked out van and pulled away from the beach house, thinking, while driving the coast, that it hurt even to push the gas pedal. He'd need help. Recruits.

# AN END TO THE MEANS

*DAVID HOBBS – AGE 32*
*Summer, 2006*

Cold waves lapped at the bare feet David dangled solemnly over the lake. An empty bottle splashed and floated gently back and forth against the wall to the man made shoreline. Joggers adhering to the prescribed mental health day graced the lakefront path sending stares in David's direction while not breaking pace. A white collar watching the world go by looks strangely out of place in such a natural setting. A few runners took note of the large cardboard box accompanying this strange person. They acknowledged the general dishevelment and were briefly mindful of the loss of a fellow worker bee. Moving on down the path, they continued their jog or bike ride and quickly forget David's predicament in their thoughts on their own employment situation.

David's toes stretched out playfully tapping the tops of calm waters. Even though it may be summer, the water still seemed numbing to David's lower half. The cool temperature soothed some of David's initial anger. Some of that alleviation could also be attributed to the whiskey David had polished off so quickly while enjoying a bright shining Sun that seemed to display such unlimited potential for a day's achievement. But now, sunbeams faded away softly into a day that David would soon like to forget.

The anger within him subsided, thanks to David drowning his blood in whiskey. Overcome by neglect and carelessness, David resolved himself to the fact that Karen, Thomason, and the AJ Quality Retail account were not immediately responsible and should not be blamed for his firing. Yes, Karen and Thomason had fucked him, and they should burn in hell forever. But David had unknowingly doomed himself by being so loyal to Lou for all those years. It seemed good work didn't necessarily pay off, and that one swift political move made by the CEO could control the fates of many people. The CEO disliked Lou even more. He had been a rebel from the heyday of advertising, a renegade in his thinking and his processes. The board disliked anyone associated with Lou, including David. He should have seen that coming. He was smarter than that. He had blinded himself with alcohol. David spotted the bottle of whiskey bobbing up and down atop the surface of the water. He swore at it silently and cursed his enslavement. His current situation had been dictated by one swift political move and by one mistake that he couldn't even render as his responsibility. David wondered if he'd ever have sobered up enough to see it coming. Amazing how so much in life was day-to-day and routine. And then after thousands of those days piled up, one simple decision could affect the lives of so many.

The CEO had beaten Lou into the ground. Lou had even acknowledged that fact at one point to David. He remembered the conversation.

"They're working me to death. Hoping I'll retire early or maybe go consult at another shop in town."

"So, why don't you?" David asked point blank.

Lou took a deep breath and looked up to David, who was standing at attention in front of his desk. "Because I have a daughter who's getting married in June. I have a son starting college in the fall. I sold my soul the first day I got into this business. It pays too damn well to do anything else anyway."

David had been picking up a lot of Lou's slack lately. They'd even begun to share the corner office. And many bottles of liquor.

"So," David pondered, "you continue to work despite the fact that you know you're not wanted?"

"Until it kills me."

It did. Lou had a heart attack just over a year ago. Maybe David was due to follow him to heaven. Or, David reexamined, if they had indeed sold their souls, heaven would not be the final destination.

David mulled his options. The papers had indeed crucified him. There was nowhere else for him to go.

What the hell, David thought, why not re-boot? Fuck it. Looking down upon the lake just a few feet below his dangling feet, he cursed again at the bottle of booze floating by temptingly in front of him. There it was hovering about. The empty bottle of which David had just polished off the contents. Empty. Just as David felt. He cursed at the alcohol pulsing through his veins, robbing his brain of cogent, rational thoughts. Suicide was an easy solution to this problem. The lake begged for him now, but David knew it couldn't happen that way. Not again.

Getting up from the shoreline in order to prevent an accident, David immediately felt the ground sway. David once again noted the FedEx box inside his shoulder bag. It was time to identify its contents, which David reasoned were rightfully his, considering he had lugged the box all over infinity and back. Bending back down to sit with box in hand, David's world spun from the turmoil of the whiskey churning its way about his brain. David stumbled to the ground awkwardly. His forehead bounced off the cement, and gravel and dust kicked up into his eyes. David tumbled blindly over the side and into the cool Lake Michigan water without much of a splash for any jogger to take note. His shoulder bag encircled him instantly, swallowing his arms in the manner a straight jacket might encapsulate its host. He'd fallen in again. Drunk…again.

Kicking loose the shoulder bag, David's arms finally broke free, leaving the bag to its apparent descent. The sunlight flickered in between waves somewhere above as the transparent surface slowly moved further and further away. The gravel and dirt floating around inside David's eyelids burned. What little light he was able to catch in between painful blinking had dimmed. His eyes opened again cleanly, and he thought calmly for a moment: he probably wouldn't even be missed for a week. It certainly would be no major loss for anyone. G&H wouldn't even acknowledge him as a missing person. Perhaps if he had still worked there, they might have. Now, David recognized that no one on Earth would notice he'd gone missing. He'd be fish food. Pulled in by some Coast Guard's gaff. They'd find the receipt in his wallet for the bottle of whiskey and sum it up as an accidental death instead of what was actually an accidental life.

Strands of light stretched through the surface and grew fainter as David sucked water into his lungs. He watched as a few remaining bubbles of oxygen burst through his mouth and immediately reversed their course moving in the opposite direction. *Damn*, he thought, realizing he was upside down. He made an attempt at righting himself while his lungs burned for oxygen and tried to dispel the water they'd been forced to hold. This was how it felt last time. He raised his arms up towards the refracting light. The last time he did this, her arms found him. Her hands pulled him up. Perhaps, he thought, she was there once more. One last shot at this world, David thought, for her. Hands reached out again, but she was not there. And despite not finding the solace of her open arms, David met with a hard iron ladder built into the side of the man made beach. His feet, which had been kicking wildly, pushed at the iron rungs of the ladder, propelling David up towards the light and a setting Sun. David, thankfully on all fours now, a shivering, coughing mess, expelled lake water and whiskey all over the cement. Joggers and bikers continued on, unknowing of just how close to death someone had come on their precious path. Laying there on the cement, after consistent breaths without coughing, and with a nod to the sky above for thanks, David offered a knowing sneer to the lake that almost buried him.

Floating by now, in place of the whiskey bottle which apparently got tired of being sworn at, David saw the FedEx box which had nearly caused his death. Instead, inside, he would find life. Finally, and with one sobered steady hand locked to the top rung of the ladder, David reached down to the lake water to grab the box he'd so dutifully carried around the city for the last twenty hours.

Ripping open the box top revealed the contents to be dozens of envelopes with addresses and keys which were apparently warehouse locations. David studied the paperwork that went along with each envelope. He realized he'd lost a contact lens in his escapade into the water. The paperwork showed that Thomason and the AJ Quality Retail account were moving massive inventory into and through Chicago, and that corporate headquarters would soon call Chicago its home. Dampened folders gave David dates and times of shipping routes, even truck drivers' names and addresses and drivers license numbers to those that would be driving the trucks all across the country. Soon there'd be dozens of warehouses in the Chicagoland area, filled with trucks overflowing with multiple millions of dollars of inventory being hubbed out of Chicago for the entire U.S. David recalled when his nostrils filled with the exotic smells of smoke and fire, and her hair, and the smells of a jungle that burned around him and almost swallowed him.

If one were so inclined, David reasoned, one could very well put a large dent into the AJ Quality Retail corporation's inventory, doing damage to Thomason and his bottom line. Eventually this would lead to damage to Karen and her fresh new agency's bottom line. And if anybody looked into the signature of delivery, they'd find out that it was somebody at G&H who signed for it. Maybe it was the intern, maybe not. But it'd be one big legal mess. Things would snowball out of control, taking all three parties involved in David's sudden turn of events straight to hell. It would be one great big last laugh. But was it right? Was it the right thing to do? David's one good eye scanned the arrivals for what he already knew. Production and inventory came from a country with mediocre if not inadequate child labor laws. David reminded himself that this minor note never bothered him when he pitched the business.

But this was "new" David. And it was time to start making things right. First he'd have to start with himself. Both physically and mentally. Watching the three parties go down would be sufficient he thought. Looking out to the water that had nearly conquered him, he thought it might be fun watching them burn. And they would burn. All three. Together. What would Jessica say? Maybe it would even get her attention. Wherever she was in this world. She'd have told him to quit being a jerk and to get a hold of himself a long time ago. But now? Now she'd tell him to get a good seat and watch them burn.

# STATE UNIVERSITY

*DAVID HOBBS – AGE 21*
*Finals - Fall Semester, 1995*

Strangled by fast food franchises, a stray fraternity house, and a lone university bookstore kitty-corner to its convenience store mate, campus town on a late Friday afternoon emitted a collective, anxious and palpable exhale. The pulse around town quickened in part due to the looming deep freeze for the state, which was in the midst of a snowfall that littered the small towns, farmlands, and cities of Iowa all the same. Nearing the end of December and with finals imminent, inches of snow mounted across the state and severe weather bulletins broke television programming announcing the bitter cold front that was to follow.

David and Jessica marched through the snow from the apartment over to the convenience mart and stopped only to giggle and throw poorly formed snowballs at one another. Gym shoes and snow boots tracked slushy muddy snow inside the store, and a clerk stood guard over an entrance that couldn't be mopped enough. David and Jessica prepared to hunker down for a weekend, which promised intense studying on David's part while Jessica exercised frequently and studied on her own from the books and papers she had David check out from the school's library. It had been a glorious Fall season. Their relationship stood solid. Frequent trips to the movies and to class shows were a staple. David even bought mountain bikes for them both, and they would spend hours and hours just riding around campus town together. David's light class load for his senior year lent itself to such free time, and it aided in the growth of their love for one another.

With slender fingers tracing the many packages of potato chips and other goodies, Jessica noted the garish display of snack foods that ran across the store. The vulgarity of it all, she noted, summed up the overconfidence and ignorance of the population in general. Jessica turned her head to say something to David and saw him pulling the grocery list from his pocket while grabbing another twelve pack of beer.

"More beer?" Jessica asked. "I thought we were good."

"One more final to go, and it's going to be a real bitch."

"Since when do you need, oh, whatever," Jessica said and quickly disregarded any further nagging.

David paid with cash at the counter. The clerk, a sleepy-eyed student with a book nearby, handed David his change. As they walked outside, the snow seemingly finished with its inch by inch dressing of the land. As the wind blew through the massive cornfields surrounding the university, the icy chill bit at exposed skin. It was a quick walk to David's apartment half a block away, and he held Jessica's gloved hand steadily as they crossed a street. David sensed Jessica's mind was elsewhere. He could tell when she was thinking of her friends. Lately, he couldn't quite tell if her friends meant the Indians back in Mexico or the ones who asked her to go there.

As they walked into an intensely clean college apartment (the result of Jessica playing housewife while David was in classes), Jessica hung up the coats, and David plopped himself on the couch lazily and cracked open a beer. He stared at the economics book that lay open on the kitchen table and cursed it silently. After the intensity of the internship last summer, schoolwork seemed like mind-numbing exercise. It seemed like he was just going through the motions. Jessica went into the kitchen and put the provisions away. David sat underneath the large picture of a sailboat that he had bought on a whim from the university bookstore. At one point last year, David had needed something to remind him of the sea. That was before Jess. When he had no one else to lure him away from the dark places his mind sometime traveled to.

"David, do you have any idea how fortunate we are?" Jessica asked.

David knew what was coming, but he tried to avoid it by playing dumb.

"What do you mean? The weatherman said with the wind chill it could be twenty below this weekend."

"What I mean is that we could have six different flavors of potato chips if we wanted, and all we have to do is walk a block down the street to the convenience mart."

"Does this mean I'm about to get the speech about how fortunate we are and how people take things for granted in this country?"

Jessica poured herself a glass of milk and took small sips. She went back to putting the groceries away.

"No, I just get a little sad at the state of things sometimes."

David, looked up to her in the kitchen, got off the couch, walked up to her, and puts his arms around her waist.

"Listen, I know you're sad. But look at what you did. Look at what you're doing. You're going to write about your time with the Indians, right? That'll do some good. That will tell people exactly how fortunate they are in this world."

Jessica had been procrastinating on an article she told David she'd write. Instead, while David was at class she chose to spend her days cleaning the apartment and working out. She'd dropped in on a few classes but never really got excited about anything. She did it for David's sake. Deep down, she knew, that article would, and could never get written.

"It's just," Jess started, "six months ago I was eating watered down tree bark and having a great time with people in a language I couldn't even understand. Now, I'm in the land of microwave burritos and taco pizza. And, I'm not sure, but I think I'd rather have the tree bark."

David held her close hoping there'd be no tears, and offered, "I promise you, when it's warm outside, I'll get you all the tree bark you want. Come on, I've got about two hours of studying in front of me, and then we can watch the Bulls game."

"Great," Jessica said sounding less than enthused.

"Okay, how about I study for two hours and then we get naked and we have ourselves one tantric boot knocking session?"

"That's more like it," Jessica said pleased.

David let her go with a kiss on the lips. He sat down with his beer in front of the economics book. Jessica, seemingly content for now, went back to her duties in the kitchen.

\* \* \*

In bed, the two lovers hid from the cold beneath the flannel sheets. A few empty cans of beer graced a milk crate that doubled as a bookshelf and a nightstand. Her purple nighty that had graced her magnificent body for almost five whole minutes lay crumpled up on the floor next to David's clothes. In between making love and snoozing away through a frosty night, David and Jessica held each other amid a whispered midnight conversation.

"Listen," Jessica began, "I just want you to know that, before, I was with some pretty bad people. They didn't seem bad at first. But they were bad."

"Okay," David responded hesitantly at the admission.

"I'm just telling you because you need to know I did some things I'm not proud of. Some things that hurt people. Really, really hurt people. I'm not proud of it, but it's in the past, okay?"

"Hey, it's okay," David responds comfortingly.

"If you want to know what I did, I will tell you. But it's because I love you that I would tell you. It's all in the past, David. Know that."

"Then I don't want to know. What's in the past is the past, and I don't want to know any of it. Let it never come up again."

"I can only hope," Jessica replied softly. "David, the people I'm with now don't hurt anybody. Just think of it as a little mischief, okay?"

"Mischief is toilet papering someone's house. Destroying a dozen dump trucks in a Mexican jungle is terrorism."

"It's no 'ism', David. Sure we have our ideas and our philosophy, but we will not bow to anyone."

"Spare me the rhetoric, Jess. It's criminal. Bottom line."

"I seem to remember someone enjoying themselves while they helped start that fire in the jungle."

David stared through the dark and found a single band of light that poked through the window, exposing one of Jessica's bare arms. The rest of her was huddled up close to him. Her bare breasts lay nudged up into his chest. She held him close. David was upset over having to continually attempt to appease her boredom.

"You're selfish enough to keep me here aren't you?" Jessica asked without malice but with a dose of concern. "Not that I'm not selfish enough to stay."

"Come on, Jess," David fired back, "we're great together! You've sat in on a dozen classes or so. Been to a few lectures. Besides, I've only got one more semester and then we're out of corn country."

"Oh, yeah, right," Jess retorts, "and then it's on to the big city. Am I supposed to follow you there, too? Will I be hiding my clothes when your mom comes to visit there, too?"

"Listen, we're good together. Let's not let this get out of hand."

Jessica rolls away from his arms to her back joining David in staring at the ceiling.

"I was only supposed to lay low," she said.

David turns to her now and runs his fingers through her hair. It wasn't the first time they'd had this argument. In fact, lately, they had been having it more and more frequently.

"They'll start looking for me, David. They will find me."

"How? We're smack dab in the middle of Iowa and..."

"I want them to find me, David."

David winced at the blow.

"So, eventually you just take off, and that's it for us?"

"No, no," she sighed. "I do love you, David."

"I know," David said, easing off a bit, exhaling at the thought of always losing this argument until he offered back, "I love you, too."

"I'll be gone, but I'll see you from time to time. Come on, Chicago is a big town. I'm sure I'll pass through it all the time. And I'll write you. I'll write you all the time."

"But eventually, Jess," David responds, "the end is always the same, isn't it? You leave."

"Listen, David, there's things that I feel I need to do."

"And I'm in the way?"

"No, no, you have a standing offer to help us, David."

"You keep saying that like I have a choice. Like I can do something else. I don't have a choice, Jess. I've got nothing else."

"That's the point. You do have a choice. We all have a choice."

They paused for a lengthy, angry kiss.

"Someday, I won't be lying here next to you, David. But I'll be with you. I'll always love you and be with you."

"I won't let you go, Jess. Never."

Deep down, they both knew it. They both knew Jessica spoke the truth. David promised himself to fight it as long as he could.

* * *

With the bitter sub-zero temperatures having departed David rejoiced to himself silently, amid his walk home, that he had finished with his last final exam of the semester. It wasn't all that stimulating an exam, but more than likely it was a success. Campus town was quiet and reserved, with the students walking around with their faces portraying that of the focused young, stressed-out student. David looked forward to a few days at home for Christmas break. He'd leave Jessica here in Iowa so he could go home and try and take care of his mother. It occurred to David that Jessica might not be there when he came back to school.

Walking up main street in campus town and within a few blocks of his apartment David caught sight of a familiar headband. It belonged to Jessica, and she wore it when she was out of the shower and needed to get dressed quickly. David noted that she was in the café that was usually reserved for beatniks and stoners. Through the window David watched her from behind. She wasn't facing him, so she couldn't possibly see him. It was in fact Jessica, leading a particularly animated discussion that probably had something to do with tree hugging, judging from the hippie-esque looking crowd.

*Well, she likes to fight and she's good at it*, David surmised, standing there in the cold, spying on the woman he loved. The group argued good naturedly, and he noted the passion from each of them. He would have liked to go inside and join them, but this was Jessica's club. He chose not to intrude. David's cold breath hit the window, temporarily shielding Jessica from his view. David recalled finding some maps on the kitchen table this morning that Jessica had probably stolen from the library.

David saw Jessica get up and go to the counter to pay for something. When she asked for something behind the counter, the barista grabbed several packs of gum, one in every flavor, and passed them to Jessica. David wanted to barge in but fought the urge so he could observe further. David then saw a well-dressed older man in a suit get up from a nearby table and walk up next to Jessica. He placed a manila file folder on the counter next to Jessica and promptly walked out of the café. Jessica grabbed the folder without hesitation (and all too naturally) and put it in her bag. David stared at the man in the suit and watched him walk down the street. The man in the suit took no note of him, despite David's eyes that tracked him as he hurried away.

"So, that's what a terrorist looks like," was all David could say. He left the window with no acknowledgment. When Jessica got home shortly thereafter, she walked in to find David sitting on the couch. A few empty cans of beer kept him company. Despite downing the beer so quickly, David still felt quite sober. As Jessica walked in, she could feel the intense stare from David.

"What's eating you?" she asked, plopping her book bag down on the kitchen table. David could see the manila file from the couch. "Exam go shitty?"

David didn't move. Slumped on the couch he instead focused on the words he'd use.

"So, who were those people at the café?" he finally asked. Jessica sat down carefully next to him on the couch.

"Friends," she answered. "Are you spying on me?"

"Friends," David both responded and questioned.

"Yes," Jessica said, "am I allowed to have friends?"

David admitted to himself he was being a little hard on her. Besides, she was in a good mood after being with her type.

"Come on, they're just a bunch of local activists. Do-gooders. The most controversial thing they can do is hand out flyers. They're harmless, and I just had to set them straight on a few things."

"And the guy in the suit. What is he? A professor friend of yours?"

"Oh, him. So you were spying on me."

"Is he…one of the gang?"

"Yes, David," Jessica responded, "he is 'one of the gang,' so to speak. But he's just a local guy. Helps provide information. That's all."

"And, uh, that file, is that your little project for you and your friends after I leave for home tomorrow?" David asked.

Jessica wanted to admit to David that the books she was checking out were a calling card, but then David might not do it anymore. She chose to address it with him later.

"David, it's just information. There is no assignment. Yet."

"You're thinking about leaving while I'm home for break."

"I can't say it hasn't crossed my mind, David. I told you I wouldn't lie to you."

"If it weren't for the interview, I would stay here with you."

"David, there are issues out there that need to be addressed."

"Where is it this time?" David asked curiously.

"Ecuador."

David continued to chug beer and swear at himself in his head. They didn't say anything for a long time. Finally, Jessica gave in, tired from watching him drink.

"Listen, David, I just want you to know that no matter what happens, from the first moment we met, you know, in the market there, I've felt what love can feel like. I've never felt this way about anyone before."

David knew it was coming.

"But David, I'm landlocked here. I'm going crazy. And there's some serious shit going on in this world, David. And I can help. I want to fight. I can't do that here."

David chugged the rest of his beer. He picked himself up from the couch and walked away from Jessica. He went to the bedroom to lay down, but mostly it was to be away from the hurt. Jessica remained on the couch. Later she would join him in bed, and although they would make love, it would be empty and meaningless.

# BURNING DOWN THE HOUSE

*DAVID HOBBS – AGE 32*
*Summer, 2006*

Welcomed by sheaths of sunlight thrown down from the sky, David stood and stared through a dirt encrusted window that had seen the wraths of many a Chicago season. The warehouse (designated as warehouse number fourteen according to the paperwork) rested menacingly on the far South Side of the city of Chicago. David could make out further filth and grime as he scanned the vacant floor inside and concluded that he had indeed found what he came for. Perfectly hidden away and camouflaged among the several dozen other surrounding factories, David deemed it a good "home base." David had spent his life living on the lake on the North Side of town among the white collars, forever dependent upon plentiful cabs and the CTA's most pristine busses. Factories and warehouses up north were dance clubs and office space. For David, this swatch of landscape brimming with factories and smokestacks was country unknown.

It had been a decent bike ride from his condominium, and thankfully most of the ride consisted of travelling along the lakefront path. The key fit the door at the back entrance perfectly as David scanned the alley for further observers. He chose the back in case there were cameras out front. The entrance to the dock in back must have been hell for the drivers to maneuver through, evidenced by scored concrete and brick bruised by countless deliveries over time. David grabbed at the chains of the manual, out-of-date door opener, and his hand was instantly soiled with cobwebs and grease. It was obvious that the place hadn't been used for years. It was their reserve, an alternate, David had discovered while examining the paperwork he had come across in the FedEx box. It was highly unlikely this place would see any of the massive amounts of forthcoming inventory that was intended to be delegated to AJ Quality Retail stores across the Midwest.

David chose to disappear. His condo, absent of pets or anything capable of dying, was left darkened and soulless which, eerily enough, was how it typically stood. David tossed a few favorite pairs of clothes as well as a toothbrush and comb inside a gym bag and slung it over his shoulder. Whatever else was needed he could pick up along the way. Besides, everything he truly needed lay aboard the *Bejeweled* anyway. Upon giving his basement storage unit one last look, he had discovered a mountain bike that was rarely used (evidenced by the gut that David sported). The tires required just a bit of air; otherwise the thing was brand new. The ride along the lake down to the warehouse had been comforting, and David recalled just how much fun it was to be out in the open air again.

The rest of the warehouse matched the welcome that David got from the door opener. Years of dirt and filth piled up on an empty warehouse floor. After spending a majority of the morning working a large push broom, David sat in the center of the warehouse floor and ate a bologna sandwich. Surrounded by utter emptiness was how he'd always undergone his days, and only now did it manifest itself physically in his surroundings.

The FedEx box sat nearby, mostly intact. David spent an hour or so sorting through the paperwork he had absconded with, placing each wet page of the schedule in chronological order across the floor one by one. With so many deliveries expected, David guessed he had enough for six months' work for revenge or retribution or whatever it was that he was doing. He would be a busy man. Each page held different drivers' names and truck numbers and a list of prospective inventory. David justified everything by noting one of the pages exposed inventory lots with quota and production broken down to the second. It sickened David to think that somewhere small fingers were making toys for American children to play with while they in turn were being worked to death. David would feel bad firebombing toys. Kids liked toys, and David had just ridden through a neighborhood where he'd seen children playing with rocks and bottle caps.

Fresh air lit his lungs on fire and sweat beaded and pulsed into his clothes. His veins still surged with blood from the spirited bike ride down to the South Side of Chicago. Apart from a trusty push broom that David had quickly grown accustomed to there was not much else to the place. *It'll be whatever it is to be*, David had decided. Blessed by no distractions it was the perfect place to plan. David took a crowbar to one of the nearby windows and heaved it open, breaking the decade or so of mold that had been allowed to accumulate, allowing the sunlight to break through and shoot into the warehouse.

It would have to be soon. *No second thoughts!* David searched for and found the inventory schedule with tomorrow morning's delivery date. David was not opposed to improvising the first time out.

\* \* \*

That afternoon he took a casual bike ride around the neighborhood and over towards the target warehouse. Research and reconnaissance, he called it. Abandoning the fluorescent lights for natural sunlight that washed a city in its warmth finally, David thought to himself, *Peace*. Despite the pressure of the game he was playing, he'd be satisfied with his choice no matter the outcome. It was his will and not someone or something else's driving him. David smiled towards a setting Sun and rode around the target warehouse, scouting exit routes while listening to the sounds of the city. The muscles in David's legs ached, and he stopped for water frequently, soaking up the atmosphere of the South Side and the neighborhoods surrounding the factories.

The next morning at exactly nine thirty a.m. David watched the semi-trailer truck with the large AJ Quality Retail block letters scrolled across the trailer back in to the dock at a seemingly impossible angle. *These drivers are talented*, he thought. The large numbers on the back doors corresponded to the numbers written by a felt pen on David's arm. The license plates matched as well, and David presumed that the driver's name would be William Morgan. David watched the driver, slightly overweight and less than kempt, plod around the dock in back. David took note of the clipboard he was handed and the many signatures it took to release the materials. The foreman began opening the back entrance doors to prepare for unloading the inventory. David was good at improvising speeches. He was about to find out just how good he was.

"Excuse me, Mr. Morgan?" David called out to the truck driver, jogging up from behind, with the same clipboard the foreman had left on a desk near the entrance to the loading dock. There were sure to be cameras around posted above in working warehouses. David pulled his ball cap down a bit lower on his approach.

"Who the fuck are you?" asked the unkempt wooly truck driver.

"Assistant," David cried, and notes his warehouse garb disguise would need work. "The boss wants you in the office in back. Says there's more paperwork."

"What paperwork?" the driver demands. "Jeez, what is it with you guys?"

"Yeah, I know," David empathizes, "Pain in the ass, isn't it?"

The truck driver grumbled off into the warehouse in search of the back office.

"Whoa, wait," David asked, "We gotta back this thing in a little more."

"You do it," the driver said and tossed the keys to David trustingly. "That's the price you pay for all this paperwork. No scratches, punk."

David caught the keys in mid-air, and the driver turned and walked away in search of paperwork but found the vending machine first.

"Right," David said, "not a scratch."

* * *

Late at night, in an empty parking lot long abandoned and buttressed by rotting concrete among the barren wastelands of once popular factories bursting with energy, David brought the semi truck to a stop. The empty warehouses lay dormant, hibernating, in wait for their eventual demolition or, if lucky, conversion to lofts and condos. The many parking spaces afforded there stayed inhabited solely by weeds instead of automobiles.

Street lights off in the distance offered tiny little light for vision. Two gallon sized drums of gasoline rode shotgun.

The inventory was never meant for destruction. That was not his intention, nor the point to David's rebirth. Production was good, Jessica had taught him. It was the effects that the production had on people that David rebelled against now, and the means in which people fought for it. The shipment, toys from somewhere David had trouble locating on the map, had taken him the entire day to unload with a lone dolly he had found in the storage room back at the home base that was warehouse fourteen. It was good exercise, David thought, tasting the salt from the sweat covering his lips. He rotted with stink and would have to find a shower soon. Perhaps on the *Bejeweled*. The last two days had seen David perform more exercise than in the last fifteen years.

The next few mornings were reserved for deliveries, David thought. With all those boxes, David would make certain that the toys would make it to parks and school playgrounds across the city where he'd seen children playing with broken beer bottles.

Now, in the darkness of the summer night, without much light around, David could just make out the AJ Quality Retail logo branded across the side of the trailer. It was now his bulls eye. David lit the end of the rag with a lighter he'd found in the glove box. The toss smacked the logo square and spit fire and light across the truck instantly. David lit another rag from another gasoline bomb and walked a bit closer. This time the bottle was lobbed inside the cabin of the truck. David made his exit quickly. Fire blasted away at the inside cabin. David took a moment to look back and grin. He even performed a small dance routine that, although quite unorthodox, David felt compelled to carry out. The truck fire lit the surrounding night's sky with smoke and flames. David walked casually away and eventually found his bike locked up nearby. For David, anything was possible now. Much more planning would be required, yet satisfaction came upon looking back and seeing a charred truck. Things would get more difficult, he imagined.

# TYING THE KNOT

*DAVID HOBBS – AGE 21*
*Summer, 1995*

Summers in Chicago were rivaled by no other city on the planet. Fine restaurants adjoining the lake positioned themselves alongside taverns with outdoor seating that adorned already crowded sidewalks. Entertainment came in the form of never ending pitchers of beer served to you by waitresses who had spent too much time in the Sun that day and who were anxiously awaiting their next cigarette break. David's butt was planted opposite Lou in one of the chairs, where no doubt it was starting to leave its impression. Lou's massive desk was an expanse of cluttered, oaken real-estate that separated the two individuals.

David Hobbs, amused by these thoughts, stared out the window of his boss's office, slightly hung-over, engrossed by the waves systematically rolling in from Lake Michigan. He had been an intern for all of one month, and all he'd seemingly done was sit in on meeting after inexhaustible meeting. But David listened and paid attention. That was what Lou had told him to do. David had also spent a good deal of time in Lou's office listening to him deal with people on the telephone. Lou's office had in fact been one of the largest offices he'd seen thus far in his travails as a lowly intern in the new business department at the Graham & Hoffman Advertising agency. David had been privileged to see many offices in the high-rise building, given that he was occasionally responsible for running storyboards down to an art director along with Lou's notes on whether or not a creative execution was on target or not. Upon scrutinizing the notes that Lou had left on the boards, David could surmise that Lou was harder on the men and much easier going on the women. Especially the pretty ones.

"Listen, Kid, you don't know shit, all right, so just sit there and listen. And read. Know what's happening in the world. Read everything you can. That will help you in this business."

Graham & Hoffman, or G&H as most employees and those in the advertising community referred to it, was the foremost advertising agency in the city and far and away one of the most successful in the country. Only a month in to his internship and David's eyes had seen things not registered yet by his college classmates back in Iowa. Thanks to an aunt who had looked after David and had excellent connections within the advertising community, David was able to be schooled throughout the summer in what it was like to work at a prestigious advertising firm. The relationship between Lou and David had so far been cordial but task oriented. What Lou attempted to present as sage words and advice now and then, David stored and vowed to revisit at a later date to determine their validity. Lou was not quite a role model and not exactly the picture of health his father had been. They certainly could not call one another friends. Here, among the halls populated by suits and creatives, David had seen plenty, and his ears had heard so much more. The world had been tarnished in his eyes yet again. David winced at the failure that was forming from the assumption that upon leaving college next year and entering the world he would find a bright shiny place. Instead of the pristine crystal clear newness of a fresh world, David had been welcomed to the muck and dredge of the city: the homeless men that shook wax paper cups for change all day. Firemen hosing off a bike messenger's blood on the street. Sarcasm, irony, cynicism and degradation due to extreme egoism, dripped from the walls of G&H, waiting to infect the young, impressionable David Hobbs who had recently completed his junior year at the college in Iowa. The pages flipped by, read, and re-read. The hours spent in auditoriums at school mattered little to him now. Textbooks were of no use here unless someone was researching a young man's eyes and the sadness they held for the naiveté that had been left behind at the school in Iowa.

Currently, Lou was on the phone with a producer discussing the selection of an animatic they were to be using in the pitch to a potential client later that afternoon. His boss, with drink in hand at all times during the happy hours, networked David well to the agency and his fellow employees at the many hangouts of the who's-who at G&H.

Lou spoke to the phone receiver. David sat patiently in what was undoubtedly an expensive leather chair.

"Yes, I agree," Lou answered. Lou said it as if the producer should have been expecting it. "That was quite a shock when they added that in there. It was a real surprise to me."

David, tired from sitting quietly all the time, decided to add some of his own sarcasm to the room for once, despite knowingly interrupting his boss while on the phone.

"A surprise?" David asked in a break from his usual silence, "you mean like the other night when I saw you arm in arm with that young woman who was not your wife."

Lou rummaged around his desk, quickly finding it absent of any rubbish to throw at David. He instead opts for the rope that stuck out of a gym bag that lay on the floor close by. He throws it at David quickly, playfully, and David catches the twelve-strand Dyneema core without fail. David had heard Lou talk sailing quite a bit on the phone, but it hadn't come up in their conversations just yet. Instead, David was subjected to random bouts of advice espoused to him amid the mute button during a creative or producer's excuses as to why they were running behind schedule.

That had been an odd night though. He had seen the two together just a few blocks from G&H as David staggered from the bar en route to the train stations. She was young and not the woman in the picture frame set amid the storyboards crowding an already muddled old desk. This girl had not seen the trials of life, and nor would she, judging by her looks, David concluded. Wrinkles had yet to force the need for frequent mirror inspection, though David suspected she was the sort to do so anyway. She was very pretty and very young. Clearly she had been out of David's league and perhaps was not even David's type. Not that David was altogether even sure what his type was just yet. He had seen them cuddled up together in their walk from a bar or restaurant, and they had not seen him. David recognized her as an Art Director on the 27th floor. He had delivered storyboards to her routinely. She was being primed, David thought. For fucking him, she would get the high profile assignments. There was still so much to learn, David contemplated, shortly after seeing them, on his train ride north to the suburbs.

David and his fellow interns usually met up after work, after they had been released, each one staggering in at odd times throughout the night and then staggering back for more odd jobs. He had formed a decent camaraderie with the other interns. Some of them weren't even twenty-one yet, but they were served at the bar anyway. They dressed professionally, and worked in the loop, so there wasn't any need to check IDs. Phone calls broke through banter among company issued mobile cellular telephones, interrupting beers in search of someone to run art work down the street to a printer or take a cab across the city to pick up a CD from an art director's collection just because he or she wasn't feeling very stimulated at the present moment. Sometimes, when the art director caught you in the lobby en route, there'd be a twenty in it for you if you also delivered the baggie full of grass that waited in the coffee canister. The fact remained that if you could suffer through the summer, then you were able to put G&H on your resume, and that was like a golden ticket to a job in the ad industry. Most had hoped they'd eventually end up back here at G&H anyway.

"You're a rather intense young fellow, aren't you?" Lou asked David, hanging up the phone, not bothering to listen to the nonstop jibber-jabber of the producer as they said their good-byes.

"Yes, I suppose so, Sir," David acknowledged. David had been staring out at the lake. He wondered if his mother was okay.

"Just listen when I tell you that everything we do here, non-stop, is for the client. In this department, it is our job to continue to bring in…clients. What that means is we do whatever it takes. I don't care if your child is sick at home. I don't care if your wife has left you or if you have to take your mother to the hospital. If you can't do the job, then I will get somebody who will. In here, there is no out there. There's too much money at stake, and this business is getting less fun all the time. The client demands, and we deliver. Or at least make it look as though we do. It takes all sorts around this company to achieve this."

"We promise…what we cannot deliver," David attempted a summation.

"Not quite. Demand, David. We demand people's best. Especially in the new business department. And when they achieve, we reward. When they disappoint, we get someone else. And it takes a lot of people to do the job, David. Whether it's me up here in this big, beautiful office, or the mailroom attendant who's delivering the contracts to be signed. It takes all sorts. And it requires eleventh-hour action. Tension, sure, there's tension. But all that is negated by being cool under fire."

"Like you are?" David asked rhetorically, perhaps now adopting a more sarcastic look upon life. While Lou espoused more all-knowings from the all-knowing, David fiddled with the rope. He could smell the lake on it.

"Like I am," Lou answered back frankly. "Hey, what the fuck is that?"

"What?" David asked shuddering, scared, and at once played innocent.

"That?" Lou shouted, pointing at the line in David's hands. "You just tied a bowline."

"Yeah, so?" David replied plainly.

"You sail?"

"Yes, I've been sailing."

"How long?" Lou asked, demanding an immediate response. Every other thing in Lou's consciousness is quickly removed so that at this point he is focusing solely on the answers David was giving him.

"I've been sailing all my life."

"No, shit?" Lou responded, disbelieving every word.

"No, shit," David admitted honestly. "Dad had me in the crew since I was five."

"So, you know your way around a boat then?"

"I should say so, yes, Sir."

"Holy Christ, you're kidding," Lou said and stared at David intensely refusing words and instead choosing to study the young man in front of him.

Lou looked around his cluttered, disorganized desk. Underneath several piles of half empty packs of cigarettes and a dozen or so storyboards that needed going over, Lou unearthed one of the gimmick bandanas from a leave-behind they had done for the cigarette company they had pitched. He threw that at David as well.

"Offering me my last requests?" David asked sarcastically.

"Put it on," Lou demanded.

David wrapped the black bandana around his head so that his eyes were covered. He took a moment to stare blankly at Lou.

"How many fingers am I holding up?" Lou asked.

Lou held up his middle finger at David.

"Knowing you, I'm guessing that it's one and that the child in you has selected your middle finger."

"Very good, but I'll take that as a yes that you cannot see. Now, tie a bowline."

David did as he was told.

"Now," Lou began again, "tie a clove hitch."

David did as he was told. Lou watched David start to tie the knot and waited until he knew for sure that David knew what he was doing.

"Reef knot," Lou commanded.

David started. Lou's demands began rapid-fire.

"No, do a round turn and two half hitches," Lou said, hoping to mix up David.

David increased his speed.

"Rolling hitch," Lou ordered.

"Against what?" David asked, not knowing precisely what Lou wanted the line adhered to.

"Here," Lou relented, throwing him another rope from his gym bag.

David did as he was told. Remarkably, all had been performed perfectly, adeptly, and not at all to David's surprise. Lou laughed at his good fortune.

"Just 'cause you know the knots don't mean you can sail, Kid. What races have you been in this summer? I haven't seen you at the yacht club."

"None this summer, Sir," David replied. "You see I have this new boss that likes to keep me at work very late most nights and weekends."

"Funny, Kid."

"Thank you, Sir," David replied.

"How about a drink?" Lou asked, swiveling his chair around, no doubt to raid his secret stash.

"It's ten a.m., Sir."

"We have to celebrate. You've just been officially welcomed aboard as a new crew member of the *Bejeweled,* my boat."

Lou brought out a bottle of vodka from the mini-fridge next to his desk. Two small tumblers clinked together as he placed them on precious open real estate on the beautiful desk. Lou started pouring.

"You're taking me on?" David asked. "You haven't even seen me in action yet."

"Doesn't matter, Kid. I just lost a good man, and the rest of my crew is worthless. Especially my kid. Maybe you can teach him something. Besides, I could use any healthy body that knows just what the fuck they're doing. And you need to learn more about the advertising business. We can talk about your future while we sail."

"I shall enjoy that very much, Sir," David said hoping he wasn't going to be babysitting the boss's son all summer.

"How come I didn't know you sailed?" Lou asked disbelievingly.

"You did, Sir. We talked about it at length in my interview. The boat I was on lost a couple good men."

"Was I drunk when you interviewed?"

"Quite possibly, Sir."

"Well, shit, what races have you been in?"

"I've mostly stuck to the Midwest. I try to hop on a crew here or there. My Dad's crew left after the accident."

"Shit, this is great news! You're still a young man. I can help mold you while you jump on board. I'll have you know our boat came in twelfth place last year in the Door County Lake to the Bay Regatta."

"How nice," David replied, avoiding an addendum that he had won the whole damn race practically by himself a few years back.

"You stick with me, Kid. I'll make sure you stay on the right track. With sailing and with this business."

Lou winked and gulped his vodka down. He poured another one quickly.

"To my new mate," Lou said and raised his glass.

David looked at the glass, chilled frosty from the ice. Sitting deadened in position inside the glass the ice cubes buddied with the clear, cold liquid poison. Perhaps the booze could add a little levity for the remaining meetings scheduled all afternoon and early evening, David thought. He raised his glass and clinked Lou's. David spilled the bristly, liquid fire upon his taste buds, feeling the sting of thorns blazing down his throat. He felt disbelief at his luck that he might have a new bond with the boss that seemed so distant to him when he had walked in to his office that morning. David missed his father and brother very much and felt that if they had met this man, Lou, they would say he was a courteous and cordial man. In the back of his mind, though, David knew that if his father were here, he would have spoken to him disapprovingly of all the drinking he'd been doing lately, and he would have sent a stern warning to be mindful of the man that sat across from him. That was easy for him to say, David admitted. He swallowed more from the glass, feeling the coldness infect his bloodstream like venom.

# DEMO

*DAVID HOBBS – AGE 32*
*Summer, 2006*

David's eyes cracked open to laser beams of sunlight blasting through the exposed windows of warehouse fourteen. He rose from the small mattress and walked the hundred yards or so to the bathroom. What once was a bleak, dirty, empty fortress (laying in wait as an alternate) still remained bleak and dirty. However, now a mattress lay in the corner with a lone blanket thrown on top. There were a few other items about that David afforded himself to comfort him in his sobriety, and for his call to action. He'd bought the coffee pot from a nearby hardware store. David was used to people always handing him his coffee. He'd set down the mattress in a dusty corner far away from the lone administrator's office on purpose. The office was used solely to park his bike, and other than that he stayed away. Looking inside at his bike leaning pristinely up against the old, metal desk, David hoped his loathing was palpable and that each and every inanimate office product inside felt his hate. David hadn't quite figured out the air conditioning, but in all honesty hadn't given it that much effort. It was getting hot outside, and the nights were sure to stop cooling off as they were. This being an alternate warehouse David supposed that he should consider himself lucky the plumbing was working. Still, David found himself sleeping comfortably at night now. It took him more than a few days to get used to going to sleep sober.

He hadn't made his own cup of coffee in so long it took him a few tries to make something that was drinkable. After a few sips from this morning's brew, he discovered it was going to take a few more tries. On the wall next to the empty, musky smelling office, David hung a large, poster-sized map detailing the city streets of Chicago. There was a small refrigerator he'd found in the office that suited his bare needs. Mostly he ate outside every day, usually stopping at a park during his late morning bike ride to eat a sandwich or some fruit. David fought the shakes less and less. His mind forced him to summon the courage to beat the demon that begged for him. David decided instead to torture himself further with another coffee.

Next to the map of Chicago the trucking schedules that David had usurped hung on a string clipped on by clothespins. They were completely dry now, and he hadn't lost a page, but he liked seeing each page at eye level, so he left them there. David looked at the AJ Quality Retail logo that hung there so prominently, and he smirked a bit. Which one was next, he thought. On the map the requisite pins jutted out from the location of each of the warehouses that would be receiving inventory. The pins were quite the bitch to put in when his hands shook. David sat for a moment and gulped more bad coffee, theorizing about the positives and negatives from his recent escapade. It might just be easier to take out a truck while parked inside the warehouse. A little reconnaissance at nighttime would tell him how many guards there'd be. His exploits hadn't quite been as popular on the news as he'd hoped due to the small terrorist group that seemed hell bent on disrupting the eco conference going on in the city right now. Today he would scour the streets of Chicago looking for exit points and safety zones with his bike around the city. David tried to remember the date on the milk he'd put aboard the *Bejeweled* the night before last. He couldn't. The alcohol was not completely gone from his brain. He hoped there wasn't that much irreparable damage done to his short term memory.

The bike had served him well, David judged, and exercise was long overdue. The Chicago summer had seen flawless weather so far. He could breathe deep and look out to the lake and beyond. He was looking for her, he thought. A discarded piece of pipe made for a makeshift chin-up bar. He could breathe strong again, tasting the toxins on his lips that he'd sweated out from his pores. Everything about his breakthrough had been going well until he found the plastic grocery bag tied to the door handle.

With his bike hoisted over his shoulder at the dock in back, preparing to lock the back door, David felt the crinkly plastic bag. The logo to the convenience store that had been blown up on that fateful night for David was displayed prominently, along with spatters of blood smeared across the crinkly white plastic. The bag had been tied to the door handle. It was a fateful night for David in a different manner than for the rest of the city, for that night was the beginning of the end for old David. For the rest of the city, it saw the head of an Ecological Conference committee blown to pieces by some radical terrorist group claiming there was too much talk and not enough action. The city had spooked and rightly so. The conference had been postponed indefinitely. Extra police and security were called in from other cities in a vain attempt to uncover the terrorists. Judging by the sleek job they'd done on the committee chief, they'd be long gone. However, opening up the convenience store plastic bag, David found a note written in brilliant red ink on a G&H yellow pad. The yellow pad had been taken from David's condo. An old list for the grocery store was written on it. Below that there was a note requesting his presence immediately at some outdoor café in the Loop. David was familiar with the spot.

David's lone act of rebellion so far had brought him little attention from the media. He'd been described as a copycat, and that was fine with him. The only damage was a few hundred thousand dollars of toys. David hadn't been concerned with the terrorists until now. David was simply concerned with burning down the Old David and restarting the fire in New David. But it seemed someone else was concerned with him now. And these were some pretty bad dudes if the news reports were at all accurate. A wheel chair bound ex-surfer hell bent on revenge for poisoning the waters he'd been surfing in all his life. David would have to go to the café and see what they wanted. On the bike ride there, David surmised that if they knew his whereabouts within the warehouse, then it was probably safe to assume they knew about the *Bejeweled*. There was no immediate escape.

The café sat perched on Wabash Ave., in between Wacker Drive and Lake St. It was nearly empty due to the fact that at nine thirty a.m. on a Thursday most people were settling in to their work day tasks. David settled himself in a chair that the waiter escorted him to. The waiter, with far too many things sticking out of his face and with tattoos of vines laced up his arms, sat him down in the corner, giving him a bird's eye view to the café as well as to the office building across the street. David's suspicions were raised by the waiter having sat him in a specific chair. Upon looking back, he noticed that there was no one else in the café. His suspicions were confirmed when the waiter returned and placed a large cup of coffee in front of him and a small, elegant-looking white box.

David sat for a moment and looked at the people rushing by. Most were probably very late to work. They looked nervous and sped their walks up around slower moving commuters. David was terrified. High traffic. High body count. He took the coffee in his hands, having deemed it safe because if they had wanted him dead they'd have just poisoned the coffee and not bothered with the box. Besides, if there was a bomb planted inside the pristine white box, David didn't want the horrible taste of the coffee he'd made this morning in his mouth upon leaving Planet Earth.

David stole a quick sip and relished each drop, recognizing that it was in fact a cappuccino and not just a drip coffee. David looked back down to the small, square white box. Non-threatening white, he thought. He asked himself if it was a trick to make him feel secure. He looked back to the cappuccino and took a deep swig, refusing to acknowledge the box.

The waiter, who stood at the entrance to the café, growing impatient while telling potential customers that they were closed, noted this. David acted nonchalantly, still sipping the cappuccino and enjoying the beautiful morning he was spending in the café. David watched the stud-encrusted, tattooed waiter respond to a phone call. The waiter dashed over to David quickly.

"May I, Sir?" the waiter asked quite clearly.

David took one last look around the famed Chicago Loop.

"Certainly," David responded at last.

As the top of the box was pulled away, David saw a small, silver device sitting atop a stack of newspaper clippings. The waiter remained at David's side and pretended to take an order. Reaching in and removing the device, David recognized it as a portable DVD player. The clippings underneath were all headlined by The Black Van Group. They were newspapers from around the world.

"Play it," the waiter said, "now."

David hit the play button and the small machine whirred to life. What came on screen looked to be discreetly done and was clearly a recording from some hidden camera. Passing through revolving doors, walking up to a security desk, a clipboard to sign in was handed over by security. The scene unfolded from above with occasional looks down to a marble floored lobby with an elevator bank behind a security desk taking employees to the heavens of some presumably immense skyscraper.

\* \* \*

The camera was actually duct taped to the top of her bicycle helmet and was completely obvious, yet everyone she came near seemed oblivious. This time around, the homeless person disguise had been exchanged for a bike messenger outfit. There she stood at the front desk in the lobby, the camera catching the innocuous name she applied to the sign in sheet for Missile Messenger service. Her forged ID was handed over. She blended right in with the rest, although she was a touch short. The large messenger bag that weighed a ton was slung over her shoulder trustingly and never searched. The security guard, busy on his phone taking orders from a higher up concerned about the security risk across the city, slapped down a label for her to apply, and she is granted temporary access to the elevator bank. Once the elevator doors open, she is the first and only one inside pressing the number fourteen. A lone businessman plodded up to the elevator doors.

"This one's full," she insisted and jabbed a finger in his fat chest pushing him backwards.

"But, but," is all he can stammer as the heavy doors close, and the elevator starts its ascent up the shaft.

Concealed inside, safely alone, she reached inside her satchel bag to grab the can of spray paint. Ditching the cap on the floor she immediately turned to spray the glass in the corner that housed a small security camera. She then punched the buttons for floors fifteen, sixteen, and all the way up to floor forty-nine. Bike messenger clothes were quickly removed and a purse was unveiled from the bike messenger bag. Upon removal her outfit revealed a short, slim girl ready for the work day. Donning glasses and pulling her hair back tightly, she then removed a large, heavy canister from the satchel that was an absolute bitch to carry on her bike.

The elevator doors opened to a young, beautiful, albeit short woman. Turning back to the canister, she yanked on the trigger, and smoke began to pour from its top furiously. She kept her satchel with her as she walked into the reception area of the office on the fourteenth floor. The camera had been pulled from the helmet and clipped onto the small purse that she held to look officious.

"Hi, there, Hon, are you with the temp agency?"

"Yes, I'm Jane. Marsha couldn't make it today."

Marsha had ideas of her own, and Will had to intercede. She was tied up and gagged in the van downstairs along with the bike messenger. Will would show mercy on the bike messenger. Marsha would probably be going for a swim soon though. Without being untied.

"Oh, great, Jane. Let me show you where you'll be working today."

She already knew she'd be working for the CEO of Baxter-Sternberg, a small company that was doing its part for corruption around the corporate world.

"Here you are. Make yourself at home. The boss is out this morning. Do you smell smoke?"

The receptionist dismissed herself amid further concerns of smoke, and Jane sat down temporarily, waiting for the alarm to go off. This blow for freedom would send corporate scum scurrying, and the money and the damage was all for show. Jane, she called herself now, started shredding random documents to keep herself busy. The smoke was strong now. Looking down the hallway a hallucinogenic haze formed, and her eyes tried to compensate. Just as she was sticking a pen inside the automatic pencil sharpener, the fire alarms blasted, awakening everyone from their peaceful delirium. At first instant, panic set in, but eventually order was restored and the employees of Baxter-Sternberg managed their way downstairs. Jane, the lone leftover, stayed behind and applied her gas mask, which she had stowed in her satchel. The smoke bore a thin haze throughout the office and was just irritating enough to Jane's eyes, where she might type a number incorrectly.

Entering the CEO's office, with his laptop already fired up, she was able to locate his online banking account from his bookmarks. Marsha had been one of theirs all along and had done a good job with research and recon until now. She got greedy though. And she lost her way.

Unrolling her right sleeve, Jane popped in the login info and several passwords to get to the CEO's account information. Unrolling her left sleeve now, she sees the other account information to where the money was being sent. Tomorrow morning, a man in the U.S. Virgin islands would walk into a bank and transfer several hundred thousand dollars to the safety of a Swiss bank account. Once Jane completed the transaction she looked up and saw the receptionist at the door of the CEO's office.

"You're not supposed to be in here!" she cried.

Jane pulled her Taser gun out from the satchel and let it fly on the receptionist, whose butt had seen too much chair time and not enough treadmill time. The golf club leaning up in the corner would have done just fine but Will stressed zero collateral damage on this mission. The camera remained on the entire time, still shooting footage.

Finally she removed an object from the bike messenger bag, at last emptying it. This time, there would be no cereal box. There was a bigger payload meant as a message for the CEO in charge of a company that flew Sheik's wives in town on the company jet just for a shopping trip on the magnificent mile. There were worse things being done in the world, but Will was infuriated by the arrogance of the Baxter-Sternberg Corporation and of the FBI for not doing anything because it would have hurt relations with America's oil producing friends. Several hundred grand was petty cash for Will, and it was likely that the explosion would not be much of a diversion to cause the CEO from taking that call from the bank. The always image-conscious Will wanted everyone to know he was still out there and that he was capable of inflicting great pain to anyone. Will wanted that known to David most of all. Jane made sure the camera got a good shot of the size of the plastic explosive.

Walking down the hallway, and through a thin cloud of smoke, Jane entered the stairwell, dragging the receptionist with her until a trusty fireman was found. She maneuvered the stairs with the rest of the throngs of workers en masse. Blending back in but smelling more of smoke than the rest, she took the stairs down, merging into the crowd at once. She walked out through the panicky lobby, still holding the camera as she exited, but pointing it through the crowd and across the street. As she walked up to the minivan, the door is opened for her to get in.

*  *  *

David sees all of this unfold on the screen. He sees a glimpse of silver hair as a hand helps "Jane" into the minivan. David looks up from the DVD player to see the waiter is gone. There was still the matter of the bomb that the camera panned to right before "Jane" left the office. David could take the player straight to the police. When he looked down again there is a note perhaps left by the waiter that states: SEE YOU SOON. BY THE WAY... DUCK!

David looks down again to the DVD player and sees that the camera is now showing David being seated by the waiter at the café. It dawned on David that this was taking place right now. He looked up again and sees a black minivan roll by. Faces smiled and waved from the driver's side window mockingly. A stunned David counts the floors of the building across the street up to number fourteen.

The northeast corner of the building between floors fourteen and sixteen blasted away. Mortar and brick from the century-old building rained down concrete shrapnel and paper all over the street and cars below. David's ears popped from the blast. He found himself under a table a moment later, showered in soot and concrete dust, bothered only by a small bump on his forehead. A vacant, gaping hole appeared as the smoke dispersed into thin air. The sounds of ambulances and fire trucks screamed while roaring down the crowded city street in David's direction.

# DRILL

Matthias stood up above the army's practice grounds in the crow's nest incensed by having to play the role of "spotter". He raised the Zeiss 10 x 25 binoculars and was offered a view of the spring fields. Matthias stood watch obediently, anxiously, and annoyed at the fact he was forced to babysit the two infantrymen whom he had graduated with the previous year. Günther and Felix inched along in the hayfield below while stalking the twin Leopard 2s that loafed about in the grass. The two soldiers were clumsy and required a spotter while the two tanks rumbled about. Drills were a constant now as deployment date approached. While Matthias' attention span waned, he ignored the field for a moment and sighted in the tree lines at eleven o' clock. He surveyed the kestrels that had returned and populated the nests made by the corvids from the previous season. Matthias noted the slight improvements they made to each nest in order to adjust for size. Matthias also noticed the silent, stalking Sun that approached from the horizon. It burrowed into a dry morning that ached with boredom.

Matthias' eyes left the practice field to inspect his boots and fatigues which he wore proudly. His uniform was spotless. Immaculate. *What a damn shame*, Matthias thought, *might even say it was a waste to have even put it on this morning.* Even the practice field below had been manicured enough so that potholes were flagged in order to avoid any careless sprained ankles.

Matthias marveled at the softness on display. Günther and Felix were even allowed a "time-out" if they got tired or stressed from laying out fake mines. If that did indeed occur then Matthias' job would be to order the two Leopard 2s to halt in order to avoid any accidents. Matthias' binoculars rose again to scan the trees where the kestrels assumed control of their new property without hesitation.

Much to Matthias' relief, deployment day was finally within sight. The desire to leave however had been tempered somewhat by the recent return of a regiment that brought with them unwelcomed descriptions of their tour of duty in the desert. Most had described their time was well spent building pools for generals and bug hunting the ferocious, hairy camel spiders that hung near the mess tent religiously. Matthias' attention to the army had been drained with the descriptions of their unwillingness to engage. Apathy consumed him now and he didn't bother to fight it off any longer. He took four more deep breaths and flexed his chest and triceps noting the soreness that seeped in from the thorough workout from the night before.

They wouldn't be allowed to shoot anyone unless fired upon first. Matthias smelled the fear held by those that were in control. *Fear of what,* he asked himself.  To be thought of as an actual, instinctual warrior? Or fear of bad PR if a civilian was hurt. Matthias thought himself a soldier and wondered what life would be like if someday he would be guided by someone that held no fear. Matthias always prided himself in the fact that he was someone that would pull the trigger on his enemy even if it were a dying man that lay before him and it meant shorting him just one last breath. A killer. He had just been trained several months by the German Army only to look forward to spending his days in a desert as a pool boy for a general that would never give him the order to fire. Worse yet, he would be described as a peace-keeper. It was disgusting. Hypocritical.

Matthias held no desire to go to battle and sit. He took four deep breaths and watched the Leopards plod in and trample the fields, trampling across stalks of hay steadily and mercilessly. Matthias looked up to the Sun and acknowledged daybreak. Günther and Felix struggled to remove the fake plastic mines from their backpacks. Matthias offered advice on the approaching tanks. He proffered quickly into his walkie-talkie that they should learn to rely on the sound emitted from the behemoths in order to plot an escape.

Matthias stood in the crow's nest and lowered his binoculars. He was trained to kill and to enforce a specific set of rules upon those weaker than he and they would abide or be killed. Unless things changed his talents would be wasted on some endless tug-of-war that would provide him more practice with a shovel than his specific skill set which the German Army had provided. Matthias watched the kestrels infect the trees. They banded together and hunted viciously and without prejudice. He watched them dive-bomb to the ground to catch the mice that roamed naively.

Matthias descended the ladder in retreat from the crow's nest. It took all of five minutes to gather his things. He was even saluted as he walked off the base. In the distance an alarm blared and an ambulance soon sounded its warnings as well. One or both of Günther and Felix had been careless. *Roadkill*, Matthias thought. A lesson learned for them and the army.

# WE ALL SCREAM

*JESSICA UPSHAW – AGE 8*
*July, 1981*

Standing sheltered in a sun-drenched suburban landscape, a three bedroom ranch sat with a large bay window overlooking its green grass accompaniment. The appropriate suburban soundtrack applied: A batted ball that flies into a neighbor's yard nearby amid moans from children. Lawn sprinklers that populated the green grass that blanketed the front yards as far as the eyes can see. Air conditioning units parked next to each and every house whirred continuously amid the blazing heat of a late summer afternoon. More background noise ensued as a chorus of dogs barked at one another with fences planted along plot lines as the mediator. Jessica Upshaw's house wedged itself between other various tract housing, nestled together neatly surrounded by suburbia.

An ice cream truck used to trolling the neighborhood nearly every day sent its tune out across the suburban sprawl. This was the sumptuous treat the youthful, eight year old Jessica Upshaw awaited as she stood peering out upon the front lawn as her older brother kicked at the trusty lawnmower, licking his lips while the ice cream truck approached.

*Perhaps*, Jessica thought, *today would be a bomb pop day*. Jessica looked up to her father, standing close behind, with every intention of getting down on her hands and knees to beg if necessary. Monitoring her older brother's progress on the front lawn, her father finally stated, "I bet if you look behind the couch cushions you might find some change that may have fallen out of my pocket."

Jessica ran to the cushions and probed underneath them. She found exactly one dollar, which was all she required.

"It's our secret, Jessica. Anytime you want a treat, check under the cushions for spare change."

Jessica waved her dollar bill triumphantly and attempted to run off after the ice cream truck.

"Tut-tut," her father muttered, stopping Jessica in her tracks. "Straighten out those cushions as you found them, please."

Jessica did as she was told. She even took the time to straighten out the cushions from the accompanying chairs that went undisturbed. She then made off to pursue the ice cream truck, which was past the house now and rumbling down the block. She stopped at the sight of her brother. He was mowing the lawn during the hottest part of the day. Her dad, sipping hot coffee, looked on.

"But, Daddy," Jessica said looking to her father drably, "what about Christopher?"

Jessica's father looked down to his drink. He sipped more coffee. Jessica would recollect that her father always sipped coffee no matter the temperature. Today it topped a hundred degrees outside, and it didn't faze him the slightest.

"Yes, what about Christopher?" he replied.

"Chris loves ice cream, too. And I only have enough money for myself."

Jessica looks out to the front lawn to see Christopher wipe a sweaty brow with a free hand while keeping the other on the rickety lawn mower.

"Your brother mows the lawn," her father states, "and I reward him for that."

"How come he doesn't get any ice cream?"

"That's because he spent his money already. Chris was careless with his baseball mitt last week. He left it at the park after I reminded him several times not to forget it. Well, he forgot it. And when we went back to get it, it was gone. So, I gave him an advance on his chores and allowance money so that he could get a new mitt in time for his next game. This is what you call 'teaching him a lesson.'"

Jessica watched her older brother looking in at them as they stood inside the cool house. For some reason, which later in life Jessica would figure as further punishment, her dad was only able to get the lawn mower started at the hottest part of the day. "Remember, the cushions," he said. "It's our little secret."

Jessica ran off after the ice cream truck as Christopher looked on. When she returned, she held a traditional sno-cone. It was not to her liking, but that was of no importance. It was Christopher's favorite. Jessica stood by near the front quadrant of the lawn and waited until Chris finished his last swipe. Upon conclusion, Jessica handed the sno-cone over to Chris triumphantly.

"Here you go, Chris," Jessica stated. "It looks like you could use this more than I could."

Chris looked upon Jessica with a sense of uncertainty.

"Dad's punishing me for losing my mitt. He made me use all my allowance and chore money on a new one."

Chris attacked the sno-cone.

"Where did you get the money?" Chris asked.

"Daddy and I have a secret hiding spot so I can get my treats!"

Young Jessica looked over to the large bay windows at the front of their house. She could see her father looking on disapprovingly.

* * *

Just a few days later, as the very first comprehensible intonations of the ice cream truck jingle struck young Jessica Upshaw's eardrums, she instantly sprang from her bed. Her smile continued to widen and giggles and laughs joined her as she sprinted down the stairs from her bedroom to return to the couch cushions to collect for her ice cream intake. Alas, after searching through the cushions for several minutes, there was no money to be found. Through the big bay windows Jessica watched sullenly as the ice cream truck rolled past her house. Her father couldn't possibly have forgotten, she thought.

Her mom had been at work all day, so it wasn't as though she could have cleaned and found the money. Only her brother had spent the entire morning watching television on the couch. Jessica peeked outside to admire the throng of children pointing at and purchasing their delicious afternoon snack from the ice cream truck. There, calmly walking from the parted horde, and abruptly about to devour his sno-cone, Christopher strolled from the ice cream truck indifferently and unaware of the eyes that spied him from the big bay windows. Apparently he had come across some money somewhere, Jessica thought.

\* \* \*

Christopher jetted through the kitchen and into the garage decked out in little league attire. The thick polyester jersey already issued beads of sweat across his torso while he began a hasty search for his mitt. Rummaging through his storage bin Christopher found his new mitt. It was stuck to the bottom of the bin and took a fair amount of prying to release. What he found, though, was something now only resembling his mitt. It certainly wasn't ready for the ball fields. It had been painted. Pink.

The car pool was honking annoyingly, both by a frustrated out-of-sorts mother and the half dozen or so children crammed inside the station wagon. Christopher walked from the garage and into the Sun, stunned by the new problem that was posed to him and not certain at all as to what could have happened. He'd certainly have to borrow a mitt for the game. There'd be no way in hell he could play again with something...pink. Chris was sure his dad would freak when he found out his brand new mitt had gotten damaged.

As Chris walked up to the car amid the giggles and guffaws form his fellow teammates, he is still having trouble reckoning what has happened. Insults and gibes were then submitted from the car as Christopher prepared for entry.

"What did you do, trade in that new mitt for a girl's kind?"

Then it occurred to Christopher.

"A girl's...mitt?"

Christopher left the carpool and the thunderous laughter emanating from the boys inside. He found Jessica in the living room, instantly fleeing at the sight of Chris's enraged face. Gym shoes pounded the wooden stairs as brother chased sister towards her bedroom and towards violent conflict. Jessica was just a tiny bit slower and was unable to slam the door shut as Chris's foot and shoulder preempted closure. Chris pounded at Jessica's bare arms. She attempted to find sanctuary on her bed, still attempting to dodge Chris's throes with pillows. Jessica resorted to tossing back barbs about whether or not he liked the color of his new mitt.

Jessica's father eventually pulled Chris off of his sister. Jessica rubbed sore, bare arms, likely to bruise. Christopher was quickly sent to his room. Jessica looked up to her father in tears presumptive of the grounding about to be incurred knowing that she disappointed him. Her father sat down with her on the edge of the bed and reassured her that everything was going to be all right.

"I'm sorry, Daddy," Jessica muddled between sobs, "I just wanted to teach Christopher a lesson."

Her father pulled her in close.

"Girl, you are going to be a handful."

# LEGGO MY ECO

*DAVID HOBBS – AGE 32 & WILL FROST – AGE 37*
*Summer, 2006*

Tucked alongside a large metal dumpster, sitting well inside an alley across the street from his next target, David Hobbs spent the latter half of the afternoon guzzling water, trying desperately to make up for the dehydration that had been mounting. Breathing heavily through a sweat-soaked t-shirt, David fought a throbbing thermometer signifying the arrival of the intense heat of a Chicago summer with multiple bottles of water. David let the water roll down his chin and splashed a bit in his palms so that he could dab his face for a quick bird bath. With the ever-present sweat destined to stick around for the length of the long, hot Chicago summer it was a fleeting bit of relief.

Stationed for cover beside the graffiti adorned dumpster with a pair of Bushnell binoculars slung around his neck for surveillance, David's body sat and soaked under an unyielding Sun. David waited and watched the inventory dispersed to the warehouse, chugging the remaining water from one of his several bottles. The afternoon route lead him to warehouse number two on his list. His reconnaissance positioned him on the West Side of Chicago and a considerable distance from the safety of David's operational headquarters. David's physical exertion caused trauma to a body not used to such stress. The surveillance here of warehouse number two begat boredom while he struggled to sit by idly under a Sun that seemingly refused to set. Cooped up in the alley David considered the recent events at the café to stave off hunger and boredom.

The terrorist organization known as The Black Van Group had wanted him on hand to witness the destruction of a corporate office allegedly guilty of trying to dissuade other corporations from joining the summit. Of course, with the corporate headquarters still in shambles, and in light of the news reports that the company was being accused of filibustering at the summit, there wouldn't be sympathy or favor from a public that purchased their product.

The Black Van Group even went so far as to provide video to David documenting the events of the bombing. They had wanted him there to see the damage done. To see how real it all was. There had been no reports of any deaths, but the news carried several shots of stunned, bloodied bystanders stumbling about the chaotic streets. Somebody not only wanted David to see how all of this was carried out, but to also be there in person to feel the blast.

David imagined the scenarios and ruled out the possibilities in his mind. He was no longer some lone, anonymous warrior fighting for his cause and clinging to newly adopted principles. People knew he was out there, and most distressing was the slightly unsettling fact that the infamous Black Van Group knew right where to find him. But David wasn't harmed, apart from the minor scrape on his forehead. There was an organization adept at using explosives following him, and if they'd really wanted him killed, it probably would have happened by now. Presently there was no "want" to have him killed. He was alive and given an example of the force they could exert. Maybe The Black Van Group simply wanted him to know he could be dead at any second.

David had his research outlined for him in the newspapers that he leafed through. They had printed a brief, albeit horrifying, history of the terrorist organization known as The Black Van Group. Its leader apparently preferred running about in black conversion vans. Murder was reserved for those corporate executives who had been guilty of negligence to the environment in some form or another. The Black Van group had admitted to various mayhem consisting of murders and bombings throughout the world, mostly against corporate officers accused of improprieties against the environment.

Numerous sightings of the Black Van Group were subsequently followed by numerous accidents to CEOs around the world.

David had interfered with someone else's vengeance plan, and apparently David couldn't have picked a worse time to have his revolution. Perhaps he was less in the way than he thought. Maybe he was considered more of an ally, or maybe he would even be asked to join forces. And after he told them, "No," David questioned whether or not they would let him live. David wondered how much time realistically he had left in the city.

Nearing midnight, and tired of the boredom and daydreaming, David watched an occasional car's headlights roll by on the vacant street. With warehouse number two directly in front of him, and since the second shift had left to cooked cars promptly at eleven p.m., the neighborhood had retreated to the stillness of a city asleep on a summer's night. Sufficiently pleased by the inactivity, and deeming the neighborhood mostly deserted, David put the Bushnells into his backpack in preparation to move quickly. After taking a leak one last time by the dumpster, David tugged his Mackinac Island ball cap down to hide his face from any cameras. With the heat of the day having blasted down upon him, and with the exercise of the vicious bike ride, he had drunk water all day, and only now was he beginning to feel somewhat rehydrated again.

Skulking across the city street, exposed to errant street lights in search of warehouse number two's dock, with nerves firing adrenaline up to his brain and his heart hammering away inside a dense chest, David pulled the small crow bar out of his back pack as he hit the dock. Peering through a window, David could make out a dozen pallets of AJ Quality Retail boxes stacked up and freshly unloaded from the truck that David had watched drop off the inventory earlier this afternoon. David jammed the crow bar into a window, jutting it loose from the crusty window frame, acknowledging his future entry point. That was all he needed to know. A return trip tomorrow evening with the largest rental truck he could find was in the making.

With only a dozen pallets, David thought he could be a ghost in two or three hours. David had noted this particular shipment was camping equipment containing mostly sleeping bags and foul weather gear. David thought that the homeless shelters would be well stocked for whatever harsh winter

weather Chicago would be in store for. David sat still and silently acknowledged that he probably wouldn't be around to see it.

David walked back across the street. Having done nothing wrong at
this point he wasn't fearful to be captured. There were no cars, and the
street lights still hummed. David breathed hard still and sweated. Despite
his watch nearing midnight it was eighty degrees outside and still deeply
humid. It was a closer look at things, which was all he needed, but he also
wanted to familiarize himself with the workers' schedules. He was confident that there were no eyes upon him in his walk back to the alley and to
his mountain bike. This would be no cheesy attempt to con another truck
driver. Despite the overabundance of news coverage devoted to the Eco
Summit and the terrorist group attacking the city, David was sure the AJ
Quality Retail folks would be on high alert after the stunt he pulled. He'd
need to get sleeker. David turned from his bike to take one last look at warehouse number two. It was his next target.

The explosion sent pillowy black smoke and flames blasting through
the sparse glass windows of the warehouse. The fire shot skyward sending
most of the warehouse's roof into the air and across the neighborhood. Bits
of glass pierced the air like scorching BBs. Chunks of cardboard sprinkled
the sky like flaming stars only to drift down harmlessly landing in the middle of the street and some even in the alley with David. The blast knocked
him from his bike and again blood oozed from the scrape on his forehead
that had scored the alley's cement ground. David could feel the heat from
the fire across the street smother him like a blanket.

David smelled the charred air with each breath he took. The smell of
fire flooded his clothes and soiled his skin once again. David looked back to
the bonfire of bricks and burning boxes and crates. Most of the walls were
still intact, but the roof was noticeably decimated, lending oxygen to the
fire. Pieces of the roof lay scattered around the surrounding streets with
their fire lingering. It'd be a heck of a fight for the firefighters whose siren
he could hear off in the distance. Stumbling for his bearings, David peddled
relentlessly for miles. He spotted the plume of smoke from the burning
warehouse being sent to the sky. The exhaust of charcoal smoke drained
above into the dark night sky as David bathed in Lake Michigan, freeing the
fire and smoke from his clothes. Riding to his hideout, he thought he might

not be as safe as he once assumed. He had another warehouse to cross off his list whether it was by his doing or not.

* * *

Not quite twelve hours later, David sat on top his mountain bike outside the convenience store close to his warehouse hideaway. David took a swig of water and braced for another scorching day. Hazy heat lopped itself on top of an already lazy breeze that came from the west. It was another hot start to a beautiful day in the city of Chicago. David piled the Neosporin on the continued scraping of his forehead, which seemed to be lengthening upon each blast. David had spent the last hour scanning the newspapers positioned with his back to the cameras outside the nearby convenience store. While there was nothing in print yet about the warehouse explosion, David was able to spy the small television behind the counter that the cashier ignored. David could see multiple fire trucks and police cars announcing their presence with obnoxious flashing lights warning of danger surrounding reporters in the background. It was clear that the fire had been put out but work was still ongoing and already it was presumed that The Black Van Group would be held responsible. David chuckled a bit and offered up, "Uh, duh."

Several cutaways dotted the news broadcast. The first was a photo of the leader of the group. A man with wiry silver hair with a leathery, pouchy face damned to look ugly. David wasn't close enough to see the caption under the image, but guessed they'd put a name there which was, according to the papers, Will Frost. Punctuating the news report was the second and third image which was that of the young woman in the bike messenger disguise. The papers presented the freeze frame video capture and posted it on the front page every day since the bombing of the office building. David studied the close-up image on the front page of the paper and then looked over through the window of the convenience store to see the television sport the picture of her again.

David, perplexed by a woman approaching the store wearing a trench coat in blistering heat, watched her as she walked across the parking lot straight into the store. David studied the young woman, who wore a raincoat cinched tightly around a small waist. Then he looked down to the newspaper. Then he looked at the cashier whose head rested lazily in his hands with some magazine laying in front of him on the counter.

She simply passed by him and walked right into the store, failing to even offer a sideways glance in his direction. Had she not been dressed in a large trench coat David might not even have noticed her unless he was being attentive to short, elfish looking women running about. It looked almost comical to David, and he would have laughed had he not guessed there was trouble brewing. David, off his bike quickly, followed her into the store.

The bright fluorescent lights inside the store sat invading and illuminating a never-ending candy aisle. The girl was in fact the one that the entire city of Chicago had been searching for. David matched her step for step, remaining five paces behind her at all times. She grabbed nothing from the aisles and simply led him into the middle of the store. David finally decided to put an end to the nonsense.

"Um, excuse me?" David said roundly, clearing his throat beforehand, shocked and awed at the gall the girl had shown. A quick tap on the shoulder brought her around and finally face to face with David. It was in fact the same girl from the DVD and from the pictures in the paper.

"All right," she said, "you got me."

A slim, sleek jaw sported a small mouth with thin lips. Her cute nose curled up a bit but punctuated the attractive young girl's face with perfection. Sharp green eyes scanned David and watched him closely. Matted, straight black hair with short bangs lined her forehead. She was a beautiful young woman, David marveled, sans makeup even.

The only major problem revealed itself when she revealed herself. Small hands undid the belt that cinched her coat. The coat, dropping open, revealed her almost naked body clad only in her bra and panties surrounded by pasty white skin with an outline of her ribs accentuating the slim frame. David guessed she weighed less than one hundred pounds easily, and the size of her breasts suffered due to apparent malnourishment. David speculated it was malnourishment by choice. No matter because he had seen all shapes and sorts, and this was not the issue. The major issue happened to be the dozen or so sticks of dynamite wrapped up and belted around her waist.

"You want the easy way," she began, "or the hard way?"

Slender, boney fingers grasped a detonator that poked through a sleeve too long for such a skinny frame. David scanned his surroundings. He was stuck deep in the middle of a mile-long candy aisle.

"Well, childhood obesity is a dreadful problem these days," he said.

"I don't eat anything with a face," she returned sharply.

"I'm afraid the same cannot be said for me," David said looking her up and down. "From the looks of your hardware a few cheeseburgers would do you well."

"Enough banter, ad man. Do I blow us all to kingdom come, or are you going with me quietly?"

"With such a beautiful day outside in the beautiful city of Chicago, why don't we leave kingdom come for another time. I'm afraid my bike is only equipped for one however."

"That's okay, mine's better."

The Suzuki Hayabusa soared down Lake Shore Drive, easily weaving in and out of slow moving traffic. Its engine screeched warnings to sluggish commuters that something big was about to fly by. She let up on the accelerator only to make sharp turns, and she hadn't bothered taking off the belt full of dynamite, despite having disconnected the detonator. David hung tight to the small waist and bones that powered the large bike past commuters daydreaming during traffic. She parked the bike inside David's warehouse war room, and he led her to his makeshift workspace. The map hung with notes surrounding each location and schedules still hung nearby too, with a big X handwritten over the pages for warehouse number one and two. The desk from the office that normally was reserved for holding up David's bike had now been confiscated and set next to his mattress. Papers littered the office floor from David having removed the desk, but David left them there on purpose, refusing to touch them.

"So, this is where the magic happens," she said. "Nice mattress."

She had tightened her coat once off the bike, but with the heat inside she felt it necessary to undo the cinch. David marveled at brief glimpses of cleavage and white, satiny underpants. David reached inside the small refrigerator and pulled a couple of bottles of water from it.

"It's hot in here. Have some water."

David handed her the water sealed in the plastic bottle.

"Have you ever tasted rain water dripping off the leaves of banana plants in a Costa Rican rain forest?"

"I'm afraid I'm all out of Costa Rican rain water. You'll have to settle for this here plastic kind."

"Given the situation, I'm afraid I'll have to accept," she said reluctantly and chugged cold water. "No air conditioning. I like it. Roughing it, are we? You're really taking this mid-life crisis well, David."

"You're very well prepared. What's your name?"

"It doesn't matter what my name is."

David stared at her skeptically.

"People here have been calling me Jane," she finally offered.

"So, what are you, the warrior-type, Jane?"

"Sort of."

"Don't eat meat. Don't eat anything with a face. Afraid of plastic water bottles. Ultra radical faction of The Black Van Group?"

"I prefer 'ultra violent.' But it beats being a washed up ad man."

"I'm not so sure about that. Being wanted for murder is a lot more dangerous than blowing a campaign or two."

"Not according to my ideals. My philosophy."

"Since when is murder a philosophy?"

"It's an organizational philosophy that we let nothing get in our way. And we've only killed two people in this city. So far."

"Ah, The Black Van Group."

"Their name, not ours," Jane said and pointed to a newspaper that lay crumpled in a corner.

"Well, just what the hell is it that you want with me?"

They baked inside the warehouse. Sweat dripped off them both.

"There are plans. And we'll be needing your help. That's all."

David sat down in his chair and rested looking up to the X that covered warehouse number two. Jane studied the entrances and exits to the stale warehouse and removed the belt of dynamite carefully from inside her coat.

"I'm no terrorist," David acknowledged.

"Neither are we," Jane said.

David chuckled.

"You believe in what you're doing, don't you?" she asked him, walking up to him in the chair. Looking down upon him. Scanning the map that he had meticulously noted upon.

"Of course I do," David said.

"I believe in Will," she said, looking away, towards the map.

"Yes, but 'He' has people killed."

Jane stepped up directly in front of David. Her jacket hung open loosely revealing underpants eye level to David and her chest open to him and welcoming.

"Only those that deserve it, David."

Jane dropped her jacket to the floor. Her skinny legs darted under the arms of the chair and on top of David so that she straddled his lap. David felt the satin from the crotch of her underpants start to press into him.

"Why don't you make yourself comfortable," David advised.

"Thank you, I will."

Her lips dived down to meet his. He tasted her sweat, and her chest rubbed into his. Their tongues slid into one another.

"You sure there's no more dynamite strapped to you?" David asked.

"Why don't you try me. See if I go off."

David did as he was told.

\* \* \*

David and Jane lay on the mattress together. He knew it was the first time he'd made love inside an empty warehouse and wondered if Jane could say the same. David also figured that it had been years since he'd made love to a woman sober. A jug of water nearby kept them company, and they munched on saltines while David, propped up on the mattress with his back against the wall, held her close to him. Jane had borrowed his t-shirt and put her underpants back on while David simply hiked on a pair of shorts. She was an intense lover, David thought, requiring constant attention, and she had preferred being on top, which was fine with David.

"I used to know someone like you," David said. "You remind me of her. Of someone and something I once had in my life. Someone full of passion and a lot of fight. Someone I loved very much."

"Mmm?" Jane mumbled through a mouthful of crackers. "I get that a lot. I never had anyone or anything."

David held her in his arms on the mattress while she munched away innocently on saltines. Bare legs slid over his occasionally, and he felt her tiny frame leaning into his.

"But it was my fault that she left," David recognized finally. "It was all my fault. My pain."

"It's okay," Jane said and rubbed his arm, throwing a kiss up to his cheek and then one to his lips. "I have pain, too."

"You mean because you killed another human being?" David said point blank.

"Don't think that it doesn't hurt. It hurts like hell, David. I mean, I'm not some sociopath. I'm a human being. But it's a war, David. These people have to know they just can't go around dumping shit all over this planet only to get away with it or get some lousy fine."

"Right, I get it. But there's ways around murder."

"I know. I heard stories about your old girlfriend. She's a good woman still. Righteous. But it's not enough. People aren't listening."

"So, where did he find you? Foster home for future anarchists?"

"You might say that. It was while I was at college. Pre-Law, if I remember correctly."

"And he found you."

"He found me."

"And he changed you?"

"I saw what had happened to him. And that changed me. He appeals to your soul. Kind of like, saying, it's okay to be angry and to take it out on those responsible, ya' know?"

"No, I wouldn't know."

"Not yet."

David knew this wasn't going to end well. "So, what am I supposed to say? Take me to your leader?"

"He's already here."

Jane rolled free from David's arms on the mattress quickly and ran across the floor to the other end of the warehouse, covering up with her trench coat in the process. Ropes dropped from the rafters. Four rather rough looking young men repelled down to the floor and quickly raised compact automatic weapons in David's direction. One young man in a flannel shirt with cutoff sleeves stepped in front of David. Curly blond hair and thick glasses sat on his face, and he sweated profusely. David didn't move from the mattress. He just sat and waited.

Bursting into the warehouse housed in rays of light from the opened back door, a silver-haired man in a wheelchair rolled the length of the warehouse floor in the direction of the gunmen and David. The mechanized motor of an automatic wheelchair echoed off the walls. Jane accompanied him from behind. As the wheelchair bound man pulled up, David noticed the blood-red eyes housed under blackened circles that shot fire at David. David sat on his mattress, still propped up idle and stunned.

"Saltines?" David asked the gunman in front glibly. Then he motioned to the man in the wheelchair.

The gunmen stood silent and at attention. They were young and gruff. Skinny, definitely not the muscle, but they looked comfortable with their weapons, and David chose not to test them.

"So, you're the one who's been naughty?" asked the silver haired man.

"From what I hear on the news, you aren't exactly a boy scout," David replied.

The man in the wheelchair laughed kindly, warmly, receptive to the barb. David noted that the man in the wheelchair in front of him looked like he was being eaten alive. His insides might have been full of sawdust and just barely able to hold up his body. His hair, silver, stringy, and thinning, ran uneven and sparse down to his shoulders. The skin on his face drooped, leaving pockets of pimples dripping and oozing with puss, and it looked like his face could fall off at any moment.

"Please forgive Matthias," the man in the wheel chair spoke. "The German Army wasn't much good for his sense of humor." His eyes set back in a skull glaring forth and fixed like orbs of red fire. The gunman in front with the cutoff flannel saluted good-naturedly, and David smiled back sarcastically. "Tell me, David, did you feel wronged...on the contract? The new account? When they promised you something and they didn't deliver? Did you enjoy watching that truck burn? Ironic, isn't it? They burned you on the contract, and you in turn burn one of their trucks. It would be totally boss if irony was your intention. Q. and I aren't entirely sold on your gallantry with delivering the toys to children."

David looked to him, not knowing who Q. was.

"Oh, excuse me, 'Jane' is her name to you, I suppose. I apologize for not allowing you the pleasure to continue with your rebellion, but we couldn't risk having you picked up by the police. And if I am going to be blamed for silly truck fires and robberies, then I want them done my way. I thought it best just to go ahead and take care of it. We can't have you running around on your silly little crusades for the police to catch."

"How come, every time I get near you or your team, something tends to blow up?" David asked.

David watched the man's mouth stumble and stutter through words. David realized this little encounter was sucking up large amounts of his energy. He spoke slower now, knowing he was getting tired.

"David, you have my sincere apologies again for destroying your second target. But I did make it up to you, didn't I?"

David didn't quite understand this response until the man in the wheelchair looked back to Jane, who smiled and nodded.

"Thanks," David said, "I guess."

He'd felt used slightly. He wondered how Jane felt.

"How is it that you all know me so well, and I don't know you at all?" David asked.

"Oh, but you do, David. You know exactly what we're all about. You read the papers, don't you."

The man in the wheel chair grabbed a stack of papers from David's desk and rode back to the mattress tossing the newspapers at David. Jane stood behind him at attention, occasionally making eye contact with David apologetically.

"Yes, The Black Van Group," the man began again. "An unfortunate nickname from the press that has apparently stuck. It is the papers' choice not mine. I merely require a vehicle accessorized for my chair which is why we choose the vans. And they aren't always black, by the way. My name is Will Frost, David. And you must excuse my appearance. I'm rotting away. Very slowly, I'm afraid. Not only is it painful to look at, but I assure you it is quite painful just to move. I understand the wheelchair is a bit cliché, but I'm afraid I am mostly unable to walk today. It comes and goes. Sometimes I can get by with a cane, and some days I feel like I could break into a jog. Sure, I could numb myself into oblivion with pain killers, but then I wouldn't have my intellect."

"So, which initials do you affiliate with?" David asked.

"We're much more than initials, David. Which do you prefer?"

"Black Van Group, huh? How about BVG?"

"BVG?" Will questioned and then immediately responded cheeringly, "I love it! We'll make sure we issue a press release that from this point on we will be referred to as the BVG."

The gunmen nodded, and Will smiled.

"I just couldn't very well leave this planet without a fight, David. Just think of us as…Mother Nature's bouncers."

"Clever," David added.

"Not really," Will responded. "Like you, it took my body being poisoned and for all of my loved ones to leave me for my realization. My self-discovery."

Will wheeled over to David's map.

"No, no," Will began, "you are the one that is clever, David. What is this we have here?"

Will looked through some of the trucking schedules on the desk.

"I'm very impressed, David," Will said and turned back to him.

"I'm pleased," David responded and chugged some water.

"You are very talented. And that anger inside you…I can help you with that, you know. I can help you unload that faggoty-yuppie-scumbag you've become and turn you into a lean mean fighting machine. Your excess, your fat, will all be gone. We will turn you into a force to be reckoned with. A sleek warrior never to be challenged by your enemies."

"I've heard this all before."

"Yes, I know. She still loves you, you know.

"Oh, how do you know that?"

One of the bouncers dropped a pile of letters in David's lap.

"You broke into my condo for that?" David asked.

"Yes, that's right. The love of your life, right? It sounds as though she's still very much in love with you, David. She was with us once. Long ago.

Not very committed to our cause, I'm afraid. The FBI haven't stopped her letters to you yet. They must think her silly enough to try and visit you."

David stood by silently as Will fanned himself with one of Jessica's letters.

"I'm afraid she's a little too busy running her own revolution right now. I hear things aren't going very well for her though, what a pity. I suppose you'd like to see her again."

"I'm not sure she wants to see me. I think I need to get my own life straightened out before joining someone else's."

"There's no way she would take you back as a big strong corporate type, is there? So, you had to pull this stunt."

"It's no stunt."

"In any case, you want your old girlfriend back. I don't know where she is exactly, but given time I'm sure we can track her down. We have various connections around the world, David, and have access to unimaginable amounts of information to what many believe are much-guarded sources. I think I can help you get her back. We can change you into what you were destined to become. A power. Someone who changes things in this world rather than rapes it. In the process you help out a worthy cause. Ours."

David gave him the benefit of the doubt for just a brief moment.

"I'm busy," he said gruffly. "Besides, it was my fault that I lost her. We were kids. We both had different ideas about life and love. And I'm not sure I'll ever be able to see her again. But, right now, I'm just trying to figure some things out for myself. It's nothing personal. I'm just trying to make some sense of my whole damned situation."

"Trust in me, David. There is method to my madness."

"You finally got something right. You are quite mad."

"Please, David, hear me out. You sold your soul to the corporate devil. The same little devils that look the other way when their chemical accidents in far off villages happen to kill tens of thousands of people. You poisoned yourself with alcohol. I've been poisoned by by-product. Hell, I'm practically dead already. My surfboard draws dust daily and will only be put to good use when it's implanted into a sandy beach as my tombstone. David, you sit here in this warehouse with your schedules, and you accomplish nothing. You sling tiny arrows against a massive concrete wall. Let me help you. I can show you how to destroy that wall."

"No, thanks," David said with a guttural monotone awaiting the four hippie gunmen to start blasting.

"You see, for starters, David, the key to a good revolution is to surround yourself with young, smart people. Fighters. Those who will go to war for you. You, David, are just one of those people. You burned a truck. Broke free from your shell. Young people, David, are filled with fire. They're all over college campuses, David. Smart people, dedicated and passionate, surround me, David. And I visited a lot of college campuses around the world."

David sat still on the mattress and prayed silently.

"Too many sit idly by while years are tacked on to useless little lives plugging away on a keyboard in some cubicle. You broke free of that, David. Did you think you'd get all those years back by striking back at them? I'm very sorry to have to be the one to tell you this, David, but those years will never return. I promise you action, David!"

"Action, huh. Does that include killing innocent people close by when your bombs go off?"

"Collateral damage is unavoidable in any war."

"And murder justified by its leaders? A man was killed solely because he chaired some eco-conference. I'm confused. You kill the conference chief but then attack a corporation trying to dissuade companies from joining the summit."

"The chair of the conference was hardly innocent, David. He was lazy and stupid. He sat on his ass when action should have been taken. Companies pilfered and profited while pissing on Mother Nature. I sent a message to the good people of the summit that we need strict adherence and action. And for those against, they will be hit and hit hard. He got what was coming to him, I assure you. As for the office bombing, well, their company was spewing jargon while pocketing some serious funds for the cause. Your cause, I'm afraid, although good-natured, is over. You have a new cause now. Mine. And that means you are to see that I am transported safely from this city."

"I see."

"No, you obviously do not see yet. That is why Matthias and the others have guns pointed at you. But, you will see…soon. I can show you video of babies wheezing last breaths, dying slow deaths from toxic fumes accidentally released from nearby factories, children covered in filth, in hospitals waiting for a doctor that may or may not ever arrive. Meanwhile executives tee off on the eighteenth hole in some paradise. You tell me who's responsible, David. Look at me! I'm walking proof!"

"Once again, no, thanks."

"What if I told you I wasn't asking anymore?"

The sound of guns being cocked echoed from wall to wall.

"Uh, oh," Will jibed. "That means things are really serious now."

The guards moved towards David. Will motored his wheelchair in front of them. Jane stood behind the entire group. David wondered if the last thing he'd hear would be the loud echo of machine gun fire and random shell casings spilling to the floor. They were boys, young, very young with the possible exception of Matthias who held the automatic weapon trained upon him expertly. They all looked as if they weren't afraid to pull the trigger.

"Well, since you put it that way."

David thought for a moment and it dawned on him again.

"It's the boat, right? You want me for my boat."

"Not just for the boat, but for your talents that lie within."

"Sadly, you're not the first person to have used me for my nautical skills."

"And if you're a good boy, then perhaps I won't be the last. You're going to sail us right the hell out of here, David. I'm terribly sorry, but your little "revolt" has been put temporarily on hold. You see, my cause is much more important."

"Have you any idea how long it will take that boat to get prepped and ready?" David begged, looking to buy some time.

"It's been very interesting to watch you evolve these last two months, David. We know the *Bejeweled* is your exit strategy. We know there are plenty of provisions aboard already. We were just on your boat this morning as a matter of fact. Think of this merely as taking your leave prematurely. Via the St. Laurence seaway I can enlighten you to our cause, and we can come back any time you like. I like the summers in Chicago. Winters are a real drag though from what I'm told."

David rose to his feet, defeated but living another day. He left the water by the mattress feeling quite full.

"That a way, Kid!" Will said slapping David on the chest. Jane smiled at David.

"You could have saved us a bunch of time and just kidnapped me from the beginning," David acknowledged. Guns were lowered. Matthias grabbed David's hand and helped him from the mattress and joined them. They left the warehouse with Will leading the group into the blast furnace of heat the Sun was laying down upon the city.

# WINTER BREAK

*DAVID HOBBS – AGE 21*
*Winter, 1995*

David sat alone in the small alcove set just off the main reception area on the 20ᵗʰ floor. It was a waiting room inside a waiting room like one of those small Russian dolls that were never-ending. The ante room to the inner sanctum. The suit he wore was still wrapped in plastic sheeting from the dry cleaners as of this very morning. It hadn't seen much use throughout college. Tearing away the clear film wrap David determined that it hadn't been worn since the day he graduated high school. That was when he monitored the looks given forth from his family and friends. Everyone had made a point to show up. But as he sat and visited with people he noted the sideways glances and mumbles about the breakdown he'd had. David knew what they were saying underneath their breath. It was about the loss of his brother and father in that horrible car accident and how lost David seemed now. David didn't stay long at his own graduation.

David had spent the previous summer as an intern here in these hallowed halls of Graham & Hoffman. David had even been in this room before. Now, though, as an almost college graduate, he mused over the interview he'd just been through. If one could call it that. David and Lou had spent the first hour catching up. Lou regaled him with the rowdy client meetings and who was sleeping with whom. David briefly mentioned Jessica or actually that "he'd met a girl" and left out the bits about how Lou's boat was used to aid and abet a criminal. The second hour he was there consisted of Lou traipsing David about the office for handshakes and introductions to various important looking people in suits that had been hired on since the summer. The only legitimate questions were concerning David's school's chances in the upcoming football bowl game. There were also brief acknowledgements and introductions to scruffy looking creative types. Some even wore shorts and t-shirts despite there being snow on the ground. They kicked around a soccer ball in an open area.

The atmosphere around the agency that day was unique. Champagne corks could be heard popping as various bosses announced bonuses to their department. It just so happened that Lou had scheduled David's formal interview for the day of G&H's Christmas party. David wondered if that had been purposeful. He was answered when Lou came stomping in. Lou's breath stunk of vodka.

"Here put this on."

Lou handed David a red wristband which he immediately sealed to his right wrist. He stopped to yank down the sleeve of the button down that didn't quite fit right.

"It's for the open bar at the party this afternoon," Lou offered.

"Does this mean I'm hired?"

"As if it weren't already a foregone conclusion," Lou said with a chuckle. He then noticed the lost look on David's face which told him that he still had no idea if he'd been hired or not.

"Yes, you're on board. You report to me the Monday after graduation, Kid!"

David looked around some more at the small waiting room. He'd made it inside. *Victory*, he thought.

"So, what, do we shake hands now, or something?" David asked quiz-zically.

Lou took David's hand strong and shook it well.

The Christmas party was at some trendy nightclub David had never heard of. News of Chicago nightlife didn't travel to the cornfields of Iowa much and David didn't much care for it anyway. It was one p.m. on a Friday and David had already buzzed himself with a few cocktails. Mostly, the departments broke off together. But the single people found one another and bunched together at the bar. It had been a good year for the agency. There was a generous check given out to all (including David) that was the Christmas bonus. As the drinking continued, and the hours passed, the incidences of backslapping and boisterous laughs persisted. Some people even stumbled into tables and missed stairs on the way down. David was introduced out loud, along with a few other rising stars, as a new employee. There were lots of girls around. Women, actually. Young women, technically. Temptation sat next to David as he hung alone tottering up against a wall in the corner. It sat there, tapping him on the shoulder telling him to go and rouse some of the ladies closest to his age but its voice eventually muted as the sadness crept in. Knowing and not knowing if Jess was back in Iowa and what she might be doing at that moment. If she were folding clothes in the apartment or repelling down the façade of a building in a great hurry after breaking into some corporate office. If she had gone, David guessed she likely would not return.

There was more booze. David finally broke away from the corner he had been hiding in. The cologne Lou had shared with him before they left the office lost its luster as David slipped and bumped into the crowd resulting in him being doused with suds and other powerfully strong clear concoctions. David eventually pressed palms with some of the suits he'd been introduced to earlier. At that point in the afternoon chuckles and guffaws followed most every conversation. David politicked some and even got some backslaps of his own. The hands on David's watch swung round and round and David eventually stopped trying to adjust his plan for catching a train home. He'd offered a drunken phone call to his Mom (also drunk) and she congratulated him on his new job. He offered no ETA on the train he'd catch to come home.

The crowd thinned a bit as the five o' clock bell rang. Those that stayed just got drunker and friendlier with each other. David wondered if they'd remember who got it on with who by Monday. David had not seen much of Lou, the future boss, until he spied him in the corner rapping with two young blonds.

"I'm sorry, Lou," David interjected clumsily, "I really should get going."

Lou couldn't hear him well enough above the ear rattling rock music.

"Yes, kid, the bar is right over there. Grab us a couple."

David was certain the leftover commuter crowd that made their way home on a Friday night could tell he was piss drunk. They rolled their eyes at the smell and the languish David dwelled in and cracked tall boys.

When Christmas was finished David put away what little lights and ornaments he had demanded his Mother hang before he came home for the holiday. It took him a few days for the hangover to leave him and when it did David took a look around the child's room he had inhabited all those years. There just wasn't much use to it anymore. Still bored he made exhaustive phone calls to other friends who'd made it home from college. They mostly slept. David fought the urge to find out if Jess had left or not. He'd picked up the phone three times and gotten as far as the 515 area code before he forced himself to surrender the device to its receiver. Mom was downstairs sleeping and was no damn good at giving advice about girls anyway. It had always been Dad and Bro. He decided he'd have a conversation with them about Jessica on the way back to school. He left a kiss on Mom's forehead who had been passed out on the couch before he left. The first train he took got him to Union Station in downtown Chicago. The second train (he waited four hours for it to arrive) took him back to his school in Iowa. The entire trip took just under twelve hours. While he sat on trains and/ or waited for them, his Father and Brother failed to provide him with any answers. He wondered if Jess was still there.

The campus bus dropped him off two blocks from his apartment. It was Ten O' clock at night and absurdly cold out. He could see there were no lights on in his apartment. His heart sank a bit at that sad fact. David turned and took the longer route home as the winter chill bit at his cheeks and face. A single stray tear had managed to escape into a blustery night. David passed the café that Jess had frequented hoping to find her ranting about one thing or another. The hastily written sign on the front door admitted they were closed during the break.

Despite the darkness inside David could see his breath in his apartment. Jess had adjusted the thermostat before she left. He waited on the couch awhile with his jacket still on and just sat there. David's head finally hit the pillow and he could smell the fragrances of Jessica's all-natural shampoo infused upon her down pillow. Before falling into a deep sleep David recalled the many times they'd gone to bed together straight from a marathon lovemaking session in the shower. There was that instant of bare nakedness they spent in between showers and covers that brought chills. They would then dive under covers in a shivering rush and would spend the next few minutes warming one another with soft caresses, touches and kisses. There they warmed one another. Her hair would still be wet and it would douse him with spare droplets, leftovers from Jessica's interim waterfall.

The next morning David made a list of things he would need to procure in order to re-stock the fridge. Thus far he'd managed to come up with coffeemate and beer. And then more beer, for the eventual breakdown which loomed. The final semester was but a few days away and he would at least need an appearance of normalcy. Things and life would have to happen like they happened before she came into his life. David's spring class load was light so he would require a diversion to satisfy his depression. Just as David cracked the fridge and debated a beer at eleven a.m. he heard the key hit the deadbolt.

David turned to face Jessica standing in the doorway. Her flowery bag which meant she had been travelling was dropped to her feet. Jessica was very tan.

"You're back," David supplemented the awe in his stare with the obvious.

"I'm back," Jessica responded happily. Her smile wide.

"How long?" David asked walking up to her and closed the door.

"What can I say," Jessica muttered, a tear forming. "I've got to lay low for awhile."

David held Jessica close. Heartbeats pounded off one another's chest. They started to kiss. It was furious despite still holding each others' initial embrace. They made love on the living room floor without any further words exchanged. David could smell the sand and the sea in her hair.

# SEARCH AND RESCUE

*DAVID HOBBS – AGE 33 & WILL FROST – AGE 38*
*August, 2007*

The three lateen sails of the antiquated sailboat pierced the late afternoon sky in a prominent display. The specially fixed triangular rig made it easy to identify out in the vacant ocean off the coast of Indonesia. It had been David who had initially spotted the old boat, a dhow, in a harbor when they first arrived in Sumatra. Will decided that the BVG would borrow it. From afar Will Frost had thought it might look like a feather dusting off the tops of the cruel Indian Ocean waves. It was an elegant, old ship, and it was a shame he'd have to sink her.

Will, eager to witness the action that was about to unfold, acknowledged the Sun dipping down gently from a skyline canvassed in crimson. It had been an especially warm day, and Will was sick of being on the boat. Thankfully, they'd finally got the damn container ship to stop. Everything had been run to perfection thus far, Will surmised, as he ordered the old ship to hold steady.

There'd been two months of research, training, and rehearsal for this operation, and it had taken only twenty minutes for the massive container ship, the *Pasha*, to come to a complete stop. With a pair of dirty binoculars and leaning hard in to the handle of his cane, deeming the situation quite dire for the *Pasha*, Will watched the three large fishing trawlers in front of the massive ship's bow circling like flies irritating a sleepy lion. Will had not only stolen the three fishing trawlers but had also made some slight modifications. M-60 machine guns were inserted to the position usually occupied by the motorized winch which lay aft of the main cabin. They had left the outriggers on in an effort to maintain the appearance of a fishing boat. Naturally that mirage was abolished once they started firing upon the *Pasha*. The members of the BVG occupying the fishing trawlers spit bullets innocently, barely denting the layers of sheet metal on the hull of the *Pasha*. But the guns were only for show, implemented merely to keep the crew busy. No, Will thought, it would take something considerably more tactile to blast through that hull.

Will watched nearly twenty or so crew members of the *Pasha* work the hoses on the trawlers. That was good. Certain members of the BVG had refused showers lately in an effort to conserve water, and despite Will's failing sense of smell, he had hoped the hoses would alleviate the B.O. Despite the fact that the *Pasha* could have easily mowed down each of the three trawlers with ease, in these waters, company policy dictated that the ship stop and surrender to pirates in cases such as these.

Certain things had begun to fail in Will's body. Going to the bathroom became mostly unpleasant, and waking up to the puss and ooze flowing from odd orifices was an experience. Colors not generally known to inhabit the insides of individuals began to leak from Will and piled up on the floor each morning. Will once proposed sleeping on a canvas to create some sort of art project before he died, and that perhaps the BVG could sell the piece upon his death. Q. didn't find it funny, though. He knew his debilitating condition wore at her more and more lately, and was breaking what had been such an excellent caregiver so far. Will wondered if he'd be able to outlive her stay. Mentally he still felt fine, but it was a bitch to travel, and boarding the boat hadn't been very pleasurable. He'd be back in his chair soon. Probably for good. Will wondered if he could consider himself lucky to have lived as long as he had. But the hate fueled him. He remembered Curly thrashing about back at the cove.

Will knew the Captain of the ship had remained on the bridge to monitor the progress being made with the hoses. Perhaps attempting to send an S.O.S. or maybe alert the U.S. Navy and too busy to notice the two Rigid-hulled Inflatable Boats approaching at high speeds from the rear. RIBs they were called for short. It would make for a nice surprise. There were plenty of surprises in store, Will thought, for everyone.

The mission started with BVG aboard the trawlers, Matthias and crew on one of the RIBs, and David and Q. (or Jane as they had all continued to refer to her after Chicago) and crew on the other. They would all rendezvous at the villa after their work had concluded. The villa had made a perfect BVG compound these last two months. The island they had found mainly deserted, empty, and dilapidated. The villas that still stood, on high ground, remained as leftovers, acne to the Earth, from the Tsunami that had laid waste to so much.

In the event the two RIBs didn't capsize in the massive wake left by the *Pasha*, then the nights without showers and sufficient drinking water would be well worth it. In the event they never saw one another again, Will and David had hugged good-bye. Like brothers. This was to be one of the more dangerous missions for David, who had undergone such an extreme transformation since Will had ordered David to sail him to safety not quite one year ago.

\* \* \*

Sunlight sifted down porously through a barren cloudless sky and landed upon a face already beset by perpetual stubble and a base tan. The two months spent in Indonesia provided everyone with layers of grit and grime forever fastened to their skin as the minute long shower they were allowed every fourth day seemed entirely ineffective.

"Everyone, please be precise while performing your duties," Will reminded all via the headset. "But please hurry. It'd be a real drag to have to explain ourselves to the U.S. Navy. Or worse, other pirates."

David watched the first RIB, piloted by Matthias, hammer itself against the hull of the *Pasha*. David turned to Jane, who sat at the rudder for the twin engines. She nodded, and David stepped forward in preparation to leave the small craft. As he rose, long, lean muscles in his arms and legs were revealed by a black sleeveless t-shirt and cargo shorts. A belly that once burdened him had disappeared, and David sprang, light on his feet, fighting the buoyancy, as he stepped towards the massive ship. His cargo shorts exposed calves that had seen many climbs of mountains and volcanoes. David was beautiful again. He hadn't been on a scale in months, but knew he was well below two hundred pounds, despite the strong biceps and quadriceps he now sported from being so active and moving around all the time. Balanced by eating only when he was hungry, and then not gorging himself, David's body was positively sleek. Sweat was constantly layered upon his body, and deodorant and frequent showers were mostly a thing of the past. His body paid the price for all the inadvertent exercise he was getting (and the probable malnourishment), exposing a long, lean figure in the mirror each morning.

Matthias and three other BVG prepped themselves for the climb up the container ship. It was apparent to David that all of the BVG in the first boat to board had some sort of military background. Matthias pointed the modified rocket propelled grenade launcher towards the railing that surrounded the main deck. It was armed with a grappling hook fastened to a rope ladder. The climb would be a bitch, but it would take under eight minutes. David, unarmed, and quite fine with that, knew there would be no ransoming of the crew and cargo from the *Pasha*. The plan was to simply send the boat off course straying from the shipping lanes eventually to run aground somewhere. Immediately upon securing the crew in the RIBs it would be David's task to set the new course for the unmanned *Pasha*. David and Will had argued on this, Will wanting it to sail directly into Ellis Island, while David chose somewhere vacant in Greenland. It didn't really matter just so long as no one was hurt.

Looking at the first group going up the ladder, David wondered what was so heavy in the back packs that they were carrying. David and Jane followed the four from the other RIB, leaving one member in each to steady the craft against the hull for their return trip with the crew. If there were hoses, Jane would take aim with her AKM and its rubber bullets.

David climbed the ladder effortlessly and took a brief moment to look out across the Indian Ocean. He saw the dhow and its three strong sails sitting out on the water very far away. David had sailed to the mainland once a week, taxiing members of the BVG in the old dhow in search of food, water, and various supplies. He knew Will was watching.

They had practiced climbing a rope ladder against a rock formation from which David still had cuts on his forearms, so the cold steel plates that made up the hull of the *Pasha* were almost welcome. The splashes of water from intermittent waves certainly were. Jane, with her AKM slung over her shoulder and looking very sexy in a dark green wife beater despite her small stature, teased David on the way up the ladder.

"Hobbs, I remember last year at this time you were just some advertising fat ass. Think you would have made it up this ladder back then?"

"Not a chance," David answered, searching for the truth, realizing she was correct to admonish him, reaching for another rung. "I'd have drowned by now."

David heard the warning shots from the crew of the first RIB signaling they'd made it aboard. Scruffy looking young militants were now rounding up the crew and organizing them by weight so they could be dispersed in the RIBs proportionately.

The voice in his ear reminds him again, "Remember, show me some quickness out there!"

Rubber soled shoes struck the main deck of the *Pasha*. They had to run quite a ways to catch up. The main deck of the cargo ship, mostly clear of containers on this run, was wider than a football field and was longer than the Eiffel Tower is tall. Capacity holding consisted of 10,000 twenty-foot-long shipping containers, but the booty on this particular run was the construction equipment housed underneath that was destined for South America. The BVG had decided that it wouldn't make it on time.

Jane, flaunting the greasy AKM against her small figure, led David quickly over to the first group and shouted at the crew in Russian. Contracted by the shipping company, there were exactly twenty crew members aboard. David followed Jane's lead and pretended to act tough behind her and the other BVG. His responsibility was up there on the bridge. The crew of the *Pasha* looked decidedly frustrated with Jane and the BVG. They appeared impatient and bothered by the disruption and not at all afraid that there was a woman and group of men waving guns in their faces.

The gun Jane toted may have been weighty for her but she'd never let it be known that she was bothered. David figured the rubber bullets hurt like hell. Jane forced them to their knees for a quick head count. David watched the members of the first boat scamper, unzipping their backpacks as they raced down into the hold of the ship. David wondered where they might be off to.

Jane continued to wave the AKM in the faces of the crew despite their annoyance.

"Can we get this over with?" said one of them in very bad broken English.

Jane walked over to the crewman who spoke and aimed her rifle in his face. She looked back to David for a moment, then raised the butt of her rifle and slammed it into the nose of the man who spoke. His nose split and bone shattered, leaving blood flowing onto the deck. David looked away from the violence and away from Jane cursing at the crew to behave or they would be shot. The crew was obedient after that.

"No more talking," Jane said in perfect Russian. After sitting with Jane for all those lessons on the laptop David's Russian was clunky but he had understood most of what was being said.

"How many?" David asked.

"We've got all twenty crew members."

"Okay," David said innocently into his headset, "let the trawlers go."

"Roger that," Will said in return.

Standing there on the vast deck of the immense cargo ship, imagining the equipment down below in the hold, David laughed a bit at the situation he'd put himself in. He'd never actually joined Will's group and didn't consider himself an official member. He was more like a consultant. Will had beckoned to David's rebellious side, preaching about the protection they were providing to the planet. Will felt that they were like brothers and had kept David on by agreeing not to kill anybody. But David kept Will at arm's length and decided to use his experiences with the BVG as pursuit of his self-discovery. If Jessica had gone through it and survived, David would attempt the same.

He had gotten away from Chicago. He had travelled the world with Will and his gang. Not so much as a single drop of alcohol had he consumed. And perhaps he would run into her. The year had forged his longing for her and clear thoughts sat bestowed within him.

So far it had been a tortuous new life. Living off barely-warmed canned goods with a scarce supply of fresh fruit. He had left Chicago without any money in his pocket, and that was still the case. Will held the purse strings, and David cared little for money now. No one questioned Will except for David on occasion, and apparently that had been a first for the group. The villa which had acted as the BVG compound had housed the twenty-five or so members. It was a considerable upgrade to any of the other dozen camps and hideouts they'd inhabited the past year. Gone were the marble floors of an executive bathroom where David spent mornings evacuating the pollutants from the night before. They had been replaced by an outhouse or a patch of bushes you hoped wasn't sporting something venomous. Clothes were borrowed from one another, perhaps picked up along the way. Sex was interchangeable as well and despite there being a few attractive females in the BVG, David had mostly passed. Except for Jane. She stayed with Will at all times. David could see the frustration mounting in her to a greater extent as Will's health deteriorated.

Will had developed many contacts around the world. An entire network of devotees stood ready to rid the planet of corporate poison. Will hand picked his soldiers for each mission and took careful consideration upon each decision. David had simply stuck around. He sailed when they needed a sailor, but mostly David was subjected to Will preaching nonsensical banter either by a campfire at night or on an oil rig in which they were smuggled from port to port. Will had done his best to convince David of the principles behind the BVG and how it must live on after he was gone. Eventually, David knew, he was going off in search of Jessica, so any anxious conviction was espoused in vain.

David's dreams of Jessica had been becoming clearer and clearer with each passing week. He had shed himself of the abscess that he had become. The alcohol, the womanizing, the general misuse of life that a human body could perform had now been inverted. It was nearing the time, David thought, where he could see Jess and not be ashamed. David had surmised a million different ways in which they would meet. He'd hoped he would see her to savor a moment before she saw him. He'd hoped to look upon her and see how she'd grown. David was sure she was still writing and perhaps, maybe, was still in love with him. David imagined the letters piling up in his empty condominium or at the post-office if he had been presumed dead. If she'd been reading the news in Chicago she may have even put two and two together.

David and Jane steered the crew down the shaky rope ladder when the explosion underneath them rattled the bones in their feet. Underneath, where millions of dollars of deforesting equipment stood, the hull shook while tons of equipment began shifting. Thick metal wires snapped free from the blast. David could hear sounds of machinery crashing into metal down below. Thankfully the blast had been easily contained by the thick metal sheeting layered on the hull. The *Pasha* screamed from aches and pains of metal twisting and bending in ways not meant to be performed. There was an awful groan from the boat like bones twisting and breaking.

David and Jane looked at each other worriedly. Alarms began to blast, and rattling sirens whined all across the span of the ship signifying a hull breach. Another more powerful explosion took place underneath yet again, and this time they were thrown from their feet. Jane wound up in David's arms and as the ship listed sharply it sent their two bodies rolling down the main deck towards the starboard railing, which was the only thing separating them from oblivion. David caught hold of the railing, and Jane flew overboard, but David was able to catch her with his left hand. David's stomach dropped as his back burned from the friction of sliding down a slippery wet deck. Not a hundred yards to his right David could see smoke pouring out from somewhere along mid-ship. Thanks to new biceps, David swung Jane's slight body up to freely plant her on the railing.

"Thanks," Jane said, pulling herself back to the safety of the deck. "That could have been bad."

"Oh, it's bad," David admitted, nodding towards the plume of smoke exiting the side of the ship. "That generally isn't a good sign on a boat."

Colossal groans made by metal shifting and scraping against itself echoed from the hull. Machinery sliding around unrestrained could be heard and the vibration it sent to the main deck made for unsteady footing.

"What's that sound?" Jane asked.

"I believe the hull is ripping in half," David said. "Come on, we've got to go."

David grabbed Jane and they ran back towards the rope ladder. David could see the split forming on the main deck.

"We got everybody down there?" David asked into his headset.

"Looks that way," Matthias responded.

"You first," David said to Jane and helped her to the ladder.

"Better be quick," Will spouted into all their ears.

"Like the man said, be quick," David shouted as he grabbed the ladder.

The boat jerked a little more to the starboard side, and David could hear the deck crumbling apart. The boat would split in half shortly. Millions of dollars of deforestation equipment would sink, if it hadn't already, to the bottom of the ocean floor. David realized that had been the plan all along.

"Sorry for the radical change, dude," Will spoke, which David could just make out, the alarms starting to go, "but if that machinery had ever found its way to South America, then I just wouldn't be able to live with myself."

The boat rocked and split. The few containers that were on deck fell in between the crevice. Jane started fast down the ladder, but stopped to look up at David who was preparing to climb down. David looked back to the smoke only to see lengthy flames where the smoke had been. David could see the bow of the ship arching up slightly. He'd been correct. The ship had split in half. In a few minutes, the bow would meet the stern as the ship folded in half only to shoot straight down taking everything nearby down with it from the force of the wake.

"Aren't you forgetting something?" Will asked David through the headset as he climbed down the ladder.

David looked down to Jane who had not moved down the ladder. She simply stared up at David.

"How many?" David shouted, referring to the crew. Some obnoxious siren covered up most of his voice so Jane relied on her headset. She knew exactly what he was asking. Water, which had been blasting through the crack in the deck, started spilling over. David recalled he had counted twenty crew members board the *Pasha* that morning.

"We have all twenty of the crew," Jane shouted above the noise, "but we're light one."

David started back up the ladder.

"David, leave him!" Jane shouted.

"Yes, David," Will mocked, "leave him!"

"Get to a safe distance," David shouted pointing at the RIBs.

"Save yourself!" she shouted.

"I am," David said resolutely, only to himself, and climbed back up to the awkwardly tilted deck of the container ship.

"David," Jane shouted for attention,

David looked over the railing of the ship.

Jane removed her headset and shouted, "He's on the bridge."

David, on the deck of the ship, sloshing through puddles of water forming everywhere, observed the stern of the ship arching alarmingly high and beginning to expose the massive propellers that plowed the boat through the ocean. Plumes of water from the breach in the deck shot jet streams of ocean water everywhere, tearing away bits of fiberglass, pounding into metal as David sprinted to the base of the bridge. There he found another metal ladder that led to the bridge which sat a hundred and fifty feet in the air. David found this ladder a little harder to climb as his hands gripped each rung of slippery wet metal.

"The consummate hero. Forever the good guy. Well, David, I feel I must warn you that..."

David tore the headset off and tossed it overboard. David continued climbing. The dhow far off in the distance sat mockingly. Opening the door to the bridge David found a man duct taped to the Captain's chair. Multiple alarms blared. The man's ankles, hands, and mouth were duct taped as well. David grabbed two life jackets from the wall.

"We're going to need these."

David seized the razor knife from a nearby desk drawer and started hacking away at the silvery, stringy adhesive. Pulling away the tape revealed a man in a sharp but much bloodied and ruffled business suit. Then David recognized him.

"Oh, Jesus," David said.

It was Thomason, looking straight at him yet he failed to recognize David.

"Please, Son," he pleaded, "you've gotta help me! They kidnapped me! Now this thing is going down."

"Here," David said, securing the man's life vest, "this may help us."

David secured his own and watched the bridge sink lower to the water. David thought he saw a dorsal fin swimming casually above where the deck had been.

"Listen to me," David shouted, "we need to jump."

David pointed to the dhow beckoning to them. Hopefully Jane would meet them halfway.

"And we're going to swim very hard and very fast towards that boat! Whatever you do, don't stop. Now take a deep breath!"

Opening the door to the bridge, and with a hundred feet to go, the two bodies dropped through the air. David dove perfectly and with proper form into the cold water. Thomason's massive body flailed until it slapped the water. David opened his eyes to see the *Pasha's* main deck completely submerged. Thomason was a horrible swimmer. Out of shape, two hundred fifty pounds or more, and plodding along dog paddling and clumsy. David grabbed him and steered him in the direction of the dhow. Thomason would be lucky to make it. David slowed his pace to match the large man. They weren't fifty feet, with probably a mile to go before Thomason quit. Out of breath, flailing, and going under. David grabbed him by the life vest and dragged him. David plowed water aside, attempting to escape the drag from the sinking ship, Thomason's arms lopped over David's neck. Thomason held on as David drove through a crossover with his right and left arm fighting torturous waves that propelled him out of any reasonable rhythm. He spoke to himself as he swam. He promised himself he'd make it. Even as his back felt like it'd break, and as every other breath shoved a mouthful of salt water in his mouth, this time, he'd make it. David's muscular legs thrust through the ocean splitting water off to the sides, keeping his eyes on the dhow and away from what remained of the *Pasha*. There would be some choice words for Jane, who had apparently been in on this cruel hoax. After twenty minutes of arms and legs pounding through unrelenting waves of the Indian Ocean, fighting the drag of a sinking ship, David could finally hear the whiney little outboards of one of the RIBs, knowing it would be Jane. David shoved Thomason up to outreaching hands and arms. David went under the water himself, out of breath and exhausted. But he reached up and caught the side of the RIB and grabbed for Jane and Matthias' hands, and they pulled him aboard. David, shirtless and fighting for air, huffed and puffed and saw Thomason shivering and cowering under a blanket. Smelling salts woke David intermittently. But he didn't mind passing out. He heard Will's voice, "you're missing the last of it, David." With Thomason known to be alive David decided he could pass out for good.

\* \* \*

David sat hunched over on a rundown cot with two dripping, sweaty towels draped over his shoulder. The humidity hadn't let up on the island, and the towels did nothing but push the sweat from the back of his neck to the floor. Jane had poured some ammonia onto one end of the towel, and it kept David from passing out. David's lower back ached. The tendons in his right bicep burned from carrying a two hundred and fifty pound man on his back while swimming in the middle of the ocean. Both shoulders felt like they'd crack if they were touched. Thankfully, his legs only felt partly sore. He was almost sure he was alone (the villa offering only a single bedroom), given a moment of solace as a treat for such a commendable action despite the worthlessness of the subject (or so Will had advocated). David was allowed his wits to return and he was just now able to discern several different voices in the great room next to him. Apparently everyone had been assembled for some sort of debriefing.

Looking out one of the windows, towards an ocean which threw waves against an empty beach below, David scanned the empty shells of broken down hotels which lay as tombstones for the mass graves full of souls destroyed by an enormous wave. A skyline stood piloted only by birds and absent the planes of tourists flocking to a tropical paradise. The ruined assemblage of villas and hollowed out hotels was left for dead, to rot, by a corporation apparently thinking bankruptcy was a better fiscal option. They were on one of the smaller islands west of Sumatra clotting a chain of islands that supposedly hadn't been hit as bad as originally thought and lay twelve miles or so away from a fresh shipwreck. The tsunami had desecrated the island, leaving only one of the villas fit for habitation. It sat on the highest ground on the island and championed its staying power and survival by overlooking the surf with views of most of the island. Not surprisingly, the island population now mainly consisted of meandering water buffalo who looked quite pleased with themselves and relieved by the removal of the mass of inhabitants. The BVG had found the accommodations more than adequate. Hell, David thought, Will had brainwashed the group into thinking a floor was acceptable accommodations.

David had swum for his life. And for Thomason's. He recalled Matthias pulling him into the dhow from Jane's RIB, smiling and anxious to show him the pictures he'd taken of the *Pasha* going down. He also remembered the sound of someone clapping. It was Will, naturally, and his "bravo's" soon followed. David, delirious, could manage only an erect middle finger as a response as they pulled him from the RIB.

The wet towel was replaced by a thermal blanket courtesy of Jane. She had also handed him a cup of maté, which David appropriately thanked her for. She mouthed an "I'm sorry" to him, and he simply nodded back in recognition of a fact of which he was already aware. Still shirtless, and with the cargo shorts replaced by a fresh pair, he added only the sandals to cover his feet, and discarded the blanket. David and Jane had become good friends. Partners even despite their introduction less than a year before and her every inclination towards murder. They had been paired on every job, and David figured Will the omnipresent mastermind was either using her as a spy or as part of hammering home how easy it was to take someone's life.

David looked up to her from his cot. She was young, only twenty-four he had learned on one occasion. Her parents had abandoned her as a child, but she was educated, smart, and had enough cunning to outsmart even the most resolute dictator. She gripped David's hand and kissed it. She stared at him, glassy-eyed, tears at the ready. He had become conscious to the fact that she'd developed some sort of crush for him. David pulled Jane into him so he could hug her. His face met her belly and her hands caressed his hair. She didn't have to say it, he knew she'd wanted to tell him sooner. But she was supposed to be Will's girl, and with Will's anger management issues, if she had told him she might have been shark food. David let go of her and let her walk back to the group lest Will grow suspicious.

David sipped at more of the maté Jane had brought to him in a porcelain cup. He stopped wondering if Jane washed dishes or not and just drank. His guess was she wouldn't have handed it to him if something had made its home inside of it, and anything else he'd just have to live with. His body ached, but he knew he was stronger for the fact. Will had burned him in the guise of some "test" or another. David was furious he hadn't seen it coming. David, looking out towards the Indian Ocean, wondered what it must have been like to see the waves come in. The island smelled like death. David soon came to the realization that people were still making decisions for him. And that wasn't satisfying at all after all he'd been through and fought against.

David joined the group in the next room leaving the towels behind, remaining shirtless, flaunting a taut stomach and tan body. Two dozen or so scruffy looking hellions sat at bay in a semi-circle listening intently to Will.

"David, nice of you to make it," Will remarked.

David said nothing and simply wandered to a kitchenette area in back of the room to pour himself a cup of water from one of the large drums that the BVG had probably stolen. They used the same water for brief showers that had a time limit. Will stood in the center of the room surrounded by his minions and leaned on his cane. In between the excitement of his victory speech, he winced every so often. There was no doubt he was in great pain. David knew what lay inside that body were chemicals and toxins that tore him apart and ate at him. He had unfortunately spent just enough time in that bay for him to rot away slowly. His friends were lucky to die quickly. The past couple weeks David had woken early to see Jane carrying out Will's bloodied pile of clothes each morning to be burned.

"You are…just in time," Will began, taking brief intervals in his speech for long escaping breaths.

"Oh," David said, half acknowledging Will's stress for the importance of David being on hand. "What am I in time for? Planning another kidnapping?"

Heads and eyes snapped over to David's direction. It was not unlike the two to argue, and everyone knew where David stood on the issue of taking human lives.

"Oh, David," Will began, "a little kidnapping never hurt anyone. Besides, thanks to you and your heroic deed, Thomason is busy sipping Mai Tai's with the crew of that ship on a more fortunate island not very far from here."

David gripped the small countertop in the kitchenette. His blood burned and he sweat anger. David felt like he wanted to tear off the countertop and beat Will over the head with it. But that would be wrong, and David's body was still incredibly sore and tender.

"Crew?" David questioned, "That 'crew' was Russian mob all the way. How much did you have to pay for them to kidnap Thomason? And what in God's name happened to the other crew that I watched board that ship yesterday morning?"

Will laughed good naturedly, knowing he'd been caught.

"The real expense went towards the device that was used to burst a hole in the hull large enough to let the machinery get through. And then the boat sank right on top of it all. A brilliant plan. Thomason was just a throw in. Like making it a combo. Do you have any idea what kinds of explosives it takes to carve out a hole in those layers of sheet metal? Besides, David, it was a mere pittance and well worth it to watch you save one of the scumbags that nearly destroyed you."

"He did destroy me. That David is over with. Gone."

*Now you're destroying me*, is what David wanted to include, but he abandoned the protest.

"It took guts to go after him, David. You'll need guts to help run our little rag tag group here."

"Rubber bullets?" David asked and looked towards Will and then to Jane.

"I'm afraid real bullets are much easier to find in this part of the world."

"Where's the original crew?" David asked.

To that question, no one was quick to respond.

"Oh, them," Will answered weakly.

"Dammit, Frost, we had a deal. No one dies. Not while I'm around."

"I'm very sorry, David. But we had to see if you were for real or not. You jumped back on board a sinking ship to save a man who had destroyed you. We're all very impressed. Personally, I had hoped for you to leave him to die so you could save yourself. After you figured out who he was, of course. I can't believe you believed the bullshit about rubber bullets though."

"What you do, Frost, I cannot."

"We sank machinery that's sole purpose was to carve out chunks of the rain forest. Excavating trees from roots thousands of years old from land that hadn't ever seen even so much as a footprint. Thanks to us, that machinery is sitting on the bottom of the ocean rather than being unloaded onto South American soil. Besides, the killing was the mob's doing, not ours. I assure you."

"But it was your plan, wasn't it?" David said and gulped water, recognizing his gym bag in the corner near the door.

"It was a small test, David. You've turned into quite the little warrior out here in the vast open world. No longer are you defeating the enemy by tapping a keyboard and practicing CYA every moment. You're one of us now, and you should have left that man there to die."

"Why?"

"Because that was what you were once. Some scumbag suit that really wasn't worth a damn. Full of booze, soiling himself while strapped to a chair, watching it all go down on a sinking ship. You should have let that man die and become a killer."

"But I saved him."

"You got lucky."

"I'm a damn good swimmer."

"Your physique saved you and that is thanks to me. Your brain was stupid and should have told your body not to get back on a sinking boat."

"I'm sorry, it's just…I won't ever be a killer."

"But you're wrong. I know you can. Imagine yourself in a subway, planting the canisters of gas that will erase the cold unfeeling people of this world. Those that are to blame for poisoning lakes and rivers, spoiling the water so we cannot swim or bathe. It really is so sad. You're ready to tear this world a new one. And it needs it. You have companies out there operating that are destroying living breathing systems. And companies suffer little while the victims suffer greatly. Why are they exempt from the law? They hurt people! I thought all I had was a skin rash. Everything they claim now is an illusion. They haven't put a stop to tearing down and breaking this planet's back. Until they do, we'll be there. Read Brown: 'Every living system on Earth is in decline.' The corporations extract, and mine, and harvest, and they do not return anything to the planet. Can you imagine,

David, blowing a hole in the Earth, tapping the Ogalala Aquifer like a keg. Drowning the American Midwest. Just look at what you've accomplished under my leadership in just under a year. You're smart, tactical in a way that I've never been. Why are you with us, David?"

"Because I thought I could help."

"Yes, and maybe you thought you could change your white collar ways and accidentally bump into your ex-girlfriend at the Eco Terrorist convention, didn't you? You dance with the devil in order to meet your loved one. David, come on! We've had some adventures, you and I. But, it's time for the big one, David, and I need you. You're good under fire, I've watched you. But it's time for my legacy. The Big Finish. The Grand Plan."

"What is it this time?" David asked, curious.

Will held up a brochure.

"Chemical pesticides and synthetic fertilizers."

"Figures," David scoffed.

David noticed another brochure on the coffee table that was for a tennis tournament in Australia.

"We're going to give the CEO of PerfectGrass a taste of his own medicine. Give him a little bath in his Olympic sized swimming pool on his private island getaway. We shall turn his Eden, his paradise, into something sullen and full of misery."

David paused and pretended to look uninterested.

"I'm not long for this world, David. I need to go out in a grand fashion."

From the looks of Will up close, David could not argue.

"You've continually said one thing but done another."

"I can help you unleash that aggression, David. I may not be long for this world, but you, you are here to replace me. The timing couldn't have been better, with us in town in Chicago and you going through your little crisis. All we had to do was steer you in the right direction, and look at you! You're jumping on to sinking ships! Helping to destroy a billion dollars worth of machinery."

The room looked up to him trustingly.

"Thanks, but I've got my own club. My own self to worry about."

"Not if I can help it."

"You can't."

Only a few feet away, now, Will and David stared one another down.

"Look, we're not in the same fight," David said. "I'm not out to kill anybody. I just want people to change."

David saw booklets for the PerfectGrass Corporation on the coffee table and leafed through them.

"You think by being Mr. Nice Guy you can win her back?"

Jane looked sharply away at this. Will and Matthias both noticed.

"You're right. I had something beautiful once. And, well, maybe I spoiled it. Or, maybe I was just fucked up still, I'm not sure. But I let her go. And now, yes, I would very much like to have her back."

"Irresponsible people in this world did this to me, David! All for the sake of money and performed so out of practiced laziness. I didn't ask to be immobilized, scarred, or for this pain! *They said I had months, David!* Well, it seems I've found things to do before my expiration date."

Will sat down exhausted in his wheel chair.

"She knows you're with us, David. She's always known."

David sat down next to his gym bag, pretending to be disinterested and scanning its contents.

"And what has she said?"

"She said that you should run the BVG upon my demise."

"Bull."

"Oh, sure she disapproves of my methods. But she's keeping an eye on you, David. She's a leader herself. And we can find her. Together. After you help me on this project."

"I'm through fighting your fights, Frost. I've got my own."

"But you've been fighting your battles, don't you see? For a year now you've kept your demons at bay haven't you? Why stop now? What have you got left in you?"

"Plenty," David responded. He looked at Will's shoes and noticed blood seeping through at the toe.

"Then do this with me. Just imagine what it would be like, David. To rule the world. Living on a sustainable land with no waste and no worry of contaminants. For people to quake when you set foot in their city. My image impairs me, I'm afraid. You see, I am not entirely without fault."

"And what if I said 'No' and that I would do everything in my power to prevent your war from happening?"

"I wouldn't recommend that."

David stood up from the floor and grabbed his gym bag. Hippies brandished weapons and looked to Will for advice. Jane and Matthias sat still with mouths agape in disbelief.

"Well, that's it then. Isn't it? If anyone cares to join me, leaving this lunatic, then by all means."

David walked past raised guns. He scoffed at the smelly children holding automatic weapons. At nineteen or twenty years old, they should have been in search of the next kegger, not plotting the murder of a chemical and fertilizer executive. *PerfectGrass*, David stored to memory…and the tennis brochure that lay nearby. David closed the door on the villa behind him and headed down the flat rocks they'd put in as steps since the staircase was deemed unsuitable. David heard the door open once again, and he stood there with his back facing the villa. He expected a bullet to find his back. Jane and Matthias came running up after him with their gym bags. David began down the rocks again, and the three of them said nothing.

Inside the villa, Will's gunmen motioned to go after them.

"No, no," he spoke, tired and agitated. His head bellowed a headache. "Put your weapons down now."

Will took a moment to surmise the situation.

"One day…one day we will reunite," he said simply and looked to the Heavens half expecting some sort of backup from above.

The gunmen closed the door on the villa. The sunlight faded to shadows crossing Will's beaten leathery face.

# COMMENCEMENT

*DAVID HOBBS – AGE 22*
*May, 1996*

The spring season's efforts to signal renewal and rebirth were lost on David. While on his route home from his very last exam he noted it would be his last walk past a library where he'd spent many a night the previous four years. Passing by the century-old buildings that housed so many classrooms that had burned much of his time and energy David offered a quick nod but never broke his stride.

Sunshine surrounded him and leaked through pesky clouds lingering through an afternoon eventually giving way to swathes of abundant sunshine blasting down upon the quad. Boys who shed their shirts at the slightest precursor to sunlight sent their gawky bodies diving after Frisbees. Girls sat nearby and smoked cigarettes and drank coffee, pointing and laughing at the odd bodies among the young men. No such joy coming from a carefree spring day surrounded David. No amount of sunlight could soften the hardened shell that housed him.

With the last of his exams complete, it was just a matter of time before donning the cap and gown and receiving a fake diploma. And leaving. With most of his official schoolwork and papers turned in, the last two weeks had seen calls and faxes from Lou at G&H. David appreciated the work showing up. It was just reviewing current campaigns and executions, but they had wanted David to be prepared right from the start. It was an excuse to avoid Jessica by diving into paperwork and reports that really didn't matter. She had busied herself closing out the utilities and other official apartment business.

David and Jessica hadn't said a word about saying good-bye. And in the morning, upon removal of the gown and toss of the cap, there was a rental car reserved and waiting for David courtesy of G&H. He had no doubt he'd be travelling alone. He recognized that he had never really asked Jess to join him in Chicago. What had started out as a romance ignited literally with passion and heat inside a little known jungle in Mexico was now quickly flickering to a whimper. There was never any chance of her coming to Chicago. She was sick of being cooped up, and it was time to set her free. David held the cage closed this long, why not torture her with another eighteen hours or so? God help the poor bastards she and her group would be after next.

David walked into his apartment to find her in the familiar flannel shirt and khaki shorts. She was cleaning up, vacuuming for the final time. David dropped his book bag and refused to say anything. He acknowledged nothing. In between questions about closing out utilities, Jessica's soft green eyes searched David for help and for the eventual discussion of the finality of it all. He provided no help with his silence and instead preferred to avoid the messiness of a real break up. They had loved each other so very much—that was certain. They would go on loving each other. But intense pain was soon to come. If there was no talk before the ceremony, David predicted he would be taking his last look at Jessica in the audience and would be handed her good-bye note at the car rental counter.

She would make a good wife, David decided. And if it weren't for her damned spirit, David could have dressed her up in an apron (a la 50's wives) and married her. She wouldn't have it now. And he knew it. The apartment was always spotless when David walked in. Usually if it were close to lunch or dinner, she'd even have a sandwich or a sensible meal prepared. The small kitchen table would be neat and clean and set. But now, with her vacation or sabbatical (or whatever it was she was calling it) finally over, there'd be hell to pay if you were fucking with the environment. Before she knew it, she'd be stalking oil company executives guilty of causing an accident arising from having too few crewmembers and setting deadlines far too demanding, causing supertankers to stray from safe shipping lanes. But her group would be there, perhaps filling an executive's Olympic-sized swimming pool with oil from the spill in response. Or perhaps the next target was still Ecuador. David hadn't seen any maps lying around lately.

"Well, you're especially crabby today," Jessica said. "Exam go okay?"

"It went fine," David offered.

David bee-lined to the fridge and cracked a cold beer. They didn't say another word to one another while David began the task of packing his clothes. Her bag was brand new, an over the shoulder flowery job, stuffed full of what she'd accumulated while enjoying her stay in Iowa. David could see the purple nighty that he had preferred poking free from underneath the zipper. All the new clothes David had bought her in the last nine months remained hanging in the closet. Most of them still had their tags on to be returned or left for the next couple that would inhabit their space. Lord only knows where she had picked up the rest of her clothes from. David pilfered through their closets and rifled through clothes while devouring a six pack in no time. Jane eventually came into the room and sat on top of the clothes piled in his suitcase. David admired her there and so desperately wanted to smile and make love to her. His anger impeded that from happening. She had added some much needed weight out here in the heartland and she looked gorgeous.

"Want to talk?" she asked.

David looked at the bedside table and noticed her incense and candles were not packed yet.

"What about?" David said gruffly and continued shuffling through the closet.

Jessica got up and walked out of the bedroom. She had been much more optimistic in terms of the breakup. David meanwhile dreaded the last two weeks of his final semester and that had been quite obvious in his attitude. He had no idea how to say good-bye to the woman that he loved. He knew she must still love him in return, because if she hadn't, no person on Earth would have put up with him these last few weeks.

David held the purple nighty in his hands now, running his fingers across the material, recounting each time he'd felt and rubbed her breasts through the soft smooth feel of the purple silk.

"Be careful," he said to it.

David shoved the nighty back into her bag.

\* \* \*

A few tense hours later David and Jessica were free from the forced claustrophobia of the apartment and outside walking in search of a suitable party to attend. There were many. Houses lining the Welch Ave. thoroughfare sported raucous crowds and loud music. Students surrounding the keg were already wearing their game faces in preparation for pending job interviews awaiting them back home. Not that there wasn't an incredible amount of drinking going on, it just wasn't as clearly evident from those about to graduate. Campus town rang with quiet excitement, and it was mostly just the seniors awaiting graduation the next morning that populated the town. It had been a quiet walk for David and Jessica, and they chose a house they'd frequented quite regularly that school year, with David hoping the line for the keg was not obscenely long.

The party was loud, and smoke stuck to the short ceilings of the densely packed living room. Jessica sat and watched David hug female classmates frequently. Jessica finally got fed up and found one of her hippie-esque friends she'd been hanging out in the café with, and the two went off in search of the keg. David hung back and spent the time chatting with a few cuties that he'd met in some Literature classes. Tonight they were especially giggly and flirty (probably due to Jess not hanging on him at the moment), and David chose to take advantage firing back a few flirty exchanges of his own. The two girls mussed his hair and massaged his arm excessively. David's eyes searched and found the keg in the corner of the room. Jessica looked away from him quickly. David continued his rap with the two girls who were euphoric due to the fact that graduation was now down to a matter of hours.

"Isn't that your girlfriend by the keg?" one of them asked. David thought her name was Lara but the twelve pack of beer already swimming about his brain impeded his memory. The music seemed excessively loud for some reason.

David thought for a moment and decided he wasn't at all certain how to answer her question.

"Um," he began, while he seized one of the cups they held and downed a deep gulp of bad keg beer, "I'm not really sure."

"She doesn't look like your type," the other girl, not Lara, or whatever her name is, said.

"Oh, well, what is my type?"

"Yes, I'd like to hear this. What is your type, David?"

It was Jessica back with the beers along with her hippie friend who, seeing the aggravation mounting, made her getaway.

"They were just asking about you and whether or not you were my girlfriend," David rebutted.

"And what did you tell them?" Jessica asked coldly. The two co-eds departed now due to the scene that was unfolding.

"I said I wasn't sure," David called out over the earsplitting bass that thumped through the walls.

Jessica was more than a little disappointed by this. Her shoulders dropped, and she looked weakened by the blow.

"You know, I've been trying to talk this through with you. You haven't exactly been very receptive as of late. As a matter of fact you've pretty much been a callous bastard."

"Yeah, well, I've had a lot on my mind," David stated and started his walk away from her.

"No, no you don't," Jessica said and grabbed his arm. "Don't you do this. Don't just blow me off, David. You chose this big party so you could avoid me, didn't you?"

"I'm sorry, I just, I don't know what else there is to say."

"It's our last night together, David. I was kind of hoping you would say good-bye."

"I know, I just, I don't really know how to say good-bye, Jess."

Jessica threw a hand up to his cheek.

"Well, generally a couple doesn't ignore one another like you've been doing to me for the last two weeks."

"You just don't see where I'm at right now."

"And you *won't* see where I'm at. Look, that's the problem. When we started this relationship it was about finally finding someone and falling in love. Now we're barely talking, and we fight all the time. And that's in between your frequent trips to the fridge for beer. That seems to be what you care most for these days. I found an empty beer bottle in the garbage can this morning. Did you really have a beer before your exam?"

"What business is it of yours? You're leaving, remember?"

"David I don't care if the anger and the ignorance is your defense. But I don't want to see you purposefully harm yourself."

The smoke piled up and collected on their clothes. Numerous conversations abounded between the young men and women of the party.

"You knew we had to have an expiration date. I was just supposed to lay low. It drove me nuts to stay here out in the middle of nowhere. If I wanted this life I would have stayed with my family. But I did it because I loved you, David. I love you."

David surrendered his mind and succumbed to the thoughts and wishes of the alcohol battling his blood.

"You know what," David started, "why don't you just go fuck one of your little activist buddies!"

David regretted it as he spouted it. And Jessica didn't even hesitate.

"How dare you. I opened my soul to you, and you treat me like *this*? Good-bye, David."

The beer was tossed in David's face so fast; she even leaned in to a nearby crowd to grab Lara's beer and threw that at him as well. David's fine motors skills were long since numbed free from their vigilance. There were laughs, but most people didn't really think it was truly out of the ordinary for a couple to fight at a college party. David surveyed his soaked shirt and swore, wiping the cold filtered foam from his brow.

His senses waded through the alcohol and through the insecurity and anger he was feeling. Through the inebriation, he forced his body to go after her.

Stumbling free from the house, David staggered into the crisp evening air in the backyard. Bumping clumsily into cheap plastic furniture David found a pool next to him which he hadn't ever noticed before until now. David thought he heard Jessica and turned around quickly. David swore at himself, vowed to run after her and beat her home, even despite the drunk he carried. He turned and decided to run after her when things went black. And wet.

His first thought as his body sank was to wonder why he'd never known that they had a pool. When he began sinking further, he struggled. David's arms flapped foolishly in an attempt to swim. The plastic lounge chair he had apparently run into spun to the bottom of the pool. Sinking further, there was one last look to the stars. The world went black and David now realized his life was in jeopardy. The alcohol continued to impede, and his lungs started to burn in search of oxygen. He had always been an expert swimmer, yet now he failed to find the surface. Before he could anger himself further, his lungs began to fill with water. David noted he was screaming underwater. He choked and grasped for the sky. His legs kicked spastically, and consciousness faded. Reality and vision fluttered in lucid images. Hands mercifully found him at last and pulled him free from the entombment and up to the surface.

David sat on a patio chair coughing and choking for a few minutes. Eventually he puked water krausened with a combination of chlorine and hops. David closed his eyes from the pain in his chest and tried not to pass out from drunkenness and exhaustion. Jessica stood behind him hitting his back until he was through coughing.

"I'm sorry," he said. "I'm so sorry."

"It's okay," she said forgivingly. "It's going to be okay."

"I'm sorry I didn't ask you to come to Chicago," David said through spit and tears.

"I never wanted you to."

David suffered chills while a breeze had picked up. Jessica found some towels that had been left out.

"I'm sorry I didn't know how to say good-bye. I thought we loved each other," David begged.

"We did," Jessica said and then thought better, "I mean, we do."

David sat back in the lounge chair with his towels wrapping him up and surrounding him. He still shook a little.

"But?" he asked.

"Not everybody falls in love with a revolutionary. It just can't happen right now, David. I'll write, David. I'll write you all the time."

David closed his eyes, and the pain from the break-up grew more intense than the pain from nearly drowning.

"You were going back no matter what," David pointed out to himself.

"That's right. As much as that hurts to say and as much as it hurts you, I have to go."

"There's nothing I could say or do to keep you?"

"Nope. You were perfect, David. We were perfect. It's just, I have to go back. There's a war out there. And they need me. Someday we'll see each other. If you believe that we belong together, then someday it will happen."

"But not anytime soon."

"I'm afraid not. But the offer still stands, David. To help. It always will."

David closed his eyes gently.

"I know it's going to hurt, David. It's going to hurt inside real bad. And we might think that this is over but if we try, if we really try, than we can think that someday we might be together again. And if you're not any kind of an optimist, which I don't think you are right now, then I'll believe. I'll believe enough for the both of us. If you can't, then I will."

Jessica stood up from the rattling lounge chair. She leaned over and dropped one final kiss to his lips.

"Go to sleep, my love."

And then she walked away.

* * *

The chill of the morning air bit into the soggy towels that surrounded him. The sunlight belted him, and David's watch told him it was past graduation. There were a few other bodies out back, passed out on the lawn, but none had been Jessica's. He grasped the cold notion that he was alone now. Dropping the towels, David raced back to his apartment amid flocks of smiling graduates in caps and gowns that passed him by.

The apartment was empty and cold. No meal or coffee awaited, just her key, which sat still on the vacant kitchen table. Sadness and darkness filled him. His pulse lessened as he knew there was no need to rush anywhere now. She'd be long gone. The bedroom sat hollow and absent of her flowery bag. His diploma would be mailed to him in six weeks, but he wouldn't bother opening it until a few weeks beyond that. There'd be letters, he thought. She said so. Scorned with guilt, a new David grabbed his suitcase and left the room only to pop back in quickly. A shell necklace, not hers, lay hanging on the bed post. There'd be no note at the car rental counter, he knew. It was time for departure. It was time to leave.

# MARCH

*DAVID HOBBS – AGE 31*
*October, 2005*

Crisp October air flooded the city streets amidst the harried workers anxious to get home to loved ones or pets. David Hobbs stared out across the city from the floor to ceiling window in his office. His eyes fixed on the twinkling warning lights attached to the antennae atop the various gigantic office buildings forewarning approaching airplanes of their might and stature. Lights from offices dotting the insides of buildings are quickly extinguished as workers depart, only to be promptly illuminated again by the janitors and cleaning people. David bit down on a pencil, sending little wooden shards rattling against his teeth. He acknowledged he hadn't eaten since lunch and figured that the art director and copywriter finishing up the storyboards a few floors below him would probably join him for some pizza. David looked back at the unusually unkempt desk and admitted the concept artwork that they had submitted previously was very good. David was excited for the pitch out in Phoenix in now…eighteen hours. The concept was funny. The previous agency had tried a critter campaign that was tired and not even remotely insightful. For a six-week pitch for a twenty-five-million-dollar account, David had his usual gaggle of the "A" team creatives and was certain that in a week or so they'd be announcing another win.

The clock on the Wrigley building announced it was just after nine, and the duo had promised him finished storyboards by seven. Currently

David hadn't any more important place to be (besides a barstool), so he didn't let the delay bother him. David looked to the streets below to see the carefree taxi cabs bobbing and weaving away from an unusual Michigan Avenue detour. David could just make out couples strolling arm in arm off to the side streets in advance of their reservations at a restaurant. Outside, David knew it was cold. Maybe in the forties. He hadn't brought his jacket when he went to visit Lou in the ICU at Northwestern just a couple of hours ago.

Walking past a med student attacking a large medical book, David noted he'd seen enough pictures of what the liver looked like after being attacked by cirrhosis. Nurses scurried from room to room and wrote furious notes. David strode the hallways of the hospital, recognizing the familiar fluorescent lights were the same design that lined the hallways of G&H. Lou hadn't any family left, so David was allowed in, and by now both shifts had come to know David well. David wasn't a bother to the staff, despite the frequency of his visits. And without family traipsing in and out of the ICU, David was sure the nurses and doctors were just thankful there'd be no one to have to apologize to. "We're sorry that your husband/father/brother smoked, ate and/or drank himself to death."

Lou lay as a small, portly lump on the mechanized bed. David noted the wheezing that emanated from Lou alongside the humming of machines even before entering the room. He nodded to the mass of tissue that sprouted tubes from various locations on his body. Encumbered by several cords and tubes, Lou nodded back slowly. On the bright side, David thought, visiting Lou during a lunch and dinner break allowed him a stop in for a quick shot and a beer at the bar before returning to work.

"You know, Kid, you don't have to keep coming here," Lou managed. "People are going to start to think that someone actually cares about me."

"I've always admired your positive attitude. It's what's kept me coming back to work every day for these last nine years."

"Yeah, that and the incredible paycheck. Don't you have work to do?"

David's butt fell into the cushion of his usual chair. It hadn't seen another visitor. David knew Lou feared the awkwardness of suddenly feeling mortal, and David's realization of that made him even more uncomfortable. On one of David's first visits he'd walked in on a nurse changing soiled linens with Lou's pale skin exposed front and center as Nurses scrubbed at nether regions.

"Just waiting on the storyboards from Grant and Jason."

"Who?"

"Grant and Jason. They're the team I've got on the project."

"Oh, right, right," Lou professed, clearly lacking the memory of a copywriter and art director he'd worked with frequently. David noticed Lou had been looking quite a bit thinner lately.

"How's the company around here?" David asked referring to the nurses.

"There's one or two lookers. But I fail to see any attraction in the female form when its covered up behind such ugly materials like scrubs."

"You'd much prefer the nurses walk around in lingerie? Maybe something out of the Victoria's Secret catalog?"

"Anything out of the Victoria's Secret catalog."

They shared a small, comforting laugh.

"Nice flowers," David nodded to an unusually large bouquet across the room. It was overcompensation from human resources for not knowing Lou was sick when David had bumped into one of them in an elevator earlier today.

"They're from G&H," Lou responded. "They must think I'm dead already."

"You're not though," David responded sharply and quickly.

Lou turned to look at David. They paused, not knowing who would say something next.

"This isn't our good-bye," Lou said, almost like he was begging it not to be.

"This isn't our good-bye," David repeated in kind acknowledging Lou's request.

"I mean, it's not like I didn't know what was happening. Christ, it was right in front of my own eyes. It's just that I didn't change."

They paused again, and silence is surrounded by strange beeps and ticks from machines.

"Where to again?" Lou asked.

"Phoenix," David answers. "Ten a.m. flight on United. It's just me and Grant doing the pitch."

David had told him the same answer at least ten times this week.

"How are the boards. Everything according to the brief? Everything on target?"

"Everything is perfect," David responded, not wishing to bog down his partner with idle details from a campaign in which he would probably never live long enough to see the final outcome.

"You've got your deck? You've got your shit together?"

"As if you had to ask."

"I know, I know," Lou said calmly and patted David on the knee. "What's the temperature in Phoenix right now?"

"It was one hundred and ten degrees today."

"Jesus, that's hot."

A nurse broke the barrier of banal conversation suddenly wheeling in a cart holding various needles and tubes, "I'm afraid I'm going to have to ask you to step out while I change some lines, Sir."

"That's okay, I gotta get back," David said and rose from the seat.

David turned back to Lou once more and shook his hand.

"You be here when I get back," David ordered.

From where he stood at the floor to ceiling window in his office David could see the hospital. A glass of vodka graced his hand now. David had been successful so far in his solo act. But Lou was his buddy. His mentor. It was odd flying with a stranger next to him. The powers that be at G&H reassured him of their confidence by giving David complete control over the creative department on new business pitches. But he missed Lou. He took a swig from the glass letting the sting of the vodka wash around his gums before allowing it to gush down his throat. He poured another glass as Security called from the lobby letting him know the pizzas were here. He'd forgotten he'd even ordered them.

David continued to stare solemnly across the city. The cold glass of vodka pressed up against his cheek. The bottle of vodka had been returned to the freezer for the moment as he knew he'd be talking to the creative team soon. High up above the city folk, safe and secure in his office and away from the city below, David felt protected from the pain as the buildings towered above. Observing the streets below offered views of the protestors, throngs of people marching along Wacker Drive in the direction of Michigan

Avenue. David was handed his pizzas by a large security guard and they munched on slices while sizing up the masses below.

"What is it this time?" David asked.

"Something about gym shoes and the Amazon."

"Ah," David said, remembering something about the large gym shoe maker being tied to ordering leather from cattle ranchers that were causing massive deforestation in the Amazon. An admirable cause, David thought. One he may have fought for if things had turned out differently. David struggled to think and eventually had to excuse himself from the guard offering him twenty bucks to take the pizza to Grant and Jason down on the 9th floor. Judging from the smell of their office from the last status meeting two hours ago, they were probably going through a serious case of the munchies. Either that or they'd gone ahead and eaten the storyboards.

After a moment, David recalled where he'd first heard about the leather demands put upon Brazil leading to deforestation in the Amazon. It was shortly after a letter from Jessica when the Times had published the photos and the story. But what was it Jessica had said that struck David as being odd and out of place?

David pulled the pink envelope from his briefcase. It was always easy to spot because it was the only thing remotely feminine in his bag. She had made the pink envelope her calling card and as generic as some of the content had been at times (she couldn't afford to be specific when she knew she was wanted and the letter itself was likely being read by various law enforcement agencies) the pink envelope always made him smile when he opened his mailbox. For nine years there had been a delivery every other month or so. Not bad, David thought. There were times her letters pre-dated "accidents" at corporate offices, job sites sabotaged with missing or damaged equipment. David noticed, despite using her varied pen names, that she'd signed "love" only occasionally, and David presumed it was perhaps a time in her life when she was in love with another man. But David thanked her quietly each time, noting the postmark from Stockholm was the same on each letter.

The line in the letter was clearly odd and quite peculiar to him from the very first time he read it. It said, "I believe I have a major issue with my gym shoes." She then went on to name the brand of the shoe and how much pain it was causing her. She never mentioned a specific body part (ankle, toe, etc.). Of course, David now realized there was never any physical harm to her body, and that it was just meant to throw off anyone who bothered to read her letter.

The protest march outside on the streets of Chicago was heading directly for a large store owned and operated by the gym shoe maker, a tourist trap really (you could get those same shoes at any store and even pay less in taxes if you bought them out in the suburbs). But David could only conclude that Jessica's allusion to the shoe and the trouble it was giving her in her last letter to him was somehow a sign that she was here in town, in Chicago, and was very likely attending, perhaps even heading the protest march that was on the streets below. It was possible she had something stronger in mind than a march. David imagined finding her out there on the street and the embrace that they would have. Stealing her away from the crowd, grabbing her and holding on to her this time, dragging her away, professing his love to her, something he should have done some time ago, somehow, and then kissing her deeply, off in some hidden alley away from the chaos.

David's fingers fumbled at the glass door to the corner curio in his office. He knew its hiding spot well. Inside one of the hollowed-out advertising awards for some dumb cough syrup campaign. David removed the shell necklace that lay hidden inside the silver trophy and stuffed it in his pocket. His fingers rubbed gently at the tiny grooves each shell had carved in its face.

David's finger jabbed at the arrow pointing down. An elevator soon announced its arrival.

The main lobby of the G&H building was layered in cold grey granite, likening itself to the color of cigarette ash. A sculpture that was apparently considered artwork stood in the center of the lobby. It looked as though someone had collected errant fenders from one of the expressways and glued them together. The CEO had wished it there, and it had been the butt of many a joke in the creative department.

There was more than the usual allotment of security guards present in the lobby tonight. No doubt they were placed there because of the march, David thought.

"They're pretty riled up out there, Mr. Hobbs," one of the guards at the front desk alerted him. "You may want to wait it out."

"Yeah, well I'm pretty riled up, too," was David's response as he flung himself through the revolving doors and outside to the chilled night.

It was an amazing crowd of about ten thousand or so. And on the street, the decibel level emanating from the demonstrators was much increased. The march was comprised mostly of students, David noticed as they passed, and all of them were shouting. Despite the drastic drop in temperature these last few days, the mostly young crowd was proud to wear their crudely designed t-shirts professing guilt upon the shoe company. Jess would be bitching about the cold, David thought. She had hated the cold weather in Iowa.

David couldn't hear what they were saying and didn't really bother to. But everything about the city had been drowned out from the crowd. There were no rampant ambulances or fire trucks, or speeding police cars running red lights. David, still in suit and tie, looked odd and out of place as he strode up and down the sidewalk spying for Jess. They smiled at him acceptingly. Begging for him to join in. David continued to race alongside. Bobbing and weaving in between cops locking up protesters who had strayed from the designated route. She would have been towards the front, David presumed, wanting to lead this thing even if it weren't her gig. David just kept looking. Begging for fate to bring them together. Wondering if it truly was time.

The march stopped exactly in front of the store and its prominent position on Michigan Avenue, which happened to be one of the most valuable pieces of real estate in the world. The press was loving it. The employees of the store, mostly kids, had long since departed after the advance warning was given to corporate through CPD. The protesters shouted and their anger seethed through their pores filling the night. Signs and slogans just wouldn't fulfill the bloodlust they all shared. Despite the bizarre and surreal feel to it all, David felt the air outside concentrated by the ever-present burning fire for a call to action. No doubt some of this sprang from the loins of the youth sharing their passion. There was no question in their minds that this shoe company would cease in aiding the efforts of deforestation in the Amazon by the time the night was over.

David saw a thousand young girls that could have been Jess. But Jessica would be at the front of the line. The commander. Leading her troops. She would be a grown woman. David had seen her pictures on the FBI's website. They had not been updated in quite a while and were blurry.

Despite the trace of frost in the cool October air doing its best to temper the sting inside the protesters, David knew it would fail, there was no doubt of that. The police, decked out in their riot gear, chomped on gum, anxious themselves, and held their batons at the ready. They were dislodging the errant protester for misconduct. Plasticuffs wrung around thin wristed kids immediately. But at the front of the line there was a man and woman leading this march. No one near even remotely resembled Jess. And a march wasn't Jess' style anyway. David thought he should have known better.

Things had been going well until a few demonstrators dug through a garbage can and found some sort of projectile to throw at the store. Bottles of water were next. Then it was rocks. And then someone found a brick (probably from some of the construction going on down the street). Then it was the garbage can itself flung through the plate glass window of the shoe store. David was astonished by how madness and chaos were so quickly realized. All sorts of things flew through the air at once. Police broke into the crowd and started beating and dragging people back to the sidewalk.

Turning around sharply, David retreated, bumping into a young girl in a green knit cap. A brunette with long, somewhat ratty curls plunged outward from underneath the cap. She smiled at David and then politely pushed him out of the way so she could toss the Molotov cocktail. David wished he could instantly transport himself back to his office at G&H, cursing himself for not staying up there to watch from a tranquil view.

Flames burst out amongst tracksuits and shiny white gym shoes. The crowd hailed a satisfying cheer. The young girl David had bumped into smiled shiftily. When David turned back around to the burning store, he noticed a rather burly Chicago police officer storming through the crowd, bashing at shoulders and ribs in order to get to them, his baton raised and ready to inflict maximum pain. David looked to the girl, who began stepping backwards, only to fall over her own feet. She lay there, rubbing a knee, with the policeman, a tank, ramming through the crowd of protesters, still advancing. David saw another garbage can that had rolled over near him and slid over to it, tossing it down in front of the rushing policeman. It was not a kind fall for the officer. David watched the policeman's ankle twist awkwardly as he attempted a pathetic gallop over the top of the rolling can. There was some shouting as he tumbled to the cement clumsily. David pulled the young woman up from the ground. She had a bloody forehead and limped badly but still shouted obscenities towards the bonfire she had begun in the storefront. David let the crowd swallow them as he carried her through to the other side of the street. At this point David was hearing the officer call for backup, and police ran past him through the crowd. News helicopters buzzed annoyingly overhead. Larger things started to go through the window of the store, now forming one collective blaze. *This was not organized,* David thought. There was no exit strategy. This was not Jess's work.

They had escaped through a barren alley, traipsing down a flight of stairs, and he had run with her in his arms for a block and a half. She cried tears of pain from a banged up knee, yet still filled the night air with her slogans. The crowd was beyond unruly now and there was no telling just how bloody it would get. The police looked thirsty for a hippie beat down.

She'd have been beaten to a pulp, and there was no sense in that. The overweight cop would suffer a sprained ankle. If it were anything worse he could only blame himself for his poor physical conditioning. And that was what David was doing currently as he sprinted through a barren alley with a young girl in his arms. And on a one way street heading north, David mercifully spotted an empty cab that stopped and welcomed them.

Scooping away the remnants of General Tso's chicken from the familiar square box of Chinese takeout, she sat at the kitchen island David recently had installed. Her elbows propped her up on the granite countertop amid little packets of soy sauce and hot mustard littered about. She'd eaten half a dozen egg rolls, the aforementioned General Tso's chicken, and two half orders of sweet and sour shrimp (one of which was David's and she had eaten while he had been on the phone with the creative team strategizing about pickup of the final boards in the morning before the flight). He was pleased to have given up his food for the young woman, he decided, and monitored the ice pack she had wrapped around her knee.

She was a far cry from the women he usually brought home. She was certainly skinny enough, but instead of fresh manicures, pedicures, and Brazilian waxes, this girl was the antithesis. She was a brunette with long curly hair, a bit unkempt, ratty jeans and sandals with no socks despite the cool temperature, and from the smell of her it had been a few days since her last shower. David walked out from the large second bathroom off the living room facing the two white leather couches. There was a window in the shower that overlooked Wrigley Field. He had deposited a pair of shorts and a t-shirt as well as a large bathrobe on top of the toilet seat. He'd make her shower and then let her crash on his couch.

"I could order more?" David asked, joining her at the island in the seat next to her. He leafed through the many carry out menus he had offered. He wanted to be as accommodating as possible to her. She was no student. This wasn't a girl from the suburbs of Chicago taking a timeout to be angry before she started college. David knew the girl in his two-bedroom condominium on the 47th floor was "one of them".

The young woman poked through the takeout menus.

"Isn't this town known for pizza?" she asked.

David, astounded but not yielding in his self-made promise to care for this young woman tonight, simply marveled at the rail thin kid that asked for more food.

"Okay," he replied, "I'll order a pizza. I'll even let you shower. Heck, I'll even let you crash on my couch. But first, you've got to tell me your name."

David grabbed his cell phone from the counter and chose the best of the pizza menus. She looked up to him. Their eyes searched one another's, finding honest souls. Inside David, she found his pain and loneliness stockpiled in a dormant heap. Her face and appearance seemed much more demure to him now than it did earlier when he held a brash young kid in his arms shouting obscenities at the police.

"It's Fiona, and no deep dish," she said to him as he began to order. "I hate deep dish."

David caught the advice and nodded his approval, stating, "Me, too."

David decided Fiona was maybe twenty years old. He ordered a large cheese and sausage pizza.

"And green pepper," Fiona begged.

He ordered a large cheese, sausage, and green pepper pizza.

David sat back down with her at the island. Fiona knew the heart to heart was pending. David geared up his more mature, older brother figure act.

"Who are you with?" David asked gently.

Fiona sat silent. Her fingers poked through the menus, and she lined up packets of soy sauce like body bags.

"Okay, how about we go this route," David pressed further. "Throwing rocks, eh? A Molotov cocktail? You know that cop would have left you on the street to bleed in front of that store."

"We just wanted to make some noise."

"Seriously, you'd probably be in a full body cast by now. And I've already got one friend too many in intensive care."

"And I'd have been there if it weren't for you," she said.

"Yeah, well, I hope it was worth it. Break a few windows. Start a small fire."

"It was worth it. That company has to pay."

"It'll be the insurance company that pays. And your argument is not with them. Nor is it with the Chicago Police Department. And it certainly isn't with some boutique gym shoe store on Michigan Avenue."

"We were making a statement," Fiona tried.

"It was a dumb statement. You need to think more. Not just react."

"Oh, and what would you do? Give them an audit?"

"No, I wouldn't give them an audit. But I would examine the argument and the situation a little more closely."

"Oh," Fiona said questioningly. "Pray tell."

"Go at their pocket books. Make them re-think the situation financially. Supply and demand, you know. If there is no supply..."

"The cows?" Fiona asked.

David nodded quickly.

"You're suggesting we kill all the cows in South America so that no cattle ranchers can sell leather to the gym shoe maker."

"No, I'm not suggesting you kill the cows. Simply borrow them. Move them to a place more...befitting. Hell, I don't know."

"And I'm sure the local villagers and guerilla leaders are going to welcome us in with open arms," Fiona remarked. "Maybe the rebels running around the countryside will throw us a parade even."

"I understand it needs work. I was just throwing an idea out there."

"You aren't just a clever ad man in a suit though, are you?"

"Right," David said, "wait, how'd you know I was in advertising."

"Sorry, but that suit screams ad exec, and this bachelor pad has power yuppie written all over it."

"Yeah, well, you may not believe this, but I was with someone like you once. A long time ago."

"Yeah?" Fiona looked up to him inquiringly, ready to hear his story.

"Yeah, and I loved her very much."

"So, is that why you brought me back here?"

"No, I guess I thought it was just the safest place for you to be."

"Sure, some ultimate bachelor pad on the $47^{th}$ floor of a luxury condominium high-rise with a doorman is the safest place. Robbed of my view of the streets by the view of skyscrapers."

"Turn on the television," David offers a large remote control.

"Nah, I'll hear about it."

"From who?"

"Never mind, that's who!" Fiona chirped back.

They paused, returning to their corners.

"So, do you expect me to sleep with you?" she asked.

"No, not at all," David responded truthfully. "What I expect is for you to shower so my couch doesn't stink like dirty, smelly hippie in the morning. There's extra blankets laid out for you."

Fiona giggled at his wry comment and flashed a young girl's smile. Despite the few odd piercings in her face and probably other places, David found her quite normal. She went in to the shower, and as David was cleaning up the carcasses of Chinese food boxes, he glimpsed a brief view of Fiona naked as she dropped her towel. She was so skinny David imagined she could have broken into pieces if she'd fallen any harder on that concrete. David, glancing at her again, up and down, was admiring her innocence as Fiona dipped herself behind the shower curtain. She had not bothered to close the door. David normally would have taken this as an invitation to join one of the random girls he had brought home, but in this instance David simply cleaned up after her mess, refusing to break the bond of trust they had built together thus far. He moved himself into the bedroom to give her some privacy. As David prepped for sleep, he recalled the first time he watched Jessica towel off, in a mirror, naked.

Later, in the quiet of the night, Fiona crawled into his bed. David feigned sleep, hoping she wouldn't try something. Thankfully, she didn't. She simply used him as a pillow. Fiona threw a small, skinny arm over his chest and hugged him. They both slept. David welcomed it, knowing he hadn't spoiled her by senseless sex. She held him tight and purred soft snores into his chest.

The next morning David woke to the Sun blasting away through unshielded windows. David thought he had closed the blinds before bed, but apparently he'd been mistaken. Or had she raised them? He recalled he had a visitor. She must have wanted the Sun to wake her, David thought. There was an empty coffee cup on the balcony that overlooked the lake and city skyline. A cigarette stub floated in the toilet. The note on the island next to the empty pizza box simply said, "Jess sends her regrets." And despite the loss of a couple hundred bucks that was missing from his opened wallet on the island, David knew it was going towards a good cause.

Overlooking Lake Michigan, Belmont Harbor, spotting the *Bejeweled* (little used lately), David joined the empty coffee cup and sat with a cup of his own and admired the Sun. It was too bad his cup was filled with vodka. He held the shell necklace up to the light acknowledging he would return it to its proper hiding spot at first chance. David figured the minutia of his trip to G&H and to the airport. He'd need to stop for cash, too. Overlooking a sedate Lake Michigan, and a Sun that prospered, he wondered if Lou had made it through another night.

# THE BLACK BOX

*DAVID HOBBS – AGE 33*
*September, 2007*

Corn stalks poised for invasion surrounded the lone highway that bisected the small Iowa town. A smattering of storefronts still stood parked within leftover buildings on the town's Main Street. The flurry of activity seen decades ago was by now undoubtedly extinguished. Barren sidewalks and empty porches sat submerged in stillness and devoid of any action. Charming weather vanes and other such gaudy lawn ornaments exhibited their prominence among the few houses surrounding the town. Further down the road, cows lazily monitored the cars zooming by on the elusive (to David) Interstate 80. About a quarter mile from town, a tiny church rose from a soft hill. It stood mightily overlooking ranch style houses, together with farmhouses and barns not far off. David guessed the church parking lot filled exactly to capacity every Sunday morning.

Faded, muted rays of sunshine pushed past the dusty curtains sending sunlight bisecting across the empty restaurant. Outside, silently on guard, a seemingly abandoned bookstore stood barren and desolate next door. This was of little surprise to anyone due to it being a Sunday afternoon in the fall. But the fact remained that each day was no different in this small Iowa town. Customers at the restaurant and bookstore, and hardware store across the street, were now few and far between. The quiet, desolate loneliness evinced by the detectable sound of the wind chimes whistling thinly with each passing breeze a staple now as the soundtrack to the death of a small town.

Sunlight spread throughout the restaurant, laying warmth upon table settings, dusty chairs, and pleather booths. It interfered little due to the absence of customers. The restaurant, only slightly dated, but considered quaint by Iowan standards, promised a full breakfast, lunch, or dinner menu at any time of the day or night. Of course, that would have required entrance to the restaurant, which would have been far from ordinary.

David hadn't been back in the state of Iowa since he said good-bye to it the morning of graduation. As David, Jane, and Matthias traveled the interstate he had frequented as a young man, the memories of school had flooded back to him. Mostly though, his thoughts were of Jessica and of the good times they had shared. She was the most beautiful person he'd met in his life, and he doubted there were many more out there such as her. Shortly after coming to that hazardous morning, realizing he was alone in the world, he left with a rental car and most of his belongings and drove to Chicago. He thought for a while afterwards that perhaps their relationship had been just one brief intersection of two separate lines speeding off in different directions. That train of thought depressed him further. Oh, he had nearly drowned the night before, too.

Pulling in to the gravel-ridden parking lot, David instantly admired the sign above the restaurant. It was "new" old-fashioned with light bulbs surrounding a giant cup of coffee and the words JOE MAMA's. David's entrance broke through the stillness of the restaurant, finding the numbing sound of Sunday afternoon television (the talking heads having a go at one another) on a flat screen television mounted in the corner above the counter. David found a single man sitting in the middle of the restaurant with his feet up on a chair (quickly removed at the sight of a customer, but eased down at the sight of the map in David's hand). The man had been watching the television intently. He was large, unkempt, but instantly sprang into action presenting himself as the kind and courteous host. The twenties-ish, pudgy man quickly stood and welcomed David into the restaurant right away, adjusting the place settings at the center table at which he had been sitting. He wore a sparkling, pristine-white chef's apron, and sported dark, shaggy hair beset in unruly curls. Stubble days-old decorated an otherwise clean face. No sooner had he welcomed David than he went to work grabbing the carafe of coffee from the back kitchen. He turned over the porcelain cup on the center table and motioned for David to sit down. He poured the beautiful smelling java quickly and expertly. Leaving Jane and Matthias in the car idling, David felt a touch of guilt as the scalding hot coffee bit the back of his throat. But it was coffee brewed with tender loving care, David thought, and he appreciated it. And he was damned tired from all the traveling.

"Can you help me?" David asked him taking a moment to survey the simplicity of his surroundings.

"I'll certainly do my best," the man in the chef's apron responded.

"That's all I ask," David said expectantly.

The man extended his hand to him. David took it, shook it, and after exchanging the hearty handshake he sat down with David.

"The name's Joe," he said. "Joe Mamaski."

"Joe…Mama?" David pieced together.

"Yes, Sir. That's me. Owner, chef, and future unemployed member of our society."

"Unemployed?" David asked. "How do you mean?"

"You don't see any customers in here, do you? I mean, you're not seeing something I ain't, right?"

"No, no customers. Besides me."

"A year ago, once church let out, we had people waiting in line down the street to get a table."

"And now?"

"I haven't had that many people this entire month."

"Well, Joseph…"

"Joe, please," he said, "my friends all call me Joe."

"Joe, my friends and I are looking for Interstate Eighty."

"You mean you're not here for the bright lights and tall buildings of our fair town? Wait, I didn't know you had friends with you! Get them in here."

"Really, we're just looking for Interstate Eighty."

"Mister…"

"It's David. David Hobbs."

"David, I'm not sure if you've caught your reflection in the mirror lately, but you look a little, shall we say, pekid. Hopefully your friends don't look half as bad as you." Joe started turning over the remaining coffee cups.

"I really shouldn't," David said.

"Nonsense. Get 'em in here."

David tossed back the remainder of his coffee and acknowledged the fact that Iowans stood true to their demand of diminutive potency for their coffee after all these years. It tasted good nonetheless. David had taken one look at the pot in the roach motel they had stayed at just outside of Pittsburgh the night before last and decided it wasn't worth it. Things had probably crawled around inside that pot.

Joe's coffee was good enough. And fresh. Aboard the cargo ship that they'd stowed away on as they traversed the Atlantic Jane attempted to hone her coffee making skills (done so without perfection sadly). They had paid the ship's captain handsomely for their travels but were forced to spend eight days together stuck in a container with bathroom and breaks for air coming all too infrequently. Apart from a brief shower in the roach motel outside of Pittsburgh, David's hygiene hadn't been what it once was.

"Go on, bring your friends in here. If they look half as bad as you, then I'm sure they could do with a cup of coffee and a meal, too."

"Is it that bad?" David asked.

"You look a little weathered," Joe said nodding affirmatively. "Kind of like you've seen a few things and places of late. Go on, get your friends in here, and you can tell me all about all the places you've been. I'll slap some bacon and eggs on the griddle, and we'll get some home cooking livening up those bones in no time."

"We really shouldn't," David protested despite the fact that a home-cooked meal was easily inviting to him and would be welcome to Jane and Matthias, he thought.

There was no response from Joe as he had moved quickly to the kitchen. David could hear the crack of fresh eggs and the sizzle resulting as yolks and egg white dripped down upon a blazing griddle. David waved Jane and Matthias in from the doorway. He relented to Joe finally, and upon passing by a mirror nearest the door agreed silently with Joe's assertion that he looked terrible.

\* \* \*

Big, beautiful golden yolks sat perched atop heaps of lean, crispy bacon, both of which accompanied big, bountiful slices of buttered toast. The yolks held just a faint bounce and jumble upon the slightest nudge to the plate. The fearsome foursome sat steady, prepared to pounce on top of their food. David noticed Joe sitting with his hands clasped, his eyes closed deep in prayer. David nudged Jane and Matthias who were oblivious. Shortly after Joe looked up, they began to eat.

"Goodness, it's been a long time since I had such a breakfast," David broke free from the forkfuls of food he shoveled into his mouth. "I truly cannot recall."

"I can't remember the last time I had an egg," Jane admitted.

Joe looked up to Jane, thinking her remark quite odd.

"She's going through a bit of a phase," David said. "I'm doing my best to alter her diet some."

"Stick around the Midwest. All the red meat will put some color back in your skin."

"And plaque in my arteries," Jane responded.

"These hash browns are incredible," Matthias remarked amid a mouthful of food he was gluttonously gnawing upon.

"Most people in these parts have forgotten how to make them. Heck, kids these days think hash browns are something that come wrapped in a wax paper and are handed to you as you sprint through the drive-in."

"What are you saying, Joe?" David chimed in. "Has your town forgotten where your restaurant is?"

"No, not forgotten. They opened up a big box store here about half a mile down the road, oh, about a year ago or so. You'll see it on your way to the Interstate. People go to that part of town now. Spend all day there. They even opened up some chain restaurants right around that big box too. No need to come back this way, I guess."

"What the hell, Joe, I mean, this is Main Street, right?" David begged.

Joe looked at David a bit sardonically. Matthias and Jane looked on.

"You say that like it's a good thing. Like it still carries weight in small towns. Heck, nobody shops around here anymore. You've only come in 'cause you were lost and needed directions. I can't imagine how you got so far from the interstate."

They'd gotten so far removed because they had wanted some distance between themselves and any crowded gas stations right along the interstate where eyes might be there to recognize them. Worse even, Jane's face continued to be plastered over news reports. David and Matthias were fortunate. But for David, he thought, Chicago was only a couple hundred miles away. It was within the realm of possibility that he could bump into a former co-worker or old college buddy. Worse yet, there were probably cameras recording customer movements and license plate numbers. So, they'd found a gas station about ten miles away complete with old man swaying in a rocking chair donning a John Deere hat. He had been asleep, he was snoring, and David had just stuffed the cash in the front pocket of the man's denim overalls. They had ambled through this town lost until they had finally agreed to stop at Joe Mama's.

"Bert's hardware store closed last week," Joe started again. "They couldn't keep up with the big box. The lady that owns the bookstore next door doesn't even bother locking up anymore."

"Well, what are we arguing here?" David began, putting down his knife and fork for the moment. "Is it the economic impact of the big box on small town America, or that small businesses can't compete with these huge, massive supply-it-all stores?"

"Who knows, probably both. I mean, I just think it's hypocritical of all us patriots to run the American Flag up the flag pole each morning but then plop ourselves in our car and go and shop at a store who's importing seventy percent of their store goods from China. I guess us small business owners suffer at the expense of the almighty dollar."

"Trust me, Joe. Those stores out there want to eliminate the competition."

"The customer suffers, too," Jane added. "I mean, they're stuck tossing back chain restaurant food with made up tchotchkes adorning the walls and the servers. Whereas, inside here, we happen to be sitting and having an intelligent conversation over a fine meal cooked especially for us."

"Good point," Joe admitted. David nodded his head in agreement. "They moved the center of town to Aisle Eleven at the big box. People think things are better because they're faster, quicker, more convenient. And they think they're getting better deals, but they're not. They're just lured in by low prices on crap."

"You mean nobody has time to stop and smell the roses because they've fallen into the trap of this big box store, with its arterial chain restaurants inhabiting its space."

"It's a new America," Joe responded. "People don't care so long as it gets done quickly and cheaply. And if they can get it all in one place, then, the hell with going to Joe Mama's that's just down the road some."

"Okay, but these are basic economic principles being practiced here, why is it wrong?" David asked.

"A week ago, when Bert's place was open, you could walk right in and talk to Bert about what kind of home fixing you needed done or whatever job it is you needed to do, and you walked out of that store with Bert telling you exactly what needed to be done, and he sold you the proper tools to do the job. Why? Because his reputation was on the line. Here, now, there's no Bert helping you at the big box. You're on your own. And if you do get help, they sell you a bunch of junk you don't need. And they don't care if your job gets done or done right. Bert would see you at church on Sunday and make it a point to ask you how your project went."

"So you believe there's a lack of service and professionalism. And people just rush, rush, rush, so it doesn't matter anyway?"

"Will these people be saying the same things about you when you close your doors?" Matthias interjected. "'Oh, Joe had great hash browns.'"

Jane looked up at Matthias disapprovingly.

"I'm sorry if I sound preachy," Joe said. "I just wanted you to know what was happening to small town America. I won't argue the economics of it. Sure, I know they're out for blood. But what I detest is that we've let them do it uncontested. We've lost touch with the little things that are important."

"Joe, you sound really pissed off," David said.

"I guess you would be, too, if all you had to keep you company all day was television."

"Joe, I don't know what it is about you, but I find you utterly fascinating to sit and talk to."

"It's nice to be listened to."

"Listen, Joe, we've sat here and pontificated and philosophized and chatted concerning life in your small town, but have you ever done more than just talk?"

"I'm afraid I don't understand."

"What I'm asking you, Joe, is have you ever done anything about it? I mean, heck, we've sat here for the better part of two hours talking and chatting, but what have we really accomplished?"

"I don't know, Guys. I guess I just leave all that up to the politicians and corporate executives to figure out. I always thought of myself as someone who would just find a cabin in the woods and wait for Armageddon to be over with."

They all chuckled a bit.

"Which is not wrong, by the way. But to me, Joe, you seem intelligent enough to know that this restaurant is headed the same way as Bert's hardware store. So, why are you still here?"

"Not sure."

"Did you ever get the feeling that there are people in this world that you are destined to meet? I guess, supposed to meet or come across?"

David looked over to Jane. She smiled shyly and looked away from David's eyes.

"Not sure I buy all that pre-ordained destiny stuff. I am a God-fearing individual myself."

"Fine, then, be it God or some other power then. Your argument, the big box that opened up, you wouldn't do anything about it? Hit back, maybe?"

"Naw, probably not. What could I do?"

The gang of three locked eyes. They knew in which direction David was taking the conversation. Matthias and Jane nodded to David.

"What if I told you," David started, "that we do things…about things."

Matthias pushed himself away from the table slowly, away from the empty plate, moving towards the television that hung in the corner of the restaurant. He started flipping through stations.

"We're out to change the world," Jane said to Joe.

"But we're not bent on destroying it first," David said. "Instead simply changing the ideas and workings of those that are destroying it."

"You mean, like my world, destroyed by some big goliath stepping on all the small businesses for the sake of the almighty dollar?" Joe questioned with a hint of sarcasm.

"Exactly," David replied. "We change things."

Matthias whistled when he found it. Joe looked up to his flat screen television. There was a picture of a young woman on the television. It was the same woman that sat across from him at the very table inside his restaurant. The news report then moved to a stock photo of the *Pasha*.

"You guys are those eco-terrorists?" Joe asked, shocked.

"No, that's not correct," David responded. "That's not us. That was someone else's idea. We have different ideas, and we're not out to hurt anybody."

"We're not bad people," Jane pleaded to Joe.

"Some of us," David corrected, "used to be, ahem, not so nice. But they have since repented."

Joe sat by idle and speechless.

"Perhaps we should go," David decides. He can see Joe thinking about who he's sitting with. Jane pushes herself away and drops some cash in the center of the table. David heads towards the door with Jane and Matthias. Once there, they stop and look to Joe who is clearly stunned.

"Are we going, or what?" Matthias asked impatiently. Jane grabs David's arm to stop him. Matthias pushes past them both to go and start the car. David and Jane look back to Joe.

"It's a whole new life out there," David said. "Trust me. It's waiting for you. I once thought like you did. That it was someone else's problem."

Joe looked up to David trustingly from his table in the center of the empty room.

"We could use a smart man. Someone clever with a good head on his shoulders."

"What do you say, Joe?" Jane began. "Are you ready to hit back?"

Joe looked around his empty restaurant. He got up from the table and started to shuffle his feet back to the kitchen. He stopped when he got to the cash register. Then he turned and looked back to David and Jane who stood at the doorway together. Joe released his apron and let it drop to the floor. David and Jane looked at one another victoriously.

Joe motioned to the cash register.

"Nope, leave it," David said. "We wouldn't want someone to think you've been robbed."

Joe took one last look at his business.

"The hell with it then," Joe said and joined them at the doorway. David and Joe shook hands. Jane is swallowed in Joe's arms by a massive bear hug. Joe turned the lights off on the restaurant. It stood empty and silent, much the same way it stood for the past year. The sign above flickered out. A lone car left an empty gravel parking lot and headed off down the road in the correct direction for Interstate 80.

"Whoa, wait one minute," David said.

"What?" Matthias asked while checking his headlights.

"Just one more stop to make before the interstate," David said.

David turned from the front seat to face Jane and Joe who sat together in the back.

"Well, why don't you lead us to the parking lot of that big box, eh? It's time for an oil spill."

It would be a minor story for the big papers. But the gazettes that surrounded small town Iowa would have a field day, David thought. The security cameras in the big box parking lot wouldn't have caught enough of a glimpse of Jane before the spray paint hit. If they were to have remained on they would have shown Jane delivering the pallet of vegetable oil on a forklift at the top of a hill. With a few swings from an axe (which Matthias had secured from aisle 14) Joe had struck his own blow for freedom. The oil sloshed its way down the hill and into the parking lot of the big box. Jane and Joe slid sideways and laughed while they pretended to be figure skaters. David and Matthias watched from afar and showcased scores written on the backs of the boxes that had held the oil. Weeks would go by before the parking lot would be passable and minor fender benders would occur. But that didn't bother anybody in the parking lot that night.

# COME SAIL AWAY

*DAVID HOBBS – AGE 31*
*November, 2005*

David Hobbs postured contempt in front of the floor to ceiling window exposing to the world a frozen, cynical, and disheartened shell. Sulking in the leather guest chair in his office, David sat, knees slightly bent, with drink in hand. The heels of his lace up oxfords pressed tightly against the glass of the window. David remained perfectly still in the dark, slumped dejectedly in the leather seat, frequenting sips from his glass of vodka while admiring the drenching the city was receiving on this Friday night. Roused by an occasional vacuum, he sipped the finality of a bottle that he had begun before Lou's funeral this morning. He finished it now and adjusted to the realization that the only people he cared about in life had been forced from his life. A sad fact realized. Dad had always taught him to do the right thing, David thought. So why had it always been so easy to do the wrong thing?

From high above David pictured the goings on below at street level: youths patrolled bars in search of booze and the opposite sex, the desire for such not being represented in that particular order. Tourists window shopped on Michigan Avenue with mouths agape at the absurdly high costs of the big city. A few blocks away, commuters assumed their sodden pose yet lingered in line for the bus despite the empty cabs flying by. The pulse and vivacity from those at ground level remained unequaled and incessant despite the tempering, cold, gray rain. David's sour mood stewed thick, tangible, and reflected unquestionably in the darkness of his office.

Such unusually late hours on Friday nights prompted visits only from those looking to dump his trash or vacuum his carpet. David remained in his gloom, parked stoically in the guest chair, and monitored the rain striking his office window, ignoring the date on his desk calendar. David instead focused on the view of a city besieged by late November rain knowing damn well what day it was. The only lights afforded him were those of the accompanying skyscrapers laying about the city. A little to the north and east stood the garish Ferris Wheel at Navy Pier which sat on a lake that David knew so well. Or, at least he used to. David supposed there were worse things to be staring at. Jagged, staccato beams of light recoiled from the sides of the vodka bottle that beseeched him on his desk. He had promised his mother he'd come out to see her. David imagined she was in quite the similar state as he was: moody and drunk.

The day had been most foul. Apparently David's mood had taken its cue from the recent weather and presented as much from the moment he walked into the office. His dark suit and dark shirt a pure reflection of the emotions David had suppressed until recently. David finished off the day with what remained of his vodka bottle, noting it was time to replenish. And there David sat. Slipping down even further into depression. Staring out his window David searched for memories between the rain drops that lay between him and infinity.

The rain had returned him to the day he stood on the dais. Again, with rain as an accompaniment, though now the sound of the raindrops was muted by a slight smattering of applause. This time, for the first time, his brother and father were absent. David stood by himself for the entire trophy ceremony alone. His foul weather gear long since ditched, he stood drenched in shorts and a t-shirt. His short hair was sopping wet. He stood on display for the hardcore masses and sponsors witnessing the trophy presentation of the Door County Lake to the Bay Regatta. David had turned what was usually four days' worth of a pleasurable diversion into some methodical, maniacal obsession. The usual team had quit on him long before the race even started for reasons David could not understand. The four mates he hired on last minute were friends from high school.

The May race was an undeniable test. Most of them had only seen small lakes in the high school sailing club, and they certainly hadn't seen the weather they'd just been through these previous four days. They hadn't even made it up to the podium yet and were still dressed in their foul weather gear. They were amateurs, David admitted, resigning himself to doing the trophy presentation alone. The reporters had attacked him directly after the finish, what with his Dad being an old timer as far as this particular race went. There were a few reporters from Green Bay and even one from Chicago where David's father had also been something of a sailing legend. David refused their questions initially in search of the podium and the awards ceremony.

It was a heavy thing to be saddled with. The trophy had already been inscribed what with David having such an insurmountable lead on the last day. He credited his expert sailing and the drive he had enforced upon his friends, most of whom spent the first day and a half vomiting overboard. The water had been rough, cold, and it rained every day. Their brand new foul weather gear, with which David had accommodated them, had been broken in to say the least. But they continued on. Taking no chances. Driving forward. His friends would later call it David's own death wish. But they did as they were ordered. And now they could share in the glory.

Upon completion of the awards ceremony and having removed himself from the podium to join the crowd (for the few that remained) David would eventually succumb to the questions of an attractive young reporter from the Green Bay Press-Gazette.

"I owe it all to my father," David said cursing the fact that it sounded generic coming out of his mouth. He meant it though. "And to my brother, too. They taught me everything. They taught me how to be such an excellent sailor."

Nearby David could still hear his mates answering questions. David expected they were still his mates, despite the heavy demands and the attitude David had used to enforce them with. That and the fact that he was a downright jerk the entire race. He would attempt an apology later, David concluded.

"It's just a hard thing to fathom for me right now," one of them said. "Winning this race...I just can't believe it. What with the lousy weather we had. And not to mention what David has been through this past week. So close, to his father and brother's car accident, you know. But it was all David. He pushed us. Rode us hard. When we were all puking overboard, he was pushing on. Pushing us to keep moving. Heck, if it weren't for him, we all would have drowned, I'm sure."

Walking past, in the direction of the hotel, David got more questions thrown his way.

"David Hobbs, young David Hobbs," the young reporter who followed began, "what does it mean to you, at the tender age of seventeen, to be the youngest man ever to win the Door County Lake to the Bay Regatta?"

"It means a lot," David admitted and then expounded. "It means I had an exceptional teacher."

The trophy in his hand was an exchange for the prayer cards he ought to have been holding. Mom was probably busy drinking herself through the post-funeral luncheon right about now.

"But, if you'd prefer I go into further detail, I'm at the Glidden Hotel."

David stayed in the hotel knowing full well the boat wasn't going back. The hell with it. Grieving would be next, he supposed. He had immediately taken a hot shower. Joining him was a cold beer. The reporter had eventually shown up, but he'd been drunk by then and at that point David had vacated any thoughts towards sex.

The trophy stood indiscriminately atop the television set. The room was lit softly with a single light. A burnt orange glow burning among the silence, David sat on the corner of the bed and said good-bye to his father. It had been David's request for his father and brother to pick him up directly after school that day. If he hadn't begged and pleaded for them to come and pick him up their route would have been changed and there would have been no need to go through that intersection. It was an intersection David was forced to go through each of his remaining days at high school.

He knew his mates were bar hopping. Passing out bad fake IDs left and right all over town. David chose to be by himself, or rather, with the trophy, with which he discussed the ins and outs of the race as if his father and brother were actually there.

"I did everything just like you taught me, Dad."

David admittedly found it odd after awhile, but after a dozen beers or so it didn't matter. And, at the end of the night, he was mesmerized by the rain still throwing itself against the window. Coming down in buckets just as the tears had.

His office window stared back at him. A pale, empty night lay before a thirty-one year old man sunken in depression finding solace at the office with his bottle. Letters from a former lover still arrived every other month or so reminding him of what could have been. David gulped the remains of the drink. He sucked the vodka off the ice cubes that had landed in his glass. David tore the entire month's page from his desk calendar, and crumbled it up, depositing it into his waste paper basket. The cleaning staff, fully aware of his drunken presence, had avoided his office the entire evening. Fresh ice cubes were secured to the glass. He'd need to venture to the convenience store across the street for more vodka. There were so many sorry memories to erase on a day already full of sorrow.

# DOWN FOR THE COUNT

*DAVID HOBBS – AGE 33 & WILL FROST – AGE 38*
*October, 2007*

Resting just inches away from his lips, he knew it was going to be bad. At this close range it smelled like burnt rust. David knew the survival rate was not in his favor. He looked down the barrel of the loaded gun that was Jane's brew swilling about the porcelain cup. He was exhausted, but knew he wasn't allowed to sleep. Smiling stupidly David took it like a man forcing the coffee past his lips.

"Sorry," Jane said meekly, honestly, after catching the grimace David made upon swallowing the molten black lava. "I'm doing the best I can with this Susie Homemaker shit."

The one bedroom cabin had served them well. Standing (or leaning, they all thought) shielded by trees on a lake about a half mile from a solitary two lane road that lay mostly unseen and unused.

"It's fine," David lied, and Joe belly laughed. Jane had demanded she make the coffee, holding faith in the theory that practice made perfect. It was apparent her homemaking skills were lacking, but she was beginning to yell at the three men when they didn't pick up after themselves.

Peeking through crusty, white curtains, David marveled at the sky, catching a billion stars laying naked above in the Pacific Northwest. A late October chill flooded the night air and surrounded the small cabin in total darkness. David admired the trees that stood surrounding the tiny cabin like soldiers at attention. He lauded their might and their disregard for the smoke from the trucks that passed by on the lonesome road. Limbs stood strong, healthy and stretched skyward. David watched headlights from an occasional car. The cabin sat just thirty-five miles from the interstate and was built mainly for a trucking route for the PerfectGrass chemical treatment and processing plant. The only other user of the road was a nearby distribution facility for a mom and pop chocolate company.

Apart from Joe, they showed their faces little around town. They spent their time instead doing what reconnaissance they could, which mostly consisted of sitting in a canoe in the guise of vacationing fishermen, pretending to fish but instead scouting the PerfectGrass facility in action.

Inside the cabin the sound of each truck passing along the road forced each of the four individuals to lock eyes. Jane would consult the trucking schedule, which was a gift from Joe who had secured part-time work on the dock at the PerfectGrass facility. The schedule had been taped to a refrigerator that may have been older than some of the trees surrounding them. Joe, as an employee at the plant, was able to attain copies of the trucking schedules, routes, and inventory. Jane checked her watch and nodded to Matthias, David, and Joe in agreement on the synchronization. Not a word was said, nor was speech needed.

With only one week to go before the tennis tournament in Australia, the press coverage had begun. Will and his remaining BVG had been quiet until David received word from one of his spotters at the airport (Joe, again, washing cars at the car rental agencies part time) that a black, handicapped accessible van had been stolen the previous night from long-term parking. Will was putting his plan into action. It was up to David and the three who'd joined him to prevent that plan from becoming successful. David cheered himself over the idea of having planted the van.

Jane sat at the small kitchen table, anxious, and not minding the coffee much, while Matthias stirred in his seat next to her. He looked frustrated and impatient. David put his coffee cup in the sink, but not before stopping to rinse out the sludge that stubbornly refused to abandon the sides of the small porcelain cup. Joe managed to polish off more than his share of the chocolate bars that lay about. David patted Jane on the shoulder comfortingly and joined the team at the small kitchen table adjacent to the quaint little living room.

"Once again," David started, adjusting his butt in the rickety wood chair, "let's take it from the top."

Jane started, "You two lay out the flares and crack the glow sticks. Act like two innocent truck drivers from the chocolate company broken down on the side of the road."

Joe adds, "Right, we're two truck drivers from the chocolate company broken down on the road, who grab the PerfectGrass driver when he comes a toddling down the road in his truck."

"Right," David adjudicated.

"Then, we switch the barrels, I take the truck and go and get kidnapped by Will and his gang somewhere along the way," Joe said.

"I'm putting you in a tight spot, Joe," David wavered.

"They're likely to be heavily armed," Matthias added blankly.

"If there's a chance before they get to you, you get the hell out of there," Jane added.

"I'll do my best," Joe said.

"That is all I ask," David responded.

"And then I hightail it to the rendezvous point with the real barrels once we've confirmed Will and his team have grabbed the wrong truck," Jane stated.

"There's thirty-five miles of quiet two-lane highway before the expressway. Somewhere in there Will and his gang are going to try and grab that truck."

"So, we let them grab the truck. Just without the right materials," Joe said.

"Correct," David points out.

"You're sure it's going to be out here?" Matthias asked. "Not on the expressway?"

With the tennis tournament in Australia a week away and the shipments for PerfectGrass going out only bi-weekly, tomorrow's truck at five p.m. was the last opportunity. Two dozen barrels of almost certainly carcinogenic pesticides and toxic ingredients mostly banned in other countries stood ripe to be plucked. Will had a horrible death in mind for the CEO of PerfectGrass, who David found out happened to be a ridiculous tennis fan with a summer home on an island off Australia. The only way onto the CEO's island was by boat or by helicopter. Will would need a boat with all that product. That was why Will had begged David to stay. He needed a competent sailor.

"The conditions of a high-speed pursuit aren't exactly favorable for what's in those barrels," David postulated. "He takes them right here. Out here in the quiet twilight with Mother Nature watching him. It goes down tomorrow night at five p.m. Right here."

"And a black van stolen from long-term parking last night is as good as any indication that Will is in town," Jane added.

"He's in town," Matthias nodded in agreement.

"Right," David said, "he's found his transportation. Too bad he's becoming a parody of his own self."

"Or maybe he's trying to throw us off," Matthias tried.

David took a moment to try and second guess. No. No way. There was too much security present for an attack on the plant itself. Will would let the goods come to him along this lone road and just steal them and the truck, perhaps already having secured his water transport at a nearby dock.

"Not a chance," David said, again breaking his train of thought, "Will is getting weaker. He's needing other people to do his dirty work now. Besides, my plan is better."

David looked up to Matthias and Jane. Joe kept eating the chocolate bars nonchalantly.

"PerfectGrass's corporate headquarters is two hundred and fifty miles away. And with the weekend ahead of us, and Joe's map avoiding major highways, we're set for a real show. The front of corporate headquarters for PerfectGrass holds a stretch of one hundred yards or so of 'perfectly' altered, genetically engineered green grass. By Monday morning, with two dozen barrels of toxic byproduct (their own) dumped upon it, it'll be months before anybody can return."

"And who'd want to after that spill?" Joe replied.

David smiled.

\* \* \*

A couple of hours later David stood at his bed and threw flannel shirts into his beat up duffel bag. A few maps were on the bed as well, which he scanned in between garments. Jane leaned up against the doorway, afraid to go inside. Matthias watched stoically from the kitchen table.

"You realize what you're doing, don't you?" Jane asked reciprocally.

"I absolutely do," David responded, blankly continuing to pack.

"You understand the ramifications of our actions."

David stopped and looked down at Jane. She was so small. So young. And less pale lately due to her changes in diet at David's request.

"'Ramifications of our actions'? Is that really you, Jane?" David teased.

"Well, since I left Will and joined your little gang here, perhaps I grew some brain cells."

"I'm told that's what happens."

"You know this isn't exactly going to endear us to the BVG. As a matter of fact, it's pretty much a declaration of war."

"Trust me when I say this," David said walking over to Jane and embracing her, "when we're through, we'll be at peace. Not war."

"Still, we're about to get on Will's bad side. And that's generally not a good place to be. People on Will's bad side have been known to wind up as fish food."

"He won't even know until it's too late."

"Why not take him on the water? You know your way around the Ocean better than the roads of the Pacific Northwest, that's for sure."

"Because that's what he thinks I'll do," David said and stopped for a moment. "Besides, there's too much risk there. If we let him get those barrels, the real barrels, and try and duke it out on the high seas, then there's too much chance that one or all of those barrels ends up in the Ocean. And that's not something I can live with."

Jane pouted and threw up her hands, pushing herself away from David.

"So, I guess it's just a suicide mission for us all then."

Jane rushed out annoyed and aggravated.

Matthias got up and prepared for bed. Joe was already snoring in the Lay-Z-Boy. David looked out the bedroom window at the nearby lake and at the trees standing guard silently outside. The smaller branches shielded those closer to the ground that waved slowly from a gentle night's breeze.

\* \* \*

She knew he wouldn't be asleep. He wasn't doing much of that lately. There was too much going through his mind. Jane lay bundled up underneath a comforter and struggled with her own thoughts that raced through her head.

"Aw, the hell with it," she murmured just under her breath.

Jane had come to the realization, some time ago, before the *Pasha* even, that she was completely in love with David Hobbs. Jane's hands and arms ducked underneath the comforter. Her t-shirt was difficult; her head momentarily ducking underneath the covers to allot the appropriate space requirement, but eventually it was removed. Thumbs found the ragged waistband of her underpants, and she yanked them down, tucking her knees up and into her chest in the process. Tiger print underpants slid past her ankles. It was her best pair and donned especially for the occasion but now with this all-or-nothing gamble he would not get to see them. Free from clothing, she resigned herself to take action. Joe snored away on the Lay-Z-Boy with purpose. Matthias's back had been turned to her, but he had been on the floor for a while, so there was no doubt he was asleep. Jane bunched up the comforter, completely surrounding any bit of bare skin below her neck, and tiptoed over to David's bedroom door. Hardwood floors froze Jane's feet, and she wondered how Matthias could sleep. The door to David's room was just barely ajar. David was sitting up in bed. In the dark. His back lay rigid against the headboard and his eyes quickly focused on her. Jane dropped the comforter.

As she closed the creaky door, the brief sliver of light shot through the room disappeared. David was offered only a momentary glimpse of Jane's bare body. Awkward and embarrassed now, Jane's eyes found the floor, and she stared at it through the darkness. Jane swore at her tiny breasts as they chilled, hoping he'd be ravaging them and the rest of her body shortly. Warmed by these thoughts Jane summoned the courage to walk over to his bed and crawl underneath the covers next to him, laying beside him, naked, for the second time in her life. David sat above the covers, though, like a statue. She heard David sigh and exhale.

Jane leaned into a cozy warm nook and stared up at him for his response.

"It can't happen, Jane."

Jane sank sharply and quickly back within her shell, although she knew that with bare breasts pressing into a man's chest that the first "no" wasn't always final.

"Why not?" Jane inquired breathily. She moved her lips up various points from his chest and neck until her eyes were next to his in the dark.

"Because we can't, Jane. Hell, I don't even know your real damn name!"

"It's..."

David had shut the creaky bedroom door behind him before she could utter her full response. To Jane, "we can't" *was* the definitive and final response. No amount of nestling and rubbing was going to bring him around. Tears began.

He did let her sleep in his bed, she recognized. So, there was that. He was accommodating her in some respect. He was on the couch when she woke up in the morning. It was apparent he hadn't slept. Jane slid on her tiger print underpants and the green 7-up t-shirt that had been set at the bedside and went to make the coffee.

\* \* \*

David put the truck in park and pressed down hard on the emergency break. He left the keys in the ignition. The hazard lights ticked to life before he exited on to the side of the road. David walked to the rear of the trailer where Matthias was waiting for him. Matthias wrenched the rickety aluminum ramp out from underneath the trailer and rolled the dolly up into the trailer in preparation for the switch.

"Nice unis," Jane said mockingly, passing by David, who begrudged her the joke. He knew he'd hurt her feelings last night.

"They came with the truck," David replied defensively, completely aware of his goofy attire.

Matthias flung open the door of the truck to reveal two dozen creamy white barrels freshly painted just a few days before. David and Joe had secured the lot numbers to the sides of each barrel and fastened the biohazard labels only just this morning.

"Think that paint job will get by Will and his gang?" Jane asked.

David took a whiff, noticing just a slight hint of fresh paint. She was smart.

"Will's sense of smell ain't what it used to be," David recalled.

Jane excused herself to the cabin of the truck. David watched Matthias set out the warning triangles on the road while he cracked neon green glow sticks to life. The October night began to peek over the tops of trees. With dusk seemingly radiating from the cold gray pavement, the trees stood witness to their tasks.

Stomping down the truck's access ramp, David closed the double doors to the trailer. As Matthias reached down to replace the access ramp, his jacket jutted up slightly, and David spotted the shiny plating of a .45 automatic tucked into the small of his back held securely in place by the waistband of Matthias's jeans. David quickly looked away, to the forest and the trees that lay close about.

Matthias and David stood in the middle of the empty road side by side. Matthias cracked flares, and as they burst to life he threw them on to the shoulder one by one. Joe came rumbling around the corner on his Vespa motor scooter. It was quite the comical sight to see Joe, such a large man, on such a little scooter. He had admitted that he was scared of anything bigger so he had been appeased. The most important action was to provide the warning to them once the truck had left the facility.

"How much time?" David asked.

"He's right behind me," Joe responded. He set the scooter off to the side in the bushes and took his place in the cabin of the truck.

It was very near dark. The light pavement of the highway lay in contrast with the invading darkness seeping down from the sky. David listened to the trees. He heard no truck yet.

"I need a minute," David said calmly, breaking the silence between the two men. He walked back to the truck. Matthias pleaded with him to stay. David kept walking. He stalked up the side of the trailer to the passenger door and opened it.

"Here, and here," Jane said, marking large red Xs on a map displaying locations where Will and his gang might intervene. Jane had scouted houses and cabins along the route with docks capable of accommodating a boat large enough to transport the stolen material. Surprised at the interruption,

Jane immediately checked the road behind her to see if she'd missed the truck.

"Joe, give me a moment, huh?" David asked.

Joe stumbled out of the cab awkwardly. He was still winded and out of breath from the expedient ride he had made from the docks of PerfectGrass. He headed back towards the rear of the truck. David motioned for him to remove a dab of chocolate which had found its way to his breast pocket of his shirt. David climbed up taking Joe's place in the empty passenger seat. Jane put her flashlight in her mouth and studied her map, avoiding eye contact with David for as long as possible. She fought the confrontation continuing to make notations for Joe on the map.

There was silence for a moment as David composed his thoughts. His hasty walk had not been long enough. Still, he struggled to concentrate. An empty road lay ahead and David stared into it.

"Listen, I just wanted to say a few things about last night," David began.

"Save it," Jane commanded, spitting the flashlight out of her mouth. "I was stupid. I was just horny, okay?"

David took hold of her hand. Jane fell back in love with him as he touched her.

"I just want you to know," David began again, sincerely now, as much as she had ever seen him, "it's nothing you have or haven't done that stopped me from making love to you. It's just…"

"You're saving yourself. For her. Aren't you?"

David looked away. He really had no idea what he was doing. He knew he couldn't hide behind bullshit with Jane.

"I'm just trying to finish what I started. I need to be clear headed. I can't have things stuck in my head when I need all of my concentration down here."

Jane challenged him again.

"I'm in love with you."

David sighed once again.

"I just wanted you to know," Jane said openly.

With her defenses laid down, David looked upon Jane in the driver's seat of the large truck and saw a young twenties-ish child with eyes lost in an unattainable love. Her lip quivered somewhat, signaling fresh insecurity. Embodied once as a monster in the making, Jane now had been reinstated with her youth. Before, upon speaking, it had looked as though she'd always had blood on her mind. Hate had lain behind those eyes as a patient predator. Now though, her eyes searched David looking for a connection. They pleaded with him in search of his loving response.

"You're too young for this. Love hasn't burned you yet."

"It has," Jane said, and then she corrected, "It is."

Jane and David looked at each other. David moved to escape from the cab. Jane grabbed hold of David and hugged him securely. For security. A tear rolled down her cheek.

"Please, be careful," she warned.

A fist pounded against the rear doors of the truck.

"Showtime," Matthias shouted from the rear.

"We'll have to continue this conversation at another time, I'm afraid."

David looked at Jane. She was defeated. Again. But she knew she had a job to do.

"I hope not," she replied, "I'm not sure I can take much more rejection."

"It's not rejection. It's…practice."

David moved to leave the truck. He stopped when he saw Jane's flashlight's older brother on the floor of the passenger side.

"Can I borrow this?" David said grabbing it and sticking the heavy Maglite in the back of his jeans.

"Hey, Joe might need that."

"I think not."

David returned to the rear of the truck where Matthias still stood guard watching the highway. A truck's engine rumbled in the distance. Joe was nowhere to be seen.

Matthias and David stood next to each other. They waited for the truck to arrive amid a silent open road.

"Where's Joe?" David asked Matthias.

"Went for a piss," Matthias responded absently. David noticed Matthias's forehead had beads of fresh sweat. David decided it was time to just get the whole thing over with.

"Where's Joe?" David asked Matthias again, firmly. They both stared at the highway. Matthias's head eventually turned in David's direction. David left one eye on the road and one eye on Matthias.

"He's in the bushes. Unconscious. I pistol-whipped him in the back of the head with this .45 here."

Matthias removed the shiny, silver-plated pistol from the back of his waist.

"And when I'm done with you," Matthias began again, "I'll probably go over there and finish him off. Just like I'll do to the driver of the truck."

"What about Jane?"

"Jane goes back."

The cool white truck proudly adorned with the PerfectGrass logo across both sides of the trailer announced itself by horn as it rounded the turn. Matthias and David faced off in the middle of the open road. Walking away from David for the moment, Matthias turned in the direction of the oncoming truck, waving his gun in the air, forcing the truck to come to a rumbling stop. David was afforded an opportunity to survey his surroundings. He saw gym shoes sticking out from the bushes off to the side of the road far from the fake chocolate truck. Matthias had knocked Joe unconscious and dragged him away from their location. Hence why Matthias had been sweating when David had returned. *Sorry, Joe*, David thought to himself, *but if I can get us out of this mess, I will.*

David watched Matthias yank the innocent truck driver from the PerfectGrass truck and march him over to the center of the road where David was standing still. Matthias was only a few feet away and well within striking distance. David heard Matthias breathing hard. He was nervous. The adrenaline incited him. He'd be tough in any kind of hand to hand combat, David surmised. Matthias easily outweighed David with his solid military build and muscle. David heard Jane getting out of the truck and was able to look back and see the quizzical look sported on her face.

"What the hell?" Jane asked honestly upset that she hadn't been included. "Nobody ever said anything about a gun."

Matthias acted frantic, flinging the gun around in everyone's direction. Jane was cool. She remained by the driver's side of the truck.

"Why are you acting like such a spaz, Matthias?" she asked. "And for God's sakes, would you put that gun down?"

Matthias raised the handgun in the air. His finger squeezed on the trigger, and very quickly the rapport of gunfire prompted nestled birds to flee from the tops of trees. David flinched at the awesome, instantaneous destruction of silence as the explosion bounced across the treetops.

"I'm in charge now, Jane," Matthias shouted while turning to Jane. He had transformed from his usual cold, menacing, intense figure into a furious, tormented giant. "Will told me you'd flake out."

David looked to Jane immediately. Jane's head dropped, broken hearted once more.

"I thought you were for real, Matthias. I really did."

Jane was being honest. David knew it now.

"I am. It's you who's lost the way!"

"What are you going to do, Matthias? Shoot me, and then this poor bastard here?" David said, and acknowledged the unnerved, innocent bystander. The truck driver looked over to David. He was unpredictable, but still frightened enough not to do anything stupid, David thought.

"For starters," Matthias answered back. The gun careened in all directions.

"Then what?" David pressed.

"Then I haul this truck and Miss Fussy Britches here back to Will. He decides."

Matthias snatched the truck's keys from the driver.

"Think about that for a second, Matthias," Jane begged. "There's a lot of badness sitting inside that truck. A lot can go wrong between here and Australia. A lot of bad things can happen."

"And you and I both know," David started, "that if Jane gets in front of Will again, he will put her down. Without even so much as a word."

"Matthias, please," Jane uttered.

"Hey, I still believe!" Matthias shouted at Jane voraciously. "Apparently you only believe in getting your rocks off with Mr. Christian over here."

Matthias lowered his arm to his side and the gun was momentarily pointed at the pavement. David hip checked the PerfectGrass driver to the ground and pulled the weighty Maglite from the back of his waist. He was able to continue his motion and clobber Matthias over the head with the heavy flashlight. Matthias fell to his knees, still clutching the gun, but blood started streaming down the side of his forehead and into his right eye. David leapt on top of the dazed Matthias, and they wrestled around the cold, gray pavement. Both right hands clutched the gun. Behind the pair doing battle, Jane ran over and picked the PerfectGrass truck driver up from the pavement and escorted him to safety behind the chocolate truck.

Matthias was quick to overpower David, despite the knock to his noggin. They were up again. Hands clutched throats, and knuckles pummeled faces. Matthias was younger, stronger, and much better built. Both sets of hands clasped over the cruel metal and yanked every which way, forcing the barrel of the gun in every direction. Grunting from both men ensued. Face to face now, with the gun at their waists, Matthias yanked down hard once, and then right back up, forcing the butt of the pistol into David's chin, knocking him backwards. David leapt forward and wrenched the gun to his side. Matthias was swung around into the barrel of the gun. David squeezed at the trigger, and the shot was fired. Both men were stunned by the blast. David let go and looked down to himself for inspection. Matthias retreated backwards. He still had the gun, but he was the one who was bleeding from his belly. David stood frozen in the road, his back to the trees and to the lake. Matthias looked down at the blood that pulsed from the ragged hole in his shirt. He looked back up to David who stood and stared questioningly at the psychopath in front of him. Matthias raised the gun and aimed at David. He aimed at three Davids. Annoyed by being unable to decide which one was legitimate Matthias instead roared and charged head on grabbing at all three in his line of vision. Matthias pushed David into a tree, knocking the air from him. They stumbled off to the ground and were sent rolling down the embankment. Their arms flailed, and Matthias sent his fists into David's face. Their bodies tumbled into trees and branches along the way as their speed and angle of descent increased. Shots rang out among the trees but the only pain David felt was Matthias's fist pounding at his face and squeezing at his throat. Scratches from branches and prickly shrubs continued as they rolled forever downhill. Random shots continued into the trees. They were slowed by slippery mud, but the two continued to roll. David did his best to shield himself from Matthias's beating. He caught sight of his own hands, which were left bloodied from Matthias's wound. The two men were swathed in mud only briefly. The water was next. David was alarmed at the thought they were already at the lake.

The coldness of the water separated them. Perhaps Matthias couldn't swim, David thought, slightly unnerved that Matthias was suddenly removed from his sight. Again, the water was deathly cold and passed quickly into his body. Just as David righted himself, he heard the shot from above. David's body recoiled backwards, and he prayed the bullet hadn't hit any vital organs. Matthias was nowhere to be seen, and now the surface was disappearing again, partially because the water surrounding him was coloring dark with his own blood. Mostly though, it was due to David's vision failing him. With only one arm operational, and struggling to put water behind him, the pain and weakness in his chest affected him now. Sadly, hands grasped at the outside air but found only the shallow, empty water. Going down again, he thought. *So cold, this water, and still no chance to say good-bye.*

\* \* \*

Matthias rose from the shallow water quickly. Moving in the tracks of the scuffle through the mud, he clutched the pain that grew in his belly wound. He meandered up the hill, shaken and beaten, following the mess of broken branches that the two had made in the scuffle. His heart was pounding. A big red dark splotch spread on the wet shirt he wore. Matthias struggled uphill. His legs were heavier than after any run he ever performed while in the military. Matthias tried to keep his mind clear. It was not a climb to be proud of. He felt himself go lightheaded. The agility he once boasted had disappeared. Ultimately he made it up the hill. As wet boots hit the pavement he stumbled to the truck, sluggishly, with the speed of a zombie. Before getting in the truck, Matthias took one last look in each direction of the road. *She's long gone*, he thought, *don't even bother*. Matthias slowly maneuvered his heavy body into the PerfectGrass truck and eventually drove off.

\* \* \*

Will had gotten out of the van when he heard the initial rounds go off. A couple of jackets lay drooped over Will's skinny, bony shoulders for protection from the chill in the air. He looked far worse than ever. Scaly skin that flaked and peeled had ceased to develop. Now there was just a thin layer of bright red skin separating muscle fibers from the outside world. His silver hair remained only in patches, and he covered his head with a ball cap he had found at a rest stop. He watched the birds soaring past and figured the battle had taken place perhaps only two miles away. *Well, at least David went down fighting*, Will thought. And then one small part of Will took a brief moment to grieve for David. That s.o.b. should have stayed on. He could have taken part in Will's greatest achievement.

Two new members of the BVG, identical twins he had scooped up as they escaped from a juvenile detention facility, stood behind Will loyally. They were synonymous with the state of Will's revolution. What once had been a band of brilliant minds recruited from universities across the planet for the BVG had lulled its way to a club of hoods that required lesson plans about the fight for Mother Earth. They held machine guns and leaned up against the black van, lazily smoking cigarettes. Will referred to the twins as Frick and Frack. They were too young to understand Will's fight. No matter. Matthias would rejoin him shortly, and his right hand man would be returned from his sabbatical. Will looked up to the sky and to the stars and then to the trees that surrounded them. There would not be many more nights on this Earth for Will. He would struggle to entrust his fight on the original members of the BVG, but not before going out with a bang.

Will had seen the puff of exhaust from the truck that was hidden by the trees around the turn. Short quick bursts of machine gun blasts shook him, and he cast angry looks in the direction of Frick & Frack. Anything for the cheap thrill of throwing bullets in the air, Will thought.

Will detected something was wrong when he witnessed the truck swerving madly in between both lanes. Loyally, the boys stood in front of Will with their machine guns raised at the PerfectGrass truck. Eventually the truck came to a complete stop quite a distance away. He instantly recognized Matthias as the sole inhabitant. Apparently Jane had gone down fighting. Too bad.

Strangely, for what seemed like a lengthy breather, Matthias refused to leave the truck. It idled for a moment and was eventually put in park. The driver's side door popped open, and only then did Will notice Matthias's slumped, jerky movements. As Matthias's boots crashed down upon the road, he almost dropped down to the ground himself. Matthias was able to right himself on the front fender which basically held his entire body up. Will waited a moment in case someone was following the truck before he set his wheelchair in Matthias's direction to greet him. Frick and Frack followed close behind.

Will saw that Matthias was soaking wet and he noticed Matthias clutching the gigantic red splotch on his stomach. Will recognized a gun-shot wound when he saw one. Matthias held his stomach in obvious pain. This was major uncool, Will thought. Matthias would require emergency care, and Frick and Frack weren't intelligent enough to know what to do with Matthias. Will looked up to the night's sky in frustration. Matthias shuffled a few feet away from the fender and his support. Will saw that most of the color in his face had drained. Matthias started towards Will again. Then he collapsed. He had delivered the goods but Matthias had gone down fighting, too, it seemed. What a pisser, Will thought.

# JESSICA – QUEEN OF THE JUNGLE

*JESSICA UPSHAW – AGE 22*
*February, 1995*

Jessica's face landed cruelly against a canvas of unblemished sand. Her body crashed into the beach, beset by exhaustion. Jessica had crawled up the shore away from the dreaded surf and attempted to right her breathing pattern. Her hands clutched at mounds of sand for safety and security in an effort just to get hold of something as she fought for breaths of air. Instead she pulled away only fading piles of sand that continued to seep through struggling, grasping hands. Jessica had fought the sea for three hours, which was hardly something she was used to. Waves lapped the shoreline now and tickled her toes mockingly. With her breathing shallow and rapid, she decided it would be an awful place to have a heart attack. Jessica rolled over on to her back, excavating the side of her cheek from the sand. Thinking she probably very much looked like a piece of breaded meat Jessica watched as her chest heaved itself in the air spasmodically. She was lightheaded, she noted, but still conscious. The sounds of waves continually pounding the surf interspersed with her gasps for air. She took a few moments to try and concentrate on slowing her breathing. She was quite certain she'd be dying soon unless she was able to gain control.

With her back now laying in the sand, and an afternoon Sun reassuring her that predators were safely snoozing away in their jungle beds, Jessica sent her toes crinkling and curling in the sand. Her breathing had begun to slow and was becoming much less intense. Jessica also took note of the stabbing pain in her lower back. There had been jellyfish out there, and that was likely the party guilty for her back pain. The muscles in her legs were stinging with pain, too, but that was just from the swim. She hadn't tried yet, but Jessica guessed that any sort of work requiring her arms being raised over her head would result in excruciating pain.

It had been awhile since she lay on a beach like this. Looking to her left, and then to her right, recognizing only the parade of fiddler crabs marching nearby as the beach's only current inhabitants, she revised her thought: maybe not a beach like this one. But it had been some time since she lay on a beach. It was four years ago on her last summer vacation with her family to sunny Southwest Florida. This was back when the most Jessica had to accomplish each day was flirt with gawky southern boys and ignore her parent's request for some direction in regards to what college she would be attending in the fall. Instead Jessica chose to remain silent and plot the timing of her departure. Her parents ignored her maturation from suburban child to woman at war, and Jessica didn't do herself any favors by barely speaking the entire week. Sometimes, she thought, there are those in the herd that simply need to rebel. Jessica thought she had the ability, and the willingness to fight, and to survive, and to keep people fighting. And winning. A scant few months after that summer vacation with her parents, she'd made good on her threats of departure. She remembered quite clearly how torturous it was to leave home: Stomping angrily out of her parent's house and hopping aboard Will Frost's van, and she had done so all without a good-bye kiss from Dad, who was heartbroken.

Will was gone from her life now. With the help of her new friends, Jessica chose instead to gather information and act upon intelligence in her battles, rather than suffer through Will's rash decisions and hell-bent vengeance campaign. His ideas and methods proved ill suited for any sustained war. Propping herself up on her elbows in the sand and admiring the ocean she had just beaten, Jessica didn't feel all that intelligent now. And yet, from a vacant beach in Mexico, still miles away from the tourists, Jessica was able to breathe in the smog and pollution from the taxi cabs and diesel oil from the charter fishing boats. It forced her to move again.

The strong Sun took its toll. Jessica would need to find water soon. No sense in reducing all that exercise into futility by dying of dehydration out here on the beach, she thought. With the ability to breathe now having returned, Jessica suspected that her body would be sore for a week. What had frightened her the most on her swim was not getting tossed into the bright pink coral reef and the possible trail of blood she was leaving in the water for potential predators (a full body inspection would be required, but only after she was able to breathe again). No, what scared her was the thought that once she hit dry land she'd be all alone. She knew she had a job to do, and that assimilation would be difficult. But Jessica was a pretty, young woman, and she'd never been alone before. Looking out towards the horizon, she couldn't even see the freighter anymore.

Raising herself from her luxurious bed of sand, dusting off the loose specks and crumbs that stuck to her sweaty thighs, she began to walk slowly, very slowly, scanning the empty beach and its contents. Fiddler crabs continued to parade in line, making quick homes in the sand further down the beach. Stray herons, apparently oblivious to the crabs, danced with the waves lapping the shoreline, and Jessica laughed at the absurdity of it all. There was no evidence of any other life on the beach apart from an occasional paw print. Her new life was inside the jungle. With people she hadn't even met yet—a tribe, native to the jungle for hundreds of years, now dwindled to a small group of thirty or so. All were not long for their current homes as the condo construction loomed and grew closer to their village with each passing day.

They had pulled her from her sleep. The bed of empty wooden pallets had been a poor substitute for the cot she had been using back on the farm anyway. They tossed her a one piece as they walked her up to the edge of the deck. Everyone watched her undress to put on the swimsuit. Her finish line was the mountain, and they told her to aim for that. Oh, and watch out for the riptide as you get close to the shore, they added. All of these instructions were being given to her amid her nakedness and the disbelief that she was actually going to be thrown overboard. Jessica begrudged them their silly little act. She had heard rumors about the initiation but never took any of them seriously. The very second the shoulder strap on the one-piece was secured underneath her t-shirt Jessica was pushed, sent overboard, plummeting through the air. The terrifying fall precluded a tremendous hit to the water which was shocking. It was a hundred feet or so off the side of that freighter. She managed to tuck in her vital appendages before she slapped the water. The adrenaline pounded about her veins, signaling every alarm in her body. Upon breaking back to the surface with salt water stinging her eyes, Jessica bobbed about the tops of waves, barely able to nod as her compatriots back up on the deck pointed towards the mountain and shouted things she could not hear. The sea in front of Jessica awaited her swim. The large freighter made its departure, knowing she'd survived the fall.

The last mile or so, with exhaustion completely consuming her, the water had tossed her body around, sometimes into a shallow coral reef. It was her initiation, of course. But she never thought they'd actually do it. They'd needed to make certain that Will's influences were completely dissolved from her stream of consciousness, every irrational thought he ingrained in her erased. And they did it. They pushed her. And now she felt terribly alone. She swam towards the mountain and the jungle, inside which somewhere she'd make friends. And enemies. Now, walking up the beach, and fully able to breathe, and with the water behind her and the jungle in front, she braced herself and entered.

* * *

Jessica soon happened upon a serene waterfall and stood at peace underneath it and without regard for the frigid water temperature that pounded the salt away from her skin. This time the breaths escaping were a blessing as the pristine water cleansed previously soiled sand-encrusted skin. An isolated rock formation sent sheets of water teeming down, rolling off the tips of her breasts. Jessica stared through the bath of ice-cold water and was offered brief glimpses of the Sun poking through the rocks above for brief warming interludes while it bore itself into an unbounded blue sky. Jessica's bathing suit and t-shirt lay presented on a cliff drying in the Sun nearby. She was fortunate for the fresh water dousing her.

From the outstretched cliff, and with a waterfall soundtrack as an accompaniment now, Jessica marveled at the view of infinity. She'd been locked away with her compatriots for a week on that freighter. Time was spent by studying the correspondence between the Mexican government and the developer who had decided to build condominiums upon the exact location where an Indian tribe was living. The short, stubby cliff oversaw the ocean from a large exposed rock jutting from the side of the mountain that was just past the alcove and her waterfall. Her swimsuit and her t-shirt dried in a scalding Sun. Jessica paused atop the cliff with her chin propped up on her knees. Her tush burned a bit on the scorching hot rock, so she moved to sit on her wet t-shirt. Jessica looked out to the ocean and saw nothing. Not even the freighter that had brought her here. She was truly alone now. Truly frightened.

Far, far below her she could make out the small town encamped into the shoreline and butting up to the very end of the mountain and edge of the jungle. Crude Americans arrived daily on the docks, and soon a large port would be built for the gigantic cruise ships importing flocks of them. Her way out, she supposed. Eventually.

The sound of a twig snapping behind Jessica's back jostled her from friendly daydreams of her family. Casually looking behind afforded her the view of a tiny brown face with dark eyebrows and curious green eyes fixed in awe and amazement. It was a child, poking her head through gigantic leaves and colossal branches. The small brown face smiled at her. This warmed Jessica at once. She smiled back and waved. Jessica picked up her clothes and slipped into her swimsuit which was nearly dry. The small brown girl was covered only with a pair of turquoise shorts that may have been decades old. Taking one last look at the vacant ocean, Jessica moved back into the jungle by the tugging of a young girl's small hand.

Folding back the brush, Jessica watched a convoy of women carrying large buckets of water traipse by along a narrow dirt path. They all carried buckets apparently having just come from a large supply of water. Jessica grabbed the bucket from her new, young friend to help. Underneath the tree tops shielding them from the blasts of sunlight, Jessica simply followed in line with the rest of the women. The dirt trail was at a constant incline, and Jessica stepped only where the other women stepped. They had obviously come from a well, and perhaps it was where Jessica's waterfall had emptied. There were about sixteen or so adult women with about six or seven children following along, mostly spilling their water as they skipped and played on the path. The adult women were nearly naked apart from a small beige loin cloth that covered each woman's pubis. It was the children who wore bits of partially torn and beaten up contemporary clothing. Jessica noticed that one of the t-shirts proclaimed the incorrect super bowl champion from a few years back. The group would whistle when one would need to stop and pee. Each woman spent minutes closely inspecting any area that they could discharge number one. Then the entire fleet would stop and wait.

Odd birds sent peculiar sounds ricocheting above the tree line while the troop they escort marched continually uphill. The adult women were thin, tall, and beautiful. Razor sharp cheekbones sat distinctly along lean faces that had seen lifetimes of manual labor. Their height was much taller than Jessica expected. Their bare breasts hung like sunken torpedoes, with stringy arms exposing bicep muscles no doubt resulting from carrying massive buckets of water around this jungle. Hardened calves sat below forceful quadriceps that propped up muscle-bound buttocks that peeked through the bottoms of their loin cloths as they walked. Jessica imagined her behind would assume similar tautness after going up and down this mountain a number of times. Apart from an occasional curious look back, the women were indifferent to her. Jessica walked behind her admirer, still holding her hand until she stopped so she could lift her up and rest her on her sore shoulders. The little girl giggled, and Jessica knew she'd made a friend.

Bursting into a clearing that had given no indication of its presence Jessica noticed about two dozen or so thatched huts. The unmistakable smell of burning animal flesh offered its welcome to the women. There was one large bonfire in the middle of the dirt compound where the men were standing. They turned away immediately from what looked like some sort of spit, where a wild pig roasted, to spy Jessica. She at once felt odd and out of place. Like High School all over again. Although the men looked her up and down, Jessica sensed that it was due to her being a stranger and did not immediately feel threatened in any way. There was a Big Wheel that looked damaged off to the side of one of the huts and apart from the t-shirts and shorts most of the children donned, it was the only thing around that reeked of the twentieth century. Jessica's friend grabbed her hand and said something incomprehensible in her dialect.

Most of the villagers wore at least some sort of cloth protecting their lower privates. Some were completely clothed in t-shirts and shorts, filthy, while some men and women walked around completely naked. All of the older women were topless. The young girl in the turquoise shorts, who couldn't have been more than six or seven years of age, handed Jessica a necklace made of shells. She took Jessica's hand and pulled her over to the group of children casting similar shells about a piece of rope. She took precise measures to show Jessica how to make the shell necklace.

One of the women who had been on the trip spoke to a withered old man near the fire. He sat in a deep, decrepit chair that might have been centuries old and watched Jessica while taking smoke from some sort of elongated pipe. Old, grey, shoulder-length hair dropped upon frail shoulders. As Jessica's back was turned and she was working, the elder man strolled away from the crowd of men near the fire. His skin refused to clutch old bones and the miniscule muscle fibers that remained. His walk to the group of girls was an arduous one, evidenced by the amount of pressure placed upon the cane with each cautious step. Jessica was tapped on the shoulder by the cane the old man used. She stood to face him. He had no teeth, and his face showed that he could have been a thousand years old. His breath smelled of some arcane tobacco, and he continued to tap Jessica about her body. Despite the awkwardness of the act, Jessica felt a strange ease emanating from the man unto her as she stood in front of him. He muddled something that resembled Spanish, but it was not clear to Jessica. The woman who was seen chatting with him earlier stood next to Jessica. The old man in front of her muttered something again, and although it was unclear to Jessica, the entire village chuckled at what he said. The women all gathered and surrounded Jessica with cheerful smiles and pats to her shoulder in obvious support. Some women put their hands on her shoulder and gripped hard. Jessica recognized that a quick prayer was said. The old man smiled and said something else. One of the women that Jessica had seen talking to the old man earlier stood next to Jessica. Everyone in the village was smiling.

"Papa says…he watched you swim ashore. He said that you are a very strong female and that you are not to be disregarded."

Jessica was surprised and relieved she wouldn't be here in the coming months completely removed from the English language, "You speak English?"

"Yes, I am at work in the town from time to time."

"I am here to learn. I am here to help."

"You will. Papa has foreseen it." They both looked over to the old man who shuffled away slowly. "That is why you are allowed to stay."

Jessica looked back to the old man resuming his position in the wooden chair near the fire. He was the only one with a chair. He smiled reassuringly at Jessica and lit his pipe.

\* \* \*

Daylight evolved into restless nights for Jessica, and she bore a reluctance to go for any walks alone, fearing she'd never return, and perhaps no one would notice or really care for that matter. When the nights turned back into day, Jessica rose from her mat and joined work along with the four other women in her hut. This included Inha, the translator. The Sun rose day after day, continuing its best to wear at them and exhaust until it dropped from the sky, leaving the tribe idle during a night involving a bonfire, a dinner, and stories told by Papa and various other men. The first few weeks, every moment of every day was exciting because Jessica had no idea what to expect. The men went out very early for their hunt and were sometimes gone for days at a time. When the men did this, Jessica was taken with the other women of the tribe to an area in the vicinity of the settlement. There she was given some sort of tool resembling a rolling pin. She followed the others' example and rolled what looked like bits of tree bark and the pulp from the tree, continually smashing it down. Occasionally women would come by and pour water upon her work, liquefying it, which Jessica would then mold into a paste. There she stood for hours and smashed at bits of broken tree. Now Jessica understood why the women had such strong, muscular, lean arms. What Jessica thought she was molding from the various trees to use as glue was in fact the tribe's dinner if the men came home empty handed from the hunt.

Recently the men had been successful, bringing back such large pigs that the village had feasted for days. Other times they brought back nothing at all. That was when they ate paste. And although edible, and quite filling, it was a delicacy that held really no taste whatsoever. There were odd looking limes growing nearby which Jessica had been told to use along with the paste.

The work was routine, but far from unpleasant. Muscle fibers fired and twitched in Jessica's arms at the end of each day those first few weeks. The women chatted with one another the entire time. Inha stayed close at times and filled Jessica in on the topic of conversation. Other times Jessica noticed she strayed further away. Perhaps on purpose and perhaps at the behest of Papa who, Jessica had realized, was the unquestionable ruler of the tribe.

The men in the village paid no special attention to Jessica. Only the older men spoke to her and advised her, and very rarely did Jessica have the slightest idea as to what the subject matter may have been. It had been almost two months since Jessica had landed on shore and joined their tribe. The hunting was going very well, she thought. One day, upon the men's return, Jessica found out why.

Jessica stood next to Papa. Her lone English speaker friend, Inha, stood nearby as well. The men marched in triumphantly with their biggest yield to date, several large pigs. Papa was told that they were forced even to let some of the smaller ones go. The old man looked sad. Jessica spoke directly to Papa.

"What is it?" she asked. "What troubles you?"

Inha translated dutifully. Jessica had begun to pick up bits of words here and there, but it was still difficult. There were also some signs that she'd picked up much more easily. She chose not to get upset about the language barrier, figuring that comprehension would come to her in time.

The old man looked out from the compound to the jungle and spoke.

"Papa says," Inha began, "that the success of this hunt is not necessarily a good thing."

"Why is that?" Jessica asked.

"Papa says," Inha began, "that the men tell them they don't need to hunt. That animals come to them shaken from their homes in the jungle by the large beasts that have invaded."

Jessica knew it was bound to come to this. The honeymoon was definitely coming to an end.

"Papa says," Inha began, "he would like to take a walk and asks if we would like to join."

Papa, Jessica, and Inha walked through the jungle, and for once, Jessica was off the path. They did not walk far before Jessica heard unfamiliar sounds within the jungle. From a familiar cliff, Jessica watched as machines mauled the Earth. Dump trucks traveled about, removing stone and dirt. It was very near the village.

"Papa says," Inha began, "we'll be leaving soon."

They were still carving out the road. They'd be up at the compound in two or three months tops, knocking down the village. Jessica burned with hate. She felt like she could pick up each truck bend it and break it free from her precious Earth. Her home for a scarce few flips of the calendar, despite the fact that she had not seen a calendar in months, and home to the tribe for a few hundred years, was dissolving before her eyes.

"Papa says," Inha began, "there is richer land out there to be discovered."

Jessica looked at the old man. Papa looked beaten and certainly not optimistic about finding a richer land. She remembered the edict given to her up on the deck of the freighter right before she was pushed in. It was to "Assimilate. And just do some damage, that's all." There was no way she could wage a war out here by herself. That was probably why they sent her here as opposed to somewhere further south.

"No, you cannot win this war here and now," Jessica started, "and, yes, you can leave, and we will tell the world what they've done to you. But we must battle. We must make them pay for what they take. And then you can leave knowing you hurt these large beasts for the hurt they caused you. I can lead your men. We may not be able to defeat them, but we can make them pay for what they've done to you and to the Earth. I can show your men how to do that. Give me your permission, and I can lead your men in battle. Then you can go."

It took Inha a while to translate.

Papa put no eye upon Jessica. He just continued to watch the trucks move around several hundred feet below him. He mumbled something.

"Papa says," Inha began, "he knows that is why you've come. He had foreseen it."

Jessica waited for permission to be granted.

"Well?" Jessica asked him from the edge of the cliff. Inha translated.

The old man turned around and began his stooped walk back.

"Well?" Jessica asked again impatiently.

Jessica turned and looked down at the two-ton trucks. *The marauders*, she thought. The large beasts were destroying the mountain. She looked back to Papa limping away on his cane.

"Do I have your permission?" Jessica asked loudly.

The old man turned back around. He'd been leaning more on his cane lately. Jessica knew the decision had been made.

There was just a slight nod of his head, and then the old man walked back into the jungle. Jessica smiled.

* * *

The hunt. It was her very first. Strict orders from Papa to the men had allowed Jessica to join. Probably a first for the tribe, she thought. And the men, it seemed, could have cared less. Only a loincloth covered Jessica's privates below. Her breasts bounced uncomfortably, and she cursed as she leapt over fallen trees. She carried a spear after proving completely inadequate with the bow and arrow. She feared not for her life out here in the jungle. Papa had a specific conversation with the men only, and it probably had everything to do with the fight that they were preparing for. They paid her no mind, and they certainly didn't help her climb over any of the fallen trees. Jessica swore at the notion that she was always forced to prove herself.

There was an immediate decisive move made to depart from the upper jungle and attack the more open spaces sought in the lower jungle floor, which was also nearer to the construction. There was much more dirt on the ground, and at least walking was easier. Jessica forced herself to concentrate on the front of the pack rather than daydream about her surroundings. Bows with arrows pointed towards the ground stood ready in the palms of the Indians. Their eyes pierced every bush. Younger men, boys uninterested in the hunt, captured large tarantulas with sticks and flicked them at one another. Jessica smiled at their play. Whiffs from the war paint that Papa had applied to her cheeks and forehead very early this morning settled in her nostrils. It gave her focus.

The group graced the jungle floor with sleek, quiet, barefoot steps. The hunt was a methodical tracing of footsteps made by the two men in the front of the pack. It was a slow pace. She had only thrown her spear three times so far. She'd been close each time. Close enough so that the men acknowledged her having strong and accurate throws. Along the way, some men discovered beer bottles strewn about trampled plants and undergrowth. Jessica had seen tracks from an ATV. The workers had apparently begun scouting out new land. Jessica looked back to the tribe gathered in a circle inspecting the bottles. They sniffed at the alcohol vapors that were left inside. It wouldn't be hard to track the ATVs and siphon off some of their gas, she thought.

It was just a slight rustle sent from some bushes off to her side. Heads snapped backwards towards Jessica. At first she had thought she had stepped on a branch, breaking the silence of the hunt. Breaking that train of thought was a large gray blur that jostled awkwardly past her feet, instantly providing Jessica's sense of smell with wafts of filth and grime from the wild animal. The two lead hunters hurtled broken limbs and loose tree stumps towards Jessica in the back of the pack. They caught up to the pig and herded it into an immense wide open berth of nearby clearing. Jessica dropped her spear to her side as everything seemed under control. Each man took turns herding the pig, some even kicking it at its side until it wore itself out and collapsed in spasms. Usually the pigs were not this slow, they said to Jessica.

By and large this was the part of the hunt reserved for the young boys to prove themselves. And usually, it was a much tougher fight. This time, with the pig breathing hard, held down on its side by one of the hunters sitting on its belly while the two elder hunters knelt down on its hindquarters, the heads of the remaining hunters all turned to Jessica, who was standing the furthest away. The group opened the circle for Jessica and motioned for her to join them at the beast. Jessica strode up to the pig, proudly donning her war paint, her breasts swaying back and forth, knowing what was expected of her now. Jessica stared down at the helpless pig, thrashing to and fro. Sweat dripped from her scalp down into her eyes, tracking her cheeks with fresh sweat. The helpless pig snorted away softly, it's little heart ready to explode. The oldest man in the hunt (not one of the two who'd been in front) held out his hand. What lay in his dirty palm was a rock, black and polished, shimmering slightly in the sunlight and shaped like a triangle. Each side of the rock held its own designated sharpness. She had seen one of these before. She had seen tribe members filet fish with smaller versions. Razor sharp. The men all said something quick to her, which Jessica ascribed to well wishes and good luck. Then there were a few chortles from the two boys that were throwing tarantulas at one another. Jessica thought it had something to do with her sex. The boys were promptly smacked on top of their heads by elder tribesmen.

Looking down at the helpless animal, Jessica reassured herself that this was the cycle of life. And that by killing this pig, it would help her lead this tribe in a victory over land robbers. Jessica could hear the bulldozers nearby. As she knelt down and placed the knife at the pig's throat, purely guessing at the point of a main artery, muscular hands abruptly grabbed both of Jessica's shoulders. Faces from across the semi-circle peered up to her and offered comforting smiles. Jessica realized she wasn't alone. The group had encircled the pig and with heads lowered, the passionate prayer was felt by chants bellowed from the chests of the strong young men. One man led and the others recited dutifully, respectfully. Jessica did the best she could to follow along. She prayed for the soul of the pig and its many blessings it would provide the village. Looking up to the men, with heads still hung low, Jessica prayed for much, much more.

# O CAPTAIN! MY CAPTAIN

*DAVID HOBBS – AGE 33*
*October, 2007*

The cold, vacuous darkness seeped inside his pores, showing no mercy, invading every parcel of existence, and forcing his soul towards bitter coldness. Her hands found him. Pulled him free from the water. His body lay limp and without fight. Intermittent visions of Jessica shaking him trying to revive him appeared. Almost at once, he recalled the pleasure he took at the touch of her lips. David stirred from the rousing her kisses always put upon him. Visions of Jessica accompanied an onslaught of pounding to David's chest. He could hear her shouting at him, "Don't let it beat you! Don't let him beat you, god damn you!" Soon, it was Joe's husky voice in the background booming about amid a few moments of clarity for David. Thinking to himself, while away, that it was good that the water was only waist high and perhaps they had gotten him out in time. Eventually sadness overcame David, for it was not, in fact, Jessica providing the genuine mouth to mouth, but Jane proving the sole owner of the breaths that infused him. Jane knelt down next to his body, exhausted and able to offer a smile at his responsiveness. Consciousness, and thoughts of Jessica, were temporary. Jane's smile quickly returned to a worried frown as she shouted at David as he occasionally slipped away. Before succumbing to oblivion, David recognized the sudden feeling that it hurt to breathe.

Joe and Jane carried him up the mountain. His rescue came in the form of a familiar face, the girl that once resembled an elf (in the guise of a murderess). A previously known terrorist, now bearing the image of some fairy, transformed to a giver of existence on the side of some small road giving mouth to mouth to someone else now reformed.

Consciousness strained against the celestial forces compelling his mind to surrender. Fading and returning vision transpired many times over. Like video starting and stopping. The outer frames of the film slipped into vision. Time temporarily turned backwards on itself. Memories started and stopped. Tragic fragments shoved their way into his brain. Suddenly pushed forward over a ledge. Reality. Back to the line of progression that is life. It's all just a violent starting and stopping action that surrounded him as his body lay limp. Caged by darkness. Vision returned meekly. Nothing seemed to link him to life. The past tense sped up to the present, waterlogged and jostled by bits of jagged darkness that invaded his vision. Then there was nothing but light. Blinding him and necessitating the closure of his eyes which led him to more sleep. Rest. Sleep this time. Motion. A car. Then propellers whined to life indicating a small plane. Then, fake light, fluorescents, no mistaking those. An oxygen mask. Pain. Needles.

Awakened by the sound of turbo diesels humming adeptly beneath him, for David, this time, awake was awake. Propping himself up on his elbows pain struck him, sharp and acute, coming from a thick bandage on his shoulder and one on his belly. His back ached from laying stiff on the hard bench. David felt other dull aches muddled about on his insides. He lay shirtless, exposing a crude sling surrounding his shoulder and arm, which still hurt, sporting wicked bruises about his chest, no doubt from Jane's resuscitation efforts. He was laying on top of a sleeping bag, with a hard bench as his makeshift hospital bed, looking out at widespread blue sea that receded behind him. White frothy waves tossing saltwater in the air fanned out. Bright Sun surrounded the boat outside. The boat moved quickly, adeptly battering through the waves.

A plastic garbage can sat near him, for puke, perhaps, but further examination revealed several bloodied bandages piled about inside. The smell of fresh oil from the engines churning underneath mixed with saltwater that splashed about. David took note of the tropical heat outside that sapped every cold drop of water that had burrowed itself within him back in the Pacific Northwest. It was a clean boat. Pristine white paint glossed the cabin. David smelled clean. The anti-septic smell rose from the thick bandage that hurt to move. He noticed another bulbous dressing that fit surrounding the front of his gut.

Jane sat next to him just below the bench on the floor of the cabin. There she sat dozing to the hypnotic rhythmic splash of the sea being spread. With one arm raised, Jane held David's hand while her face planted sleepily in the other. She only freed his hand after determining he was truly revived. She turned around quickly with just a few feet separating her face from his.

"You," David said quietly. His first words in days.

"Me," Jane responded with eyes swollen heavily from lack of sleep and from the dirge of tears she'd been shedding.

"You're here…with me?"

"Yes," she answered simply.

"You're not there…with him."

"Nope," Jane said and used her free hand to wipe excess tears and snot from her nose.

"I had to be sure," David said. "That's why I couldn't tell you every-thing."

"I'm not sure what you mean? Are you sure now?"

"Yes," he said softly.

"Good, so am I," Jane dribbled tears which David wiped away gently.

"I was happy to see you naked," he said, offering a tiny smile while memories returned slowly.

"I guess not all that much considering you wouldn't have sex with me."

David laughed. His first since returning to the world, and his body convulsed with pain. He left the comment to be cleaned up once he returned to normal. Internally, he wondered if one could build up an immunity to drowning provided he or she go through the experience enough. David wondered how many more times it would take.

"Don't try and move too much," she said. Her hands found his bare chest. Tiny fingers caressed him gracefully yet firmly assisting him back down on the bench. "I'll help you up in a little while after I change your bandages. The water has been a little rough."

"I'll say," David responded. "I realize that we're on a boat. But would you mind telling me exactly where we are?"

"Somewhere in the middle of the Gulf of Mexico. We have some friends up top that could give you a better location."

"Where'd you get the boat?"

"You mean this old thing? This one hundred ten foot U.S. Coast Guard cutter that we, uh, borrowed? It's a gun boat. The Coast Guard decommissioned a dozen of these a year ago or so after they failed to meet spec. I suspect they'll miss it but won't exactly go insane looking for it. As for your recovery, while some of our doctors were patching you up, you missed a little excitement. For the record, South Florida is probably not somewhere I'll be visiting anytime soon."

"A gunboat, eh?" David asked rhetorically tossing a sly eye down to Jane.

David knew what the deck looked like without even opening his eyes. Twin .50 calibers mounted on the bow that provided serious protection.

"Just in case," Jane said.

Jane was referring to Will's army. David wondered how careful Jane had been.

"I didn't know who else to call," she said.

"What do you mean?" he asked. "How long have I been out of commission?"

"Out for one day. In and out for three more."

David listened to the waves crashing thunderously across the hull.

"Thanks," David said honestly. "Thanks for everything."

"Don't thank me," Jane replied. "I was only taking orders. I had no idea what to do."

"Who gave you orders?" David asked quizzically.

It was a question she did not answer, and one which David did not immediately know the answer to. Peeling back some of the bandages David recognized clumsy stitching, or stitching performed under harsh conditions, and done so quickly. Indeed, he had missed some excitement.

"Is that driver okay?" David asked.

"The driver is fine. We got him out of there. And Joe has been on a steady diet of Tylenol ever since Matthias gave him the knock to his noggin."

"Matthias!"

David summoned the recent memories of the man who tried to kill him.

"Matthias's body was found in the middle of the road. No truck, though," Jane admitted sadly.

David smiled again and remained motionless. Will had lost his best man and his best girl at David's expense. *Here's hoping that Will presumes I was killed,* David thought and prodded his shoulder, and his belly, both of which provided dull aches.

"Entry and exit?" David asked, pointing shoulder to belly.

"So I'm told," Jane responded.

There was a vial and a sealed plastic bottle of water within arm's reach of David. Painkillers, he presumed, which David would force himself not to use. He'd been numb for three days already, and he didn't need anything else furthering the fog.

"I'm not going back to him," Jane blurted out, "in case you're wondering."

"I'm wondering where you're taking me. And no, I did not think that you would."

"But he will come after us," Jane retorted.

"Perhaps," David responded.

Jane took a moment for courage.

"I didn't tell the FBI everything," she started, "I just told them what to look out for."

David turned his head so he could look straight at her.

"Wheelchair accessorized vans…recently reported stolen," David rattled off. "Black is preferred, but he'd settle for first available."

"They know about the tournament. Now they just need to wait it out. The FBI have that CEO in a safe-house somewhere."

David knew that, for Will, the island vacation home of the PerfectGrass CEO was accessible only by boat or helicopter. The ferry would have been too obvious. There were too many people to notice him along with none too many places to hide. He would go in by boat, David knew, but he'd go in with his own crew. The FBI might not grab him in time before he dumped the barrels on the land. More importantly, though, Jane did the right thing. She saved a man's life.

"That's good news," David responded.

"But the bad news is Will is still running around with two dozen barrels of highly toxic chemicals."

Joe had kept quiet, he acknowledged. He was fortunate to have run into him when he did. David smiled at Joe's job well done.

"Well, let's let the FBI take it from here," David said indifferently. He was still tired. "Still, you're orders from him were to kill me. Orders he had set up long in advance if ever I should secede from the union. Why didn't you? And why is the FBI giving you orders now?"

"I saved you, *we* saved you, because I realize what you are. What you mean to me. And what you have. It's just too bad it's with her! And, that's something I never had! But I wanted it! I still want it."

"And you can! You can have that life. You'll find someone."

"I'm turning myself in, David. I'm going in. Just as soon as I drop you."

"What? Why? For protection?"

"Nope. It's for me. If I do this, if I really, really do...repent, then I'm doing it full-on and with nothing on my conscience. I know I'm looking at jail time. Maybe I can help. Maybe my story can warn younger, impressionable kids. Hell, I'll probably be locked in a room spilling my guts about the BVG for some psychotherapist to take notes on and analyze."

"But you're different now!" David pleaded.

"You taught me, David, to do the right thing. And that people can change. Look at you! Look at what a fat ass you were little more than a year ago."

Jane got up and pushed her lips to his. David recognized this as a goodbye kiss, and Jane did not hold back. She winced at the realization that this would be the last time she'd be close to him. David failed to protest, instead allowing her to savor the few remaining moments they had together. She let go reluctantly.

"When we first met," David began, as Jane wiped tears away from her cheek with her shirtsleeve, "back at the warehouse, Will referred to you as Q. What did he mean by that?"

She appreciated the question. Appreciated that he had remembered.

"It's short...for Qarlee," she answered. "Qarlee with a Q."

"Qarlee...with a Q. I think that is a very pretty name."

"Thanks," she said and sobbed again. "I don't think anyone has ever told me that."

Qarlee rose. She stared at his feet shying away from his eyes. Quickly, she leaned down and dropped one last kiss on David's cheek. Then she popped up and moved to leave the cabin.

"Wait," David stopped her. "Where are we headed?"

Qarlee halted at the doorway, refraining from turning around to look at him and stepped from the cabin out to the Sun.

"The FBI wasn't my first phone call."

Darting back inside the cabin, Qarlee looked at David and then back out to the Sun before providing anything further.

"She told me to bring you back to her."

David lay motionless for some time.

# RUN AGROUND

*WILL FROST – AGE 38*
*October, 2007*

The biohazard warning symbol stared menacingly at Will who took a certain satisfaction at having something so deadly so close at hand. The barrels sat strapped together on the deck, secured safely inside the large boat. Will had checked the lines himself. He had wanted to travel in style on this, what would probably be his last trip, so the BVG had secured a yacht. This was going to be his legacy. What he went out on. From the bow of the boat, with one knee raised forward, and with a regal stare out across the Ocean, undaunted by any sea spray that might attack what was left of his face, Will imagined he looked much like Washington crossing the Delaware.

There were only six barrels aboard. That was all they would need to fill the Jacuzzi. Every half minute or so Will allowed himself a peek over at the barrels that were close by. They weren't going anywhere. Will just liked the preeminent feeling of righteousness that flooded him when he studied them. Will had so wanted to caress them, but thought better of it figuring the BVG would have him committed or perhaps just push him overboard, which was his standing order in case he turned stark raving mad. Instead, he spoke to them.

"You are babies," he stated, "the genesis. Tools…of retribution that are born to a new Earth. Finally unconfined and unrestricted to unleash holy hell upon humanity's ignorance. My legacy. Justice served upon the guilty, justice for what was done to me and to all the others by cold and callous hands."

Will chuckled to himself a bit merely by the thought that he should be writing down all of these insane poetic meanderings for some memoir to be auctioned off some day. Will's eyes focused back upon the vacation home in the distance. A fifth home, used sparingly by the CEO of PerfectGrass, mostly for this time of the year when the tennis tournament was occurring. Assembled with the profits from the poisons and toxins spread about bright green lawns that flooded suburbia. Will admired the squared off angles of such a modernist home carved out from a mountain and overlooking the mainland from afar. Day and night, not a bad view to be had. Unless of course you were floating face down in your pool, Will mused.

They hadn't needed all the barrels. Just a few would suffice for a toxic bath intended for the CEO, his lovely wife, and their prize winning Chihuahua (which would be lucky to survive the kidnapping given the patience Frick and Frack had displayed thus far). They would take plenty of photos to populate the web, Will expected. Three corpses floating face down in their own toxins that they had produced and profited from. It would be an enduring legacy. The rest of the barrels would provide comic relief as they would likely find their way to some massive spill at some ludicrously overpriced all-inclusive resort. That would certainly make things dramatic enough. Pain was the only example people seemed to learn from. They would see pain. *The world needed examples set forth and to be honest*, Will thought, *it just wasn't worth a damn anymore*. Why not reboot?

The yacht the BVG motored in was easy enough to operate once the skipper was shown the damage a bullet to the owner's head could do. Turning away from the modern luxury of the island getaway for the PerfectGrass CEO, Will instead focused on the surf and the beaches nearby. He was soon to be relieved of his misery, he knew that much. Will wondered if he'd make it north of the equator ever again. He recalled his days in the water: Straddling his board, kicking his toes in the Ocean from sunup to sunset. Amped up in a barrel. Ending up in the inlet. Messing around with Liza, Dooby, and Kenny. This was of course back when the hate didn't fuel him. Now, this hate was the only thing keeping him alive and moving forward. He would continue living for as long as possible in order to destroy those responsible for hurting others. But his ideas would live on forever. He made damn sure of that.

His time had been reduced to only about three or four hours of consciousness a day. The master suite in the yacht dripped blood and puss. His eyesight was failing, and his skin burned with every speck of water that hit him. His gaunt face now exposed skin that was paper thin, dull, and lifeless. Will could see the outlines of his muscle fibers contracting. And yet, he would enjoy watching the couple be given a bath in the poisons that they were producing. He would stand by as close as possible in ecstasy over their screams of pain. Jealous of the fact that they were at least forewarned of the immense pain they would know and the fact that they wouldn't linger with the poisons for a decade or more. They would need to find the pool supplies in order to force them under. The crew, the BVG, pulled their Hazmat suits free from their packaging and got dressed. Will acknowledged a few bloody handprints on the wall left by the original owners of the yacht. Frick and Frack had no clue as to the definition of the word "subtlety". *Getting close now*. Will could see the dock. He marveled at the gall the art deco house and the modernist approach displayed out here in nature all alone.

Moored and docked, busy feet pounded the dock. A wheel chair was unfolded after Will is helped off the ship, but he ignored it.

"Thank you, no," Will said opting for his cane. Will knew there'd be no getting himself free from that chair. Will watched the dozen or so BVG invade the house. House staff members were rounded up, dropping towels and cleaning products in shock over the invasion. Guns were waved, but these nice service folk were to be spared. Will noted there were five staff members when intel had told him there were only three. *Interesting*, Will surmised, not putting too much stock into it. *There is no dog running around, which is also interesting, but photographs have the wife sporting the dog in her purse at most showcase events*. The tennis championship was certainly an event in which to parade her prized Chihuahua. Yippy little thing photographed well, Will recalled, almost as well as the plastic wife had in all those magazines. Will smirked at the boys and girls in Hazmat suits running around the house.

Frick and Frack (the intel) were hopefully en route with the CEO and his wife tied up in the trunk. All they had to do was grab them directly after the ferry from the main land had dropped them off. There was never any security here, so Frick and Frack could prove themselves with this one. So far, they had proven to be trigger happy, idiot kids.

Will ambled up the dock to pool side. He returned his gaze upon the ocean and the view. What it must be like to wake to this beautiful scenery. What he wouldn't do to go surfing just once more. And then Will imagined the people with emphysema as a result of a careless mixture of the PerfectGrass product performed by someone who didn't even need a college diploma. Noting that he felt lightheaded after so much movement, Will chose to expedite things. He looked to the yacht and to the BVG donning full Hazmat suits that remained waiting to unload. Will had ignored their pleas and opted only for the gas mask. The damage had been done to this body, Will ruminated, long ago.

A legacy, Will thought. The BVG. The justice served to those responsible, careless, and ignorant. What a shame Matthias and Qarlee were no longer around to see it. And David, well, poor David. *What is your legacy, David Hobbs?* Will thought to himself. *Ad man? Executive poisoning the world with endless clutter of wasted ad dollars and poisoning his soul with booze. An adman who saw the light? Unable to live with himself any longer. Afraid of what he'd become, choosing instead to fight to save the world, but only if it's done so in a responsible manner. And all the while in search of his one true love. What are you but just a dead man with no one left in this world that gives a damn about you? You are useless.*

Will's entire crew was covered head to toe in their protective suits. The pristine pool would have taken too long to drain. Instead, nods come from the BVG at the Jacuzzi that it was ready to be filled with the liquid poison. Will nodded to the two men on the yacht. They began to unload the drums. Boots stomped the dock as dollies rolled by. Will continued to survey the house from the deck near the Jacuzzi. Will smirked at the irony displayed by the PerfectGrass logo stenciled beautifully alongside the barrels and directly beneath a biohazard logo. Will noticed the house staff looking down to him from the large floor to ceiling window which displayed from a great room. They were curious and studied the BVG's each careful move. It was odd not to have a woman in the bunch, Will thought.

A report is in. Frick and Frack are non-responsive. They should be in the Mercedes by now and en route. Will looked to his wristwatch, and despite the larger face, he still could not tell what time it is.

Frick and Frack had probably lost patience with the dog and had stopped on the side of the road to argue about which one of them could punt the dog over the cliff. They would have been easy enough to grab, and Will had gone through the plan a thousand times. Nothing could possibly have gone wrong. And now the CEO and his wife would suffer the same fate that Will had suffered. Only the agony would last just a few minutes, whereas Will's had burned him alive from the inside out for ten years and more.

The stolen drums of pesticide were deposited next to the Jacuzzi. Members of the BVG handled each barrel. Will turned and looked out to the Ocean. *Legacy*, he thought, as thin lips portrayed a smile. *Peace*. Then he nodded. BVG members cracked open the drums and toppled them over spilling the contents into the nearly empty Jacuzzi. Liquid gushed from the spouts. It was a beautiful release for Will. Embattled and tortured, he felt free as he waited for the toxins to attach themselves to every living thing in its radius. But as he watched the liquid pour into the tub, he knew at once that something was wrong. The liquid, much more viscous than originally anticipated did not exactly flow from the barrels. It was thick and syrupy. And brown. Dark brown. At once Will imagined all the errors he could have made in transport. Will quickly theorized the main problem: temperature and storage. All possible scenarios ran through his head which was clouding over with improbability, frustration and derision. What had gone wrong? These were not the toxic chemicals that he had predicted. He avoided all his hypotheses apart from the obvious, and only until those had been stubbed out did he realize what had transpired. The BVG kept pouring, too dumb to understand that the toxic chemicals were not there, and that the contents were far from dangerous. Will ripped off his gas mask and angrily shouted at the BVG to stop.

Will hobbled over to the very side of the Jacuzzi, leaning down slightly for closer inspection, despite the many protests. If he had held any sense of smell, he might have been able to qualify it. His taste buds, also, had long since been extinguished. The proof would come upon intake. His body wasn't used to such high doses of dextrose.

"Is that...?" a BVG began, removing her mask.

Will swabbed two fingers full of the dark brown liquid. He inserted them into his mouth. He was immediately proven correct.

"Chocolate," Will responded. "Syrup."

"Oh," she said. "Is it okay if we take our masks off now?"

"It is unless a chocolate allergy poses a risk."

The others began removing their masks. Will looked down to the large Jacuzzi filled with chocolate syrup.

"Fondue," he cried and snickered to himself. He swore he would shoot the first BVG that laughed at him.

Other members of the BVG were now helping themselves to the chocolate syrup in the tub. Will turned to the house. He watched as the house staff expertly disarmed his BVG and gave them the beat down of their life. Plasticuffs came out. Will imagined the "staff" were now identifying themselves as the FBI.

"No, not yet," Will said, pleading to no one in particular. No one was listening. They were either being cuffed or enjoying chocolate. "I'm not finished yet!"

Will saw the flashing lights atop the swarm of cars approaching pulling off the side of the mountainous road towards the house and into the driveway. An army of police approached him while his soldiers ate chocolate. Naturally it came to him. The mom and pop chocolate company in the Pacific Northwest that neighbored the PerfectGrass distribution facility. *Very clever, Hobbs*, Will decided. A helicopter fluttered behind Will near the yacht. He could see the M-16s pointed at him. The BVG quickly dropped their weapons without a fight. The army was so close to Will now. He turned to the Ocean, and tried imagining where his surf board might be. Then he collapsed.

# TWO DAYS BY BOAT

*DAVID HOBBS – AGE 33*
*October, 2007*

Sleep this time. Genuine sleep, that is. Not sordid consciousness or broken bits of reality splicing in and out erratically. That ordeal was over with, David proclaimed. Now, there was just honest-to-goodness rest. This time someone else was piloting the boat, which David was glad for. He was able to renounce the charts, the maps, and their present course for the ability to just sit and pass the time acknowledging a cloudless sky overhead and blue water encompassing the horizon.

Joe had stolen the barrels. Barrels full of chocolate syrup destined for a cannery. He had convinced the PerfectGrass driver that his truck was already loaded and ready to go before the real pesticides could be loaded. It worked perfectly. Thanks to Joe and his homespun Americana honest face that was enough to convince that driver that he was all set. David had managed to save the CEO's life with barrels full of chocolate syrup. He would have given anything to see the look on Will's face when the barrels had been cracked open. When Joe eventually told him of the conversation between the driver and he, it was not far from what David had imagined would take place. The real bitch was forging the right serial numbers on the chocolate barrels so that the driver would be sold without any sort of close inspection.

The sunlight freed him from his stupor and incited the impatience and anxiety over seeing her. The boat allowed for only so much pacing, and David steadied a hand against the railing amidst the recovery of his sea legs. Qarlee simply stood watch, overseeing their progress on the GPS while a man not known to David steered the boat Southwesterly. Each time he stepped out back to take a look, she greeted David with her back turned to him. Qarlee answered David's few questions with one-word replies that were mostly inaudible. David stared out blankly at the world that was now in his rear view mirror. David's worries, consisting of the mess he'd made of himself the last dozen years or so, were being left behind in the form of sea spray. David admired the fish jumping out from the Gulf waters amongst the waves and wake given off from the brusque-moving boat. A dolphin escort ensued, and it made David smile. Qarlee kept her distance and remained next to the stranger at the helm. They stood above deck with access from a ladder. With his shoulder in a sling and his legs still a bit weak David dared not make the attempt at a climb. The sling was removed and pitched off the back of the boat quickly and without reservation. David wouldn't allow himself to be seen in such a weak state. He certainly wouldn't have it be the first image pressed upon Jessica. Qarlee knew this, too. She shuffled her feet above and still presented her back to him. His imminent departure from her life cut her.

The Gulf of Mexico waves parted as the "borrowed" U.S. Coast Guard cutter pressed through Mexican waters. David was on his way. At long last, he'd be with the only woman he truly ever loved. She was, in fact, just about the only woman in his life that ever gave a damn about him. Jessica had found him a dejected despondent shell of a person out there in that jungle. David had made his sacrifices recently. But was it really a sacrifice if it meant finding out who you really were? Or who you always should have been? David supposed that the idea was that you weren't supposed to dump everything to feel nothing. The numbness wore off as soon as the alcohol began to disappear. And that was it. It all came rolling off. Regret was left behind in the waves that the boat had pounded through. And he did what he could to suppress the tears of guilt, and deemed a short breakdown as an apparent necessary part of his transformation. His life had taken only a slight side track. And now, he was a new man, prompted by the push out the door from someone who cared so little. But David knew it began long before that. Jessica had planted the feelings within him. They festered. And, finally, they surfaced, humanizing a shell of a man who, without having known her, lord knew if he'd still be around this Earth. So, she had saved him twice, he thought. It was all thanks to her. Even as just a memory kept him wanting, as cards and letters arrived rather infrequently, David knew she was his mate. Apparently she knew it, too. And with every memory of her keeping him longing, the power of the soul was revealed. The effects it could have. All of it. This was her effect. And now he felt as though he owned his life and could get on with it as opposed to just waiting for death.

Before dawn, on his last day aboard, David studied a sky peppered with hazy pink clouds. A savage Sun began to evolve, ready to unleash hell upon this part of the Earth. As land approached, David recognized the mountain immediately. They didn't even bother docking (Qarlee's orders). Joe bear hugged him and waved stupidly. And with her back to David still, having borrowed one of his t-shirts, she rubbed a sleeve across her nose and both eyes. She simply said, "Get out."

David jumped from the boat onto the dock and watched the cutter muscle away. Turning to the town, David saw no one else in sight. He recalled watching a mountain burn from that very spot on the dock which was just prior to their hasty getaway so very long ago. The cutter moved away quickly, and Qarlee finally turned around. She and David exchanged stares. David imagined Qarlee busily imprinted his image to memory right then and there. Her lips curled up slightly and forced a reserved smile. David imagined, hoped rather, it was not to be the last he ever saw of Qarlee.

The market place was unequivocally different from the bustling, burgeoning town he had seen years ago. At this early hour David watched as charter boats returned from chumming, and townspeople crept outside quietly to sweep up dust and dirt kicked up from the previous night's exploits. Gone were the shops selling trinkets and tchotchkes. They had been replaced by stores with abundant bright lights inside and showy names offering themselves upon their storefront windows. Shopkeepers were exchanged for young men and women sharply dressed, holding keys to packed display cases. The irony of course coming from above the stores, where heads still poked free from windows in an attempt to check the weather. David sat down in a wicker chair looking haggard and thirsty, but knowing it was too early for the restaurants' first crews to arrive.

Tiny steps battering the cobblestones, echoing down an empty street, first alerted him. Rising from his chair, he looked to the street. There, he listened to the feet that expertly managed a cramped street fixed long ago. He watched her appear from around a corner on the hill above and thought that she must have been fake and that life was perhaps engaging in one final cruel trick. David forced his mouth shut, stunned, shocked, and in awe from the very sight of her. The imagined words he had been preparing on the boat the last two days were quickly dismissed. It was the actualization of her presence that forced every excuse and every apology he thought necessary to flee from consciousness. She watched him leave his chair and enter the street to face her. Appearing only slightly older than his memory, with just a strand or two of gray hair, now she didn't pretend not to see him. Jessica continued her approach. When she was close enough, David watched her smile, and he lost hold of his world. She appeared before him with genuine surprise evidenced by her mirroring the total shock that David so obviously articulated on his face. His look said he was sorry, and his hand shook as he deferred to the shell necklace which he pulled free from underneath his t-shirt. When she was close enough to see it, words became unfathomable for David. He simply seized hold of Jessica. Clutching her tight just as he should have done near the pool. Jessica laid one hand upon his cheek tenderly while the other tussled his hair.

"I knew," she said. "I always knew."

Jessica sported only a wrinkle or two more than in the memories David had been playing over and over in his head.

"You were right, Jess," David said. "You were always right. I never should have let you go."

"I couldn't break you then. But I've got you now. You're with me now."

This time the embrace failed to cease. And this time they both clutched at one another.

"I meant to be in Chicago a few years ago. I got a little tied up. I sent a friend though. She said you still cared. That you had the fire in your blood."

"My God, Jess, I can't believe I've finally found you."

"There's still work to be done."

"I'm ready," David acknowledged.

"I have many stories to tell you."

"I'm sure that you do. I want to hear each and every one."

At last they kissed. It was most welcome to David. His transformation completed by meeting the lips of the woman he was allowed to love again, and her embrace was the finite ending to a harrowing and wearisome journey.

David held her close. He would never let her go again. And at once David looked to the sky where the Sun burned away on a day that saw two lovers finally reunite.

# REUNION

*PRESENT DAY*

Blistering fire seared his palms and felt as though he had carried hot coals. Sweat bit his eyes. David Hobbs looked above and saw a circle of daylight. Entombed in the smokestack and with just a couple of hundred more feet remaining, David fought the ferocious heat. One hand clutched the rope for survival, and the other carried a pipe with a gasoline doused shirt that had been tied to it. David's feet and legs locked around the canvas rope while certain death waited for him below. If he survived the fall, there was little chance of being extricated once the factory was buried.

David pulled the Zippo from his pocket, transferring rope and pipe to one hand most carefully. He flicked the top open and ignited the lighter. The tiny flame still prompted enough light to show the rainbowing colors of the toxins that had permanently adhered to the walls of the smokestack like graffiti. David lit the gasoline dampened shirt and waited for the fire to catch hold. He released the pipe, watching the flame trickle underneath him. The lead pipe fell and pinged against the sides of the smokestack clumsily until he heard the metal clank at the base. He could hear the pipe roll out to the open factory floor where a bath of gasoline would be ignited. David imagined the blue flames washing over the machinery, and traversing about the length of the factory floor to the executive offices. David smiled as a glow appeared below. Beaten and somewhat dazed from the intense heat, it provided David just enough impetus to continue.

Smoke quickly joined him in his climb towards the light. David's part was over with. The only thing that remained was to hope the smokestack held against the blast, and to make it out alive. Far above, Jessica had a bird's eye view, and it was her turn for action. It would have been a terrific sight for her, David thought. He subsequently heard the unmistakable sound of three thuds of dynamite detonating from within the Earth. Placed in their strategic positions and timed right, the engineers assured Jessica they would achieve their desire. Living things hustled and scurried, leaving swaying branches as their footprints. The factory would be completely buried, leaving only the smokestack for oxygen to fuel the fire inside. Then there were five much louder, denser thuds. David imagined the sight the toucans made seeking refuge in the air. The shockwaves and tremors flowed beneath the Earth, causing the smokestack to sway unsteadily and bathe David in dust, dirt and soot. He climbed a bit more urgently now. Then there were the three deafening blasts.  Ear rattlers. Triggers, though, in reality. Exposed dynamite that was meant to elicit the landslide. Save for a few ant hills the creatures would have all sought flight by now. David could hear the Earth start to flow and bits of dirt shrapnel fell into the smokestack upon him. *Just gotta make it to the light*, he thought.

Birds retreated to the sky as dirt and mud slid away from one mountain to swallow up the factory. The jungle slid over as though it had been pulled on a rug, broken bits of Earth ejected from the mountain rolling over to cover the factory. The mud and Earth slammed into the cement walls, laying their berth upon the roof as a blaze inside melted machinery to the floor. Mud, dirt, and leaves piled up outside concealing the barren factory. Very quickly and quite perfectly, the mountain annexed the plot of land where the factory stood. Stuck in a fetal position along the rope, wincing as the smokestack swayed six inches, David held tight. Chunks of Earth and dirt came flying down at him. When it was quiet, David resumed his climb with a bit more gusto.

David Hobbs just gritted his teeth as the fire roared below. God only knew what awaited for him topside, he thought, but he kept climbing. David realized now. He knew now. He knew that he did the right thing. Embarrassed by the thought of his fat ass in a chair sitting at a desk just two years ago, his palms ripped and calloused now from climbing a rope to daylight. He did so joyously because it was what he believed in, and he thought it was the right thing to do. Just look where that had taken him: in the middle of a Costa Rican jungle, climbing a rope for his very life. Hoping the love of his life was at the other end. And he lived a life without regrets. David offered a chuckle as more dirt showered him from above.

Jessica trod gingerly across fresh Earth and dirt, minding her steps as she approached the smokestack. The ground she traversed gave way softly, marking each virginal footstep across new Earth. There were only two or three feet left of the smokestack visible that jutted up from the ground. Jessica watched and waited for him, and at long last, two familiar hands gripped at the lip of the smokestack.

David could hear the flames below and the heat began to burn at the bottoms of the rubber soles of his gym shoes. David climbed up. His muscles were besieged by every movement until he was over the lip of the smoke-stack and finally there was rest knowing he was removed from any danger. Jessica ran to him. David, completely fatigued, let his hands free of the rope so he could feel the ground and the fresh Earth on which he lay. Looking off to the side David lay witness to a mountain with a portion removed. From all appearances, the factory had been completely covered. David lay flat on the ground, drained by his climb, and craned his head over his shoulder to see plumes of smoke that had begun to rise from the smokestack. His shoulder throbbed as he looked to it, acknowledging a scar barely noticeable now beneath the dirt and soot. Jessica held him despite the shared dirt that was rubbing off on her. Only one other time in her life had she been happier to see him.

"How's that for an initiation?" David asked in between gasps of breath.

"Oh, shush!" Jessica exclaimed and kissed him fervently.

David appeared much worse for the wear, but he smiled, knowing he would make it.

The two lovers floated away on the canoe, and as David rowed, he watched Jessica admire the surroundings. Jessica watched as birds and other creatures returned to their usual state. Headed towards the coastline, they floated away across the smooth river, surrounded by a jungle that hummed with life.

# ACKNOWLEDGMENT

I would like to acknowledge and give thanks to the work done by Paul Hawken in his book *The Ecology of Commerce*. The specifics presented in his book are startling.

# AUTHOR BIOGRAPHY

Jeremy Bobrowski grew up in a suburb of Chicago. After graduating from Iowa State University he went to work for one of the world's leading advertising agencies. By day, Jeremy still toils away as a mild mannered advertising executive. But at night, he turns into super fiction writer guy. Jeremy lives in Chicago with his wife (from whom he takes orders) and his two year old son (from whom he also takes orders). His love for Chicago is clearly evident in his writing. Jeremy is also the proud father to a pesky cat named Wrigley. Jeremy is not a Cubs fan.

Now Available on Amazon.com
in Paperback and Kindle Edition

9167929R0

Made in the USA
Charleston, SC
16 August 2011